By JAMIE FESSENDEN

NOVELS
Billy's Bones
By That Sin Fell the Angels
Murderous Requiem

NOVELLAS
The Christmas Wager
The Dogs of Cyberwar
Saturn in Retrograde
We're Both Straight, Right?

Published by DREAMSPINNER PRESS
http://www.dreamspinnerpress.com

Billy's Bones
JAMIE FESSENDEN

Dreamspinner Press

Published by
Dreamspinner Press
5032 Capital Circle SW
Ste 2, PMB# 279
Tallahassee, FL 32305-7886
USA
http://www.dreamspinnerpress.com/

This is a work of fiction. Names, characters, places, and incidents either are the product of the author's imagination or are used fictitiously, and any resemblance to actual persons, living or dead, business establishments, events, or locales is entirely coincidental.

Billy's Bones
Copyright © 2013 by Jamie Fessenden

Cover Art by Lou Harper
http://lharper.deviantart.com/gallery

Cover content is being used for illustrative purposes only and any person depicted on the cover is a model.

All rights reserved. No part of this book may be reproduced or transmitted in any form or by any means, electronic or mechanical, including photocopying, recording, or by any information storage and retrieval system without the written permission of the Publisher, except where permitted by law. To request permission and all other inquiries, contact Dreamspinner Press, 5032 Capital Circle SW, Ste 2, PMB# 279, Tallahassee, FL 32305-7886, USA.
http://www.dreamspinnerpress.com/

ISBN: 978-1-62380-941-6
Digital ISBN: 978-1-62380-942-3

Printed in the United States of America
First Edition
July 2013

Dedicated to my mom, Judith Rennie,
the best therapist I've ever known.

ACKNOWLEDGMENTS

In addition to my mother, who looked over the therapy scenes for me, I'd like to also acknowledge the help of two other therapists who were kind enough to read the novel and offer insights: my stepfather, Robert Rennie, and my friend, Robert Stiefel.

AUTHOR'S NOTE

When Kevin at last remembers the details of a particular night in his childhood that he'd suppressed, the entire scene is written out for dramatic purposes. In reality, people with suppressed memories rarely recall the entire thing this clearly and may uncover bits and pieces over time without ever recalling all of the details. Also, the unique circumstances of Kevin's past make it necessary for him to remember what he's suppressed. This isn't always the case, and often therapists prefer not to delve into them, unless there is a specific reason to do so. Forcing someone to recall something he or she has suppressed can sometimes cause additional trauma.

Warning: this story contains scenes which might be possible triggers for survivors of childhood abuse.

One

KEVIN DEROCHER was just thirty-two when he walked into Tom's office, newly married, a baby on the way, and the collar of his red flannel shirt pulled up in an attempt to hide the bruises around his throat caused by hanging himself in his garage. He was a lean, quiet man with a shy smile and a disheveled appearance—unshaven, with a tangle of chocolate-brown hair, as if he'd scrambled out of bed too late to even grab a comb. When Tom shook his hand and looked into those sleepy, soft hazel eyes for the first time, he was struck not by the pain he often saw in his client's eyes, but by the confusion he saw there, as if Kevin had no idea why any of this was happening.

"So, Kevin," Tom said when they were seated in the overstuffed, faux leather chairs, "how have you been for the past few days?"

Kevin crossed his legs, as if trying to find a comfortable position, and then immediately uncrossed them again. "Okay, I guess."

"Good. How's your wife... Tracy, right? And the baby?"

"The baby's not born yet," Kevin replied.

Tom already knew this. It had been Dr. Belanger's opinion when he'd counseled Kevin at Androscoggin Valley Hospital, that learning of

Tracy's unplanned pregnancy had been the trigger that led to Kevin's suicide attempt. Kevin had denied it. Of course. Having a child is supposed to be one of the happiest moments of a man's life.

It doesn't usually lead to suicide.

"I understand that," Tom said pleasantly, tugging the short black hair of his beard between thumb and forefinger. "I simply meant, how is the pregnancy coming along?"

Kevin shrugged. "It's fine."

Tom realized he was thirsty, so he stood and went to the water bubbler in the corner. "Would you like some water?" he offered, holding up an empty paper cup.

"Yeah, sure."

It wasn't until Tom carried both cups back and set them on the slightly battered coffee table that Kevin volunteered, "I think she's mad at me."

"Your wife?" Tom settled back into his chair and smiled at him. "Mad about what?"

"Trying to kill myself."

"Has she said anything?"

"Not really," Kevin said. He crossed and uncrossed his legs again, looking at his cup on the coffee table without seeming to focus on it. "She hardly talks to me at all now. She spends most of her time after work visiting with her mom."

Tom didn't feel comfortable doing couples counseling since he'd never been married. The state of New Hampshire had legalized gay marriage this past year, but Tom wasn't even dating anyone. He generally referred people with marital trouble to his colleague, Sue Cross. But in this case, talking to Tracy might provide some valuable insight into what had happened, so he offered, "Do you think it might help to have Tracy join us for a session?"

"No."

"Well, it's an option if you decide you'd like to do that later."

"How many times do I have to see you?"

This was just an outpatient follow up since Mark Belanger hadn't felt Kevin's short stay in the hospital was enough to really help him. They'd released him when they believed he was no longer a danger to himself, but they'd never ascertained what the real issue was. That could take months, if not years. But Kevin couldn't be forced to continue counseling.

"Why don't we talk about that at the end of the session?" Tom asked. He suspected Kevin would simply get up and walk out if he gave him half a chance. "Right now, I'd like to talk about why Dr. Belanger referred you to me."

When Kevin just stared blankly at his cup of water, Tom asked him, "Would you care to tell me what happened a couple weeks ago? On that Sunday?"

Kevin sighed and leaned forward to take a sip from the cup. "We went over that about a million times in the hospital. Didn't they write it down for you?"

"Dr. Belanger did send me some notes. But I'd like to hear it from you."

"I don't really remember."

"So the case notes say."

"Well, they're right," Kevin said, irritated. "Tracy went out shopping for baby clothes or something with her sister. And I was feeling pretty low—"

"Why?"

"I don't know. I just was."

"I'm sorry. Go on."

The story Kevin told wasn't much different from what Mark Belanger had written. Kevin had decided to have a beer, and then a few more. His feeling of being "a little low" worsened until, in his intoxicated state, the depression seemed insurmountable. Then he went out to the garage, stripped completely naked, and hung himself by tying one leg of his blue jeans to a crossbeam and the other around his neck, and then stepping off the tailgate of his truck. He didn't fall far enough to break his neck, and the way he'd tied the pants leg still allowed a trickle of air into his throat. So he didn't die. He just hung there, choking. He passed out after a few minutes, but the medics estimated he dangled for ten or fifteen minutes before someone driving along the road in front of his garage saw him and called 911.

"Why do it naked?" Tom asked.

Kevin shrugged and downed the rest of his water. "I don't know. It must have seemed right at the time." He paused and then glanced up at Tom with a slightly mischievous smile. "You want to hear something gross? About when they found me?"

Tom had a pretty good idea what was coming, but he said, "Sure."

"I guess I was… kind of…." Kevin made a gesture, as if he was flipping Tom off, but he kept his hand balled into a fist.

Tom laughed. "It's apparently not uncommon for men who are… hanged… to get erections. Don't ask me why I know that. I read it somewhere."

"That's kind of fucked up," Kevin said, but he was still smiling. "I suppose I'm lucky I didn't take a dump while I was hanging there. I heard *that* can happen."

"I've heard that too."

"Now that would have been *completely* undignified."

"Oh, absolutely!"

It was a sick joke, but it cracked both of them up. And the fact that Tom was willing to laugh along with him about the whole fucked-up mess, both of them snickering like high school kids or younger, seemed to put Kevin more at ease.

"Can you remember anything else?" Tom asked when they'd settled down.

Kevin leaned back into his chair and seemed to give the matter serious thought for the first time since the session began. "I couldn't breathe."

Tom was tempted to rib him further—"I've heard hanging can cause breathing trouble too"—but he sensed this was more than just a continuation of the joke. "Do you mean… *before* you tried to hang yourself?"

Kevin nodded. "I remember that's why I started drinking—because I couldn't breathe. I thought maybe I just needed to relax."

That seemed an odd reaction. Unless it was something he'd experienced before and this was how he handled it.

"Have you had that trouble breathing in other situations?"

"Now and then. But it's no big deal. I mean, I know they're just panic attacks."

Tom tried to remember if he'd come across any of this in the case notes. He didn't think so. The notes were on his desk, but he didn't want to interrupt Kevin to go read through them. "Were you diagnosed with panic attacks in the past?"

"I figured you knew that," Kevin said. "I was sent away when I was a kid."

"Away?"

"Hampstead Hospital. For a couple months."

Hampstead Hospital had excellent programs for children and teenagers, including inpatient treatments for depression, post-traumatic stress disorder, and a host of others, including psychotic disorders. "Those records wouldn't be part of your file at Androscoggin. Do you recall what you were being treated for at Hampstead?"

Kevin shrugged. "Like I said. Panic attacks."

"How old were you?"

"I don't remember. Thirteen, maybe?"

"What was happening at that time?"

Kevin had begun to fidget again, crossing his left leg onto his knee so he could wring his ankle with his hands. "Do I have to sit?"

"No. Go ahead—stand up; walk around a bit."

Kevin practically jumped out of the armchair. As he talked he circled the office, glancing at the books in the metal racks on the walls, at the water bubbler, at Tom's desk before stopping at the window that looked out onto the streets of Berlin. "My mother says I was pretty out of control. Fighting with kids at school, breaking things in the house—like dinner plates and... this stupid wooden boy taking a piss in the garden… shit like that. I was yelling at her and my father all the time and locking myself in my room. And I think I ran away once…."

"Your mother told you this? You don't remember it?"

"Not really. I mean, I remember kicking that pissing kid to pieces."

"Why did you do that?"

"I was sick of looking at his *ass*." Kevin grimaced and turned back to face Tom for a moment. "I mean, why do people think those damned things are cute? Why is it cute to have some little kid mooning you all the time?"

Tom had to laugh again. "I don't know. I think they're pretty tacky."

"No shit."

"Do you remember your time in Hampstead?"

"No," Kevin said thoughtfully as he watched the cars on the street two stories down. "I had to go in the summer, 'cause they didn't want me to miss school. I remember being pissed about that. They were afraid I'd run away, so I was never allowed out on the grounds without a nurse. I hated it."

"Anything else?"

"Nothing very clear."

This guy is just one big, giant defense mechanism, Tom thought. He'd counseled other patients who were reluctant to talk about themselves before, but Kevin was combining that with humor and a disarming frankness. Perhaps even a shocking frankness, not that Tom was particularly shocked. But he suspected that, if he were female, Kevin might even become flirtatious. All to direct attention away from what he didn't want to talk about—why he'd attempted suicide.

Forty-five minutes later, they'd covered topics ranging from Kevin's fairly average childhood, growing up in rural New Hampshire, to meeting his wife in the local diner where she was waitressing, to his job as a handyman. Kevin had no qualms about telling Tom about his sex life, including how often he masturbated ("I mean, is that normal, considering I'm married?"), even though Tom hadn't really asked. Nothing was sacred.

Except why he'd hung himself in that damned garage.

The session ended, and Tom had a sense they'd made a small amount of headway, perhaps, but nothing very significant. He liked Kevin, was charmed by him. If he were being honest, he was even somewhat attracted to him. But the man was an enigma. Was his memory really that fragmentary? Or did he simply say "I don't remember" whenever he didn't want to talk about something?

As they shook hands at the door, Kevin looked directly into Tom's eyes with those soft hazel eyes of his, his heavy lids disconcertingly like those of a man sated from sex, and smiled that shy little boy's smile. "You're a lot easier to talk to than Dr. What's-his-name at the hospital."

"I'm glad you were comfortable."

The handshake seemed to go on a little too long, Kevin's eyes holding Tom's until Tom began to wonder if he wasn't above flirting with a male psychologist, after all.

When Kevin finally released him, Tom asked, "Will I see you next week?"

"Sure," Kevin replied, but Tom knew he was lying. They went through the motions of finding a day in Tom's appointment calendar that worked with both of their schedules, Tom writing it in with a ballpoint pen. Then Kevin walked out of the office.

Tom wished he could have done more. He hoped Kevin was past the crisis that had led him to hang himself, but he couldn't be sure of that. All he knew for certain was that he would not see Kevin Derocher again.

Two

Three years later

THE house was perfect: two upper floors and a finished basement with a wraparound porch and a deck in the back, all sitting on eight acres of lawn and forest. It had electricity—Tom wasn't a complete Luddite—but there were no streetlights on the road. He'd be able to sit on the deck at night and look up to see nothing but the silhouettes of pine trees and the starry sky beyond. As Tom walked through with his real estate agent and took in the hardwood floors, the fireplace in the living room, the pellet stoves in the dining room and the basement, the washer and dryer, the hot tub on the deck—a friggin' *hot tub!*—and the current owners' poodle dressed in a ridiculous sweater with snowflakes on it, Tom knew he had to have it. Not the poodle—the owners were taking her with them, and anyway Tom was picturing a German shepherd or some other big dog he could rassle with. But he wanted the house. More than he'd ever wanted anything in his life.

Four months later, after some haggling on the price, it was his.

He moved in the day after closing, sleeping on a mat in the upstairs bedroom. He hadn't bothered to bring any furniture from his old apartment in Berlin. He wanted everything to fit in with the rustic, country look of the place. Maybe Shaker furniture. Or he could scavenge some furnishings from antique stores. Or maybe he'd just go around to local yard sales and see if any of the old farms in the area were selling off anything decent.

He'd paid a moving company to transport his packed belongings from Berlin to the house, and he took Friday off from work to oversee that. He found it amusing that the supposedly straight young men working for the company were so blatantly showing off their muscles for each other—and for him—as they stacked boxes onto each other's backs, three high, and cheerfully carried them up and down the stairs. Was it as sexual as it looked? Or perhaps, at thirty-five, Tom was already a dirty old man. He did his best not to ogle them, but it wasn't easy when they insisted on taking their shirts off.

That evening, he decided it would be nice to use the hot tub, but that proved to be more challenging than he'd expected. The previous owners had drained all the water out, which was probably for the best, so it would have to be refilled. But the inside of the tub had some kind of scum buildup that would have to be scrubbed off before Tom would feel comfortable letting his bare ass rest against it, and it had already been a long day. So instead, he sat on the deck as night settled in, drinking a couple beers and listening to the howling of coyotes in the forest.

On Saturday, he buckled down and scrubbed. His clothes were completely drenched by the time he'd made sure all the soap was out of the tub, but he just took them off and got a little thrill from puttering around his yard in the nude, knowing there were no neighbors to see.

He filled the tub with water again and spent some time figuring out the right balance of chlorine and other chemicals. Then he flicked the power switch on the wall to turn the water pumps on.

Nothing.

He flicked it off and on again.

Still nothing. Well, not entirely nothing. Tom heard a faint humming sound coming from underneath the hot tub. But that was it.

The hot tub was dead.

"THE water pump is burnt out."

It had taken a week to find somebody local who serviced hot tubs and another four days to get him out to the house. Now, the guy had the side of the hot tub opened up and half the pieces on the deck, and he was shaking his head as if the whole thing was hopeless.

"It was running when I looked at the house, four months ago," Tom said, as if that would somehow make it not broken now.

"I'd guess somebody flicked the switch on when it didn't have water in it," the man observed. "Then they left it on."

That could have happened at any time since the thing was drained. It was possible Tom had done it himself when he was going through the house, opening doors, checking locks, switching things on and off. "Okay," he said, "how much will it cost to replace it?"

"The pump? Maybe a couple hundred. Maybe less. But look at this." The repairman indicated the mess of wiring and duct-taped tubes underneath the tub. There was even a standard power strip—one that couldn't possibly be rated for the voltage and current the hot tub demanded—with something plugged into it. And the cement underneath was damp. "None of that's up to code. If anyone found out I repaired something that badly cobbled together, I could lose my insurance."

"Can't we get replacement parts?" Tom asked, tugging at his beard and struggling to keep the dismay out of his voice. "And then put it together right?"

The repairman shook his head. "They don't make this model anymore. You'd have to look around for used parts, and that's not really something I do. I'd recommend just buying a new one."

But Tom wasn't interested in spending several thousand dollars to replace something he'd never really had to begin with. A hot tub would have been wonderful, but it wasn't really necessary. It just pissed him off that he'd *thought* he was getting one with the house.

The repairman seemed to sense that Tom wasn't interested in replacing the old hot tub, so he dug his wallet out of his back pocket and fumbled through it until he came up with a business card. He extended it to Tom. "Look, if you really want to get this up and running—safely—I have a friend who does general handyman work for a living. He isn't certified for servicing hot tubs, specifically, but he's good with plumbing and electrical. And he won't screw you over."

Tom took the card and puzzled for a moment over why the name on it seemed so familiar. Then it hit him: he'd seen the man as a client once, years ago, after a suicide attempt.

Kevin Derocher.

TOM debated whether he should call Kevin, feeling he might be violating the professional relationship between a therapist and his client. But Kevin had seen him only once, three years ago. And it was just to get the goddamned hot tub fixed. So he gave in and dialed the number.

If Kevin recognized Tom's name, he gave no sign. He was busy for the next week, but agreed to come out the weekend after. So it was just under two weeks later, on a Saturday morning in early June, that a beat-up black pickup truck with a covered truck bed and the words Derocher Repairs stenciled on the sides pulled into Tom's long, winding driveway, and Kevin Derocher stepped out of the cab.

He hadn't changed much. Still lean, his chocolate-brown hair still unruly, as if he'd just gotten out of bed, and his face still looking like he could use a shave. He was wearing faded jeans and a plain white T-shirt. As he started to climb the front steps to the porch, Kevin caught sight of Tom coming out of the house and stopped dead.

"I remember you," he announced, flashing the cute, shy smile Tom remembered. "I was wondering why your voice sounded familiar."

Tom came forward and shook his hand, grinning. "You didn't recognize my name?"

"I never remember names. But I kind of remembered your voice—all soothing and shit."

Tom laughed at the ribbing. "How have you been, Kevin?"

"Okay." Kevin glanced away and ran his hands through his tousled hair, suddenly looking uncomfortable. "I mean, things are different. Tracy divorced me, after she miscarried the baby."

"I'm very sorry."

"Probably for the best," Kevin said with a shrug. "I wasn't much of a husband. Probably wouldn't have been much of a dad either."

The temptation to psychoanalyze that statement was strong, but Tom resisted it. "Why don't I show you the hot tub?"

He took Kevin around the porch to the back deck and showed him the disaster. Kevin crouched down and practically crawled inside the damned thing, which caused Tom to fret about the spit-and-glue electrical connections under there. If Tom had known he was going to do that, he would have run inside and pulled the breaker. But Kevin somehow managed not to fry himself. He stood up again, wiping his dirty hands on his jeans.

"That's all kinds of fucked up," he said.

"I've noticed."

"I'll make up a list of parts we need. You'll have to order the pump online—I'm not paying for it out of pocket. But I can get all the plumbing and electrical pieces."

"You think it can be fixed?" Tom asked hopefully.

"Anything can be fixed, man. As long as we can get the parts."

"And it won't be a watery, electrocution Tub of Doom?"

Kevin laughed. "Not unless you want it to be."

They went inside, and Kevin helped Tom find a replacement pump online. It ended up being just $125 plus shipping, and it could be there by the end of the next week. Tom felt his excitement at having a hot tub beginning to revive. The more rational part of his mind told him it was a silly extravagance, but the rest of him kept picturing himself steaming in the hot water, late at night, looking up at the stars.

While Tom entered his credit card information, Kevin wandered off a bit, drifting aimlessly around the living room. There wasn't much to look at since there was still no furniture and all Tom's books and other belongings were stacked in boxes throughout the house. The laptop itself was sitting in the middle of the room, and Tom had to sit cross-legged on the floor in front of it to use it.

"Nice place," Kevin commented.

"Would you like to take a tour?"

"Sure."

So Tom took him through the house. Even mostly empty, the large rooms and golden pinewood paneling on the walls felt comfortable, and Tom delighted in another excuse to show the place off. His coworker, Sue, had been the only person to come out and look at it, so far. He didn't have a ton of friends, and even his family wasn't inclined to fly out from New Mexico until he had a guest room set up. But Kevin seemed properly appreciative, whistling often in admiration as they went from room to room, down and up the cool spiral staircase that led to the basement, checking out the Jacuzzi tub in the upstairs bathroom, talking about which of the upstairs bedrooms would be the guest room and which one Tom intended to turn into a library.

When they were in the master bedroom, where Tom had his sleeping bag laid out on a mat used for camping, with nothing more than a lamp near the bed and a pile of books, Kevin asked, "You're going to live here by yourself?"

Tom shrugged and prepared to do the gender dance if necessary, avoiding the pronouns "he" or "she" if he was forced to talk about relationships. It had been a tedious necessity since he'd become a professional therapist. "Yeah. It's just me."

But Kevin spared him the dance, simply grinning and saying, "That's the way to do it. You can call me a dick, if you want, but I don't really miss my ex all that much. Not that I hate her or anything. But I guess I'm not cut out to live with someone else."

"I'm not going to call you a dick," Tom replied with a smile. "Some people just like a lot of time to themselves."

"Is that why you moved all the way out to East Bumfuck?"

"I can't stand living in Berlin." Tom had grown up there, and in his childhood, the paper mill had blanketed the small city with smoke that reeked of chemicals and rotten eggs. There was no escaping it. The mill had shut down in 1994, which had been financially devastating to the area, but supposedly the air and the Androscoggin River that ran through the center of the city were cleaner. It still reeked of rotten eggs to Tom, and it always would.

Kevin stepped over to the window, where he could look out upon the long driveway. "Don't get me wrong. Tracy is a good woman, and I hope she's happy. She's seeing the owner of the diner she works at now. Hell, she was seeing him even before we divorced."

Tom cringed inwardly. So many men slandered their ex-wives with accusations of infidelity, it was a cliché—one he found repulsive. But what he said was, "You think she cheated on you, but you still call her a 'good woman'?"

Kevin turned back to face him, smiling a little wistfully. "Things weren't good between us. I can't blame her for finding someone else. I knew what was going on with her and Lee, and she knew that I knew. It just didn't matter by that point."

This was beginning to feel like a therapy session, and Tom wasn't comfortable with that. He found Kevin interesting as well as cute. Maybe if they became friends, it would be appropriate to have conversations like this. But for now, the guy was supposed be fixing his hot tub, not unloading on him.

Fortunately, Kevin realized he'd crossed a line and quickly backpedaled. "Sorry, you don't want to hear all this shit."

"It's fine," Tom lied.

"I've got to get going. Thanks for showing me around."

Once again, as they shook hands, Tom felt as though the contact went on just a few seconds too long, and those soft, bedroom eyes seemed to be peering deeply into his eyes. Perhaps that was the way Kevin always shook hands.

"My pleasure," Tom said.

"I'm busy next Saturday, but I can come over Sunday, if you have the pump by then."

"That would be great."

Three

THE water pump arrived by UPS the following Thursday. Tom came home from work and found it sitting on his front porch. Fortunately, the only likely thieves in the area were a flock of wild turkeys that sauntered across his driveway as he was pulling in.

Replacing the pump and fixing all of the duct-taped PVC pipes and dubious wiring took nearly all day on Sunday. Tom did none of it, of course, but he hovered nearby in case Kevin needed help with anything—he didn't—and to keep the man company. It was a hot day, and a beer would have been nice. But Tom wasn't rude enough to sit there drinking a Smuttynose without offering one to Kevin, and he didn't know if Kevin drinking while working on electrical wiring would be a good idea. So he mixed up some artificial lemonade from powder and brought that out in iced glasses, feeling like a ridiculous parody of Donna Reed.

But Kevin seemed to appreciate it. Or at least he appreciated the gesture. "This kind of tastes like battery acid," he commented after a swig. He screwed his face up at the sour taste, but he was smiling. Tom was beginning to learn that Kevin enjoyed ribbing people.

"Yeah, it does," Tom admitted. "I'm afraid I don't have much in the house yet. The only thing in the fridge, apart from water, is milk and beer."

"I don't drink while I'm working. This is fine."

He chugged the rest of it, sweat dripping off his hair like an actor in a Gatorade commercial. Tom couldn't help but steal a glance at him, while Kevin's eyes were closed. The man was grubby and dripping with sweat and extremely sexy. More, he seemed unaware of his sex appeal. Or perhaps he just didn't care, unlike the guys Tom knew at the gay men's group in Berlin, who seemed to think of nothing *but* their appearance.

Tom couldn't spend too much time leering at him, or Kevin would eventually notice. So he took his glass of lemonade and sat down in one of the deck chairs.

"Thanks," Kevin said as he set the glass down on the arm of another deck chair.

"No problem."

Kevin returned to his work, and Tom sipped his own lemonade—if you could call it that—slowly. After a few minutes of trying hard not to be caught staring at Kevin's legs—runner's legs, jutting out from jean cutoffs, lean and muscular and dusted with fine brown hair—Tom got up and went into the house to retrieve a book. He found one of his old favorites, *Ordinary People* by Judith Guest, and settled back into his deck chair to read, feeling a bit like a wealthy asshole, kicking back while "the help" went about its business. But he knew he'd just get in Kevin's way if he tried to assist him.

After another hour or so, Kevin announced, "Well, it's almost done. But I'm starving."

Tom thought about his empty kitchen and offered, "Well, I've got some frozen burritos and Hot Pockets. I think I've got the stuff for peanut butter and jelly sandwiches...."

"You're in the country, man," Kevin chided him. "You need a gas grill out here on your deck."

The idea was appealing. "How much would that set me back?"

"Depends on what you get," Kevin said, taking his shirt off and wiping the sweat off his face with it. His chest and stomach muscles were nicely defined and lightly covered with the same fine brown hair as his legs. A darkening trail led down from his belly button into the top of his shorts, which hung low on his hips. Tom's mouth suddenly went dry, and he tried to take a sip of his lemonade, only to find the glass empty.

Kevin tucked his shirt into the front of his shorts, which only served to pull the waistband away from his taut stomach and reveal a bit more hair traveling downward... and a conspicuous absence of underwear. "A good one might go for five hundred or a little more."

"Where can I get one?"

"I'll tell you what. Why don't we take a break and drive into town? There's a good diner we can grab lunch at. Then I can take you to the hardware store, if you have time, and you can look at what they've got."

The boundary between "contractor" and "friend" was beginning to blur, but Tom couldn't say he minded. He liked Kevin, and if the man was interested in hanging out with him a bit, that wasn't a bad thing. Provided he wasn't a gay-basher or something. Eventually, Tom's orientation would have to come out in the open if they became friends—even just casual friends. Being gay wasn't something Tom felt the need to announce to everybody he hired to fix things around the house, but he refused to be closeted in his own home.

THE town of Stark had a very quaint bed-and-breakfast called the Stark Village Inn, located near the covered bridge that crossed the Ammonoosuc River. Together with the Stark Union Church on the other side of the bridge, it presented a very picturesque scene, but one noticeably devoid of anything resembling a diner. It turned out that by "town," Kevin had actually meant Groveton, which was less than ten miles down the road from Stark. There was a place Kevin frequented called Lee's, a small, typical New England diner with cheap prices and enormous servings. He insisted on driving since Tom had no idea where to go.

"I should warn you," Kevin said as he parked his truck directly under the unlit neon sign of the diner and pulled the emergency brake, "Tracy works here."

Tom laughed. "She's your ex, not mine."

"It's cool. We can run into each other in public without getting into a fistfight or anything like that."

The inside of the diner was bright and clean, and Tom warmed to it immediately. Hopefully the food was good because he suspected he'd be eating here a lot. Kevin led him to a booth near one of the front windows, and almost before they'd sat down, he gave Tom a conspiratorial smile and said under his breath, "Here she comes."

Tracy was a lovely woman, with reddish-blonde hair, cheerful blue eyes, and a nice smile. She also had a figure a girl ten years her junior would have been proud of. Tom could certainly see why a straight guy would be drawn to her. She came over to the table as soon as she'd caught sight of Kevin and greeted him. "Hey, sweetie. Who's your friend?"

The smile she turned on Tom was flirtatious enough to make him uncomfortable, especially with Kevin watching, but Kevin didn't seem to mind.

"Tracy, this is Tom Langois," he said. "He just moved into a house in Stark, and he hired me to fix some stuff."

"Well, you did good there," Tracy told Tom. "Kevin can fix anything."

There appeared to still be some affection between the two of them, and Tom was glad of it. Warring exes were tedious. Tracy left a couple of menus and said she'd be back in a minute with some glasses of water. But before she wandered off, she asked Kevin, "Can I have a word with you in private?"

Kevin excused himself and went off to talk to her, while Tom did his best to keep his curiosity in check by skimming through the menu. It was all pretty typical New England diner food—burgers; all-day breakfasts with three-egg omelets, pancakes, and plenty of bacon; steak tips; steak dinners; biscuits and gravy; chicken-fried steak with gravy; pork chops and gravy; basically, anything that could be covered with gravy, cheese, butter, or all three. Not a place to hang out if you were watching your weight or your blood pressure. In fact, some of those things, like biscuits and gravy and chicken-fried steak with gravy, weren't traditionally from New England, but the locals had enthusiastically adopted them because they fit the theme.

Kevin came back alone, and he looked a little agitated, but he didn't offer an explanation, and Tom wasn't going to press him for one. He just pretended to be fascinated with the menu for a couple more minutes until Tracy returned to take their order. Kevin hadn't even bothered to look at the menu; he just said, "Same thing I always get," and Tracy wrote something down on her pad. Tom ordered the steak tips and fries.

When they were alone, Kevin said quietly, "She's pregnant again."

It didn't sound as if he was happy about it, but Tom couldn't just sit there staring blankly at him. He tugged at his beard a moment and then simply said, "Ah."

Kevin was silent for a long time before he seemed to rouse himself. He took a deep breath and let it out slowly. Then he made an attempt at smiling that wasn't entirely successful. "That's good. I'm happy for her. For both of them."

He picked up the saltshaker and fiddled with it, but Tom noticed his hand was trembling, almost imperceptibly. Tom resisted the completely inappropriate urge to reach out and place his hand over Kevin's. He was more convinced than he'd been a week ago that Kevin had wanted to have a baby. Perhaps he'd been conflicted about it, but part of him was still grieving over the loss.

When Tracy brought their food over—it turned out what Kevin always got was a cheeseburger and fries with a chocolate milkshake—they ate in silence. The steak tips were good and plentiful, if a bit on the salty side, and the "fries" were real sliced potato wedges instead of cheap frozen fries. Tom had no doubt he'd be back.

Kevin's brooding continued through the entire meal and paying for it, so Tom was expecting they'd simply head back to his house rather than shop around for grills. He wasn't even sure Kevin would stick around to finish the hot tub that afternoon. But Kevin drove him to a local hardware store, as he'd promised, and once inside, he seemed to shake the dark mood he'd slipped into.

"You don't want any of these two- or three-hundred-dollar jobbies," Kevin said, waving a hand at some of the low-end grills dismissively. "The igniters will die on you after the first year, and the whole mess will fall apart a year after that."

He led Tom over to some of the more middle-range grills. These were a far cry from the simple charcoal grills Tom remembered cooking burgers and hot dogs on when he was a kid. These things were big stainless steel monsters with four long propane burners and automatic ignition switches.

"Do I really need something this big?" Tom asked.

"Well, I don't know, Tom. I haven't seen how big it is. But I thought we were talking about grills."

Tom rolled his eyes at him, and Kevin flashed him a grin.

"Do you have a grill like this?" Tom tried again.

"No, I can't afford shit. I just have a fucking hibachi on my porch. But this is what I'd get, if I could afford to get a nice grill."

In the end, Tom bought the grill. He wasn't sure why, but he trusted Kevin not to steer him wrong. Or maybe he was just developing a stupid crush on the guy. He'd have to watch that, before it got him into trouble.

But then again, he'd just spent almost seven-hundred dollars on a gas grill he wasn't sure he needed. Maybe he was *already* in trouble.

BY THE time they got back to the house, it was pretty late in the afternoon. Tom had half hoped Kevin would hang around a bit longer after finishing up on the hot tub, maybe have a beer. But either Kevin was still in a bad mood after learning about Tracy's pregnancy, or perhaps he just had a life. Once he'd finished the job and popped the side panel back into place on the hot tub, he told Tom, "That should do it. Just fill it up again, turn it on, and let the water heat up. You'll be all set."

Tom wrote him a check for his labor, and Kevin left. Standing alone on his back deck and listening to the truck pull out of his driveway, Tom felt ridiculously lonely, as though he hadn't spent the last ten years of his life living alone anyway.

The grill sat in two cardboard boxes on the deck, alongside a squat little propane tank, but he didn't feel motivated to assemble it. Instead, he took Kevin's advice and filled the hot tub. By the time it was full and the chemicals had been added, it was beginning to get dark. He stripped naked again and brought a book out onto the deck to read by the spotlight overhanging the deck, but he couldn't concentrate on it. All he could think about was Kevin shirtless and the fact that he clearly hadn't been wearing underwear under those cutoffs. It wasn't long before his dick started to demand attention, so he put the book down and turned the spotlight off. Then he stretched out in the deck chair and jerked off unhurriedly under the clear night sky.

When he was ready, he stood up and walked to the railing, so he could spew his seed out into the darkness. He couldn't remember exactly what was below the deck on that side, but hopefully it was just grass he was squirting onto.

Then he went to check the hot tub. The water was still ice cold.

Four

THE next morning, the water in the hot tub felt somewhat warmer, but only lukewarm. Was this normal? Did hot tubs always take this long to heat up? Tom was tempted to call Kevin, but it was pretty early. Tom had to get to work, anyway. Maybe it would be hot by tonight.

At lunchtime, Sue Cross offered to pick up takeout from Wang's Garden on Main Street, and the two of them ate in her office. Sue was several years older than Tom, though he'd certainly never asked her about her age. She was a no-nonsense woman who knew how to rock a business suit, and she'd put more than one belligerent, misogynist client in his place during her long career as a therapist. But she seemed to regard Tom as an opportunity to flex long-disused motherly instincts.

"You really shouldn't be seeing a guy you've treated," she cautioned as she doled out portions of pork fried rice onto two Styrofoam plates.

"I'm not 'seeing' him," Tom hedged. "He's straight. I just hired him."

She snorted. "How many straight men have you fallen for since I've met you?"

Too many, Tom knew. But that was beside the point. "I already know I have a long history of being an idiot. But I've never *dated* any of the straight guys I've had crushes on because they were—oddly enough—straight."

"It's not a healthy obsession."

"I'm not obsessed, and stop psychoanalyzing me," Tom snapped, fishing around in the paper bag the food came in to see if there were any chopsticks. There weren't. Just the short plastic forks he hated. "I don't fall for straight guys *because* they're straight. I just happen to like guys who are a little rough around the edges."

"Surely you're not saying all gay men are effeminate," Sue chastised, taking her seat and dragging her plate across the desk to bring it closer.

"Of course not. I've met a few men—a few *gay* men—I found attractive. But one was a total jerk, and I slept with the other three. It didn't work out."

Sue pursed her lips in an expression of mock prudishness. "You slept with all three of them?"

"Well, not at the same time."

"In any event," Sue said, "you shouldn't be *friends* with somebody you've treated either."

"I saw him once, three years ago. I think we're well past him thinking of me as an authority figure."

Sue merely raised her eyebrows skeptically since she was busy chewing.

"Besides," Tom added, "neither one of us sought the other out. Destiny just threw us together again."

He realized he'd unintentionally phrased it as if the situation was romantic, and he cringed. But fortunately Sue's cell phone rang, and she was too busy answering it to notice.

WHEN he got home from work, Tom checked the water temperature again on the hot tub. It was definitely warm now, but still not hot. He double-checked the time and decided it was early enough to call Kevin. And this was a legitimate reason, wasn't it? The hot tub might not be working properly.

Fortunately, Kevin didn't seem to mind getting a call. "I don't know," he said. "Sometimes they take a while to heat up, 'cause there's so much water in there. But maybe the heating element is going. Do you want me to swing by and take a look?"

"Sure. When?"

"Right now, if you're not busy."

That threw Tom for a loop. He hadn't expected an immediate response. "Um… I don't want to put you out.…"

"It's up to you," Kevin said cheerfully. "I'm just sitting around the house bored."

"Oh. Okay. Sure." Then, feeling like a total idiot, Tom asked, "Hey, have you had dinner yet?"

It was seven o'clock. Of course Kevin would have eaten. But he was surprised when Kevin answered, "No. You want to grill something?"

"Uh… yeah. We could do that."

"All right!" Kevin said enthusiastically. "Give me a half hour."

As soon as Tom hung up, he realized he didn't actually have anything in the house to grill.

HE DROVE to Groveton in a panic, hoping there would be something open where he could at least buy hot dogs. He drove around until he stumbled across the Groveton Village Store, which was still open, and there he managed to pick up some raw hamburger, cheese, buns, and ketchup. He also grabbed a couple six-packs of beer. Unfortunately, by the time he got back to his car, a half hour had gone by. It took another fifteen minutes to get home, and by then Kevin's truck was already in the driveway and Kevin was sitting on the porch steps.

Shit.

Kevin stood and grinned as Tom got out of his car and popped the trunk. "You didn't have any food in the house, did you, you dumb shit?"

"No," Tom confessed sheepishly, pulling several plastic grocery bags from the trunk. "And it gets worse."

Kevin approached the car and saw the two six-packs, so he lifted them out. "How?"

"I haven't put the grill together yet."

Kevin shook his head and slammed the trunk closed. "Jesus."

IT DIDN'T take long to put the grill together with Kevin helping. It took a little longer to stop feeling like an ass, but Kevin seemed to find the whole situation amusing. So after a couple of beers, Tom relaxed and settled into the pleasant, easy feeling of hanging out with another guy. It wasn't something he experienced often.

The burgers were delicious, but far better than that was simply sitting back in a deck chair, drinking beer, and talking about nothing much with Kevin. Tom wished the evening could go on forever.

At one point, Kevin roused himself from his chair and said, "Fuck. I haven't even looked at the hot tub yet."

Tom wasn't so sure he cared about that, at the moment, but he watched as Kevin lifted the cover and stuck his hand in the water.

"It's warm," Kevin commented.

"I know it's warm. It just doesn't seem *very* warm."

Tom dragged himself out of his stupor and joined Kevin at the tub. He stuck his hand in the water and swished it around. It did feel a bit warmer than he remembered. Not as hot as he would have liked, but certainly comfortably warm.

"It's an old tub," Kevin said. "Sometimes they can take a couple days to warm up completely. But I'd say it's warm enough to take a dip in. What do you say?"

This took Tom by surprise. It hadn't even occurred to him that Kevin would want to use the hot tub. "I don't have a swimsuit."

"Dude," Kevin said with a laugh, "you don't wear a swimsuit in a hot tub."

If Kevin hadn't been there, Tom would have had no problem stripping naked, but it bothered him to think about the two of them being naked in the tub together. Not so much because he couldn't control his erection—he hadn't had any trouble keeping things under control in gym showers since high school—but just because it felt dishonest. Kevin felt comfortable with the idea of getting naked in front of Tom because he was assuming Tom wouldn't be looking at him with any kind of sexual interest.

"Look," Tom said slowly, "this isn't something I would normally tell you until we were better friends…." He balked at going further, but Kevin was looking at him curiously now, expecting him to finish what he'd started. Tom took another swig of his beer. "I'm not… straight."

For just a moment, Kevin looked confused. Then he frowned and said, "Oh."

He walked away from the hot tub, leaving Tom to set the cover back down onto it. Kevin opened the last of the beers and went back to his deck chair before taking a long swallow. It was clear he was disturbed, though Tom couldn't tell if it was the kind of disturbed that would nip off their budding friendship.

"I didn't think it would be fair to let you undress in front of me until I'd told you that," Tom explained.

"Yeah. Thanks."

There didn't seem to be much to say after that. Tom went back to his chair, and they drank in silence for several minutes until Kevin stood up and announced, "I'd better go before I'm too tired to drive home."

"Are you safe to drive?"

"I'm fine, man. I'll see you."

"Okay."

Tom felt his spirits sinking as Kevin walked around to the front of the house and drove away. He hadn't really done anything wrong, he knew. But there were probably better ways of breaking the news to a new friend. Or maybe Kevin was just a homophobic asshole, and he would have bailed no matter what Tom did.

But Tom still felt as if he'd blown it.

Five

"I WARNED you."

"No," Tom replied with a long-suffering look, "you did not warn me that he'd freak out when I told him I was gay."

Sue waved a hand dismissively. "Not in those precise words. But I warned you about chasing after straight men."

"I wasn't chasing him. I had no delusions about him wanting to sleep with me." Tom couldn't deny he'd *wanted* Kevin to sleep with him, but he knew that was just a fantasy. A lot of men—gay and straight—fantasized about sleeping with attractive friends. It was harmless, as long as they knew it would never be more than a fantasy. "Certainly I didn't make a pass at him."

"No…," Sue said, but she sounded skeptical.

"You're not saying I should have just gotten naked with him, are you?"

Sue shook her head and absently brushed a stray tendril of her graying hair back into place behind her ear. "Absolutely not. You were right to be honest with him, before you found yourself in a more awkward position. I'm just saying you shouldn't be wasting this much energy fretting about a relationship that you know is never going to go anywhere."

"I'm not allowed to have a male friend who isn't gay?"

"Oh, Tom," Sue said in her best maternal tone, "you know you wouldn't be this upset if you weren't falling for the guy."

He frowned at her, but he couldn't think of a response because they both knew she was right.

TOM checked the hot tub again when he got home from work. It was definitely as hot as he expected a hot tub to be now. He considered taking the cover off and soaking for a while, but as soon as he thought about it, he remembered Kevin's sudden about-face the night before, and he no longer had any enthusiasm for the idea. Maybe later.

The grill was still covered in hamburger grease, so he spent some time cleaning it. But again, he couldn't muster up the desire to hang out on the deck by himself. It was ridiculous that Kevin's bad reaction was putting him in such a funk, but he couldn't help it. Tom tried reading for a bit, but he couldn't concentrate, and eventually he just went to bed early.

He had a weird dream about Kevin hanging out with him, drinking beer and laughing. Tom stripped naked and climbed into the hot tub. Then he watched, with growing arousal, as Kevin stripped down, too, revealing the lean beautiful body Tom had already seen most of, but with a substantial endowment that was perhaps a bit exaggerated, fully erect. Kevin climbed the steps to get into the hot tub as Tom's breathing grew heavy in anticipation.

Then, as Kevin dropped into the water, he suddenly jerked to a halt in midair. His body hung there, swinging slowly from side to side in a strange motion, his penis erect and twitching. Tom looked up and realized Kevin was hanging from a rafter that jutted out over the hot tub, dangling from a pair of blue jeans that were tied around the rafter and around his neck. His face was turning blue, and his eyes were bulging out as he made short gasping noises in his throat.

Tom awoke, drenched in sweat and terrified.

By Friday afternoon, Tom had grown tired of moping around his empty house in the evenings. He hadn't been motivated enough to unpack anything, and his aversion to the grill and the hot tub had become simply ridiculous. He decided to check out Lee's Diner again. It would get him out of the house, and he'd at least eat more than the junk food he'd been surviving on for "dinner" all week.

Of course, it was possible he could run into Kevin there. Tom wasn't sure if he was dreading that or secretly hoping for it. But he decided that, if Kevin's truck was in the parking lot, he could always keep going and find somewhere else to eat.

This was a lie, of course. Kevin's truck *did* turn out to be in the parking lot, and Tom pulled in anyway. It was hopeless. He might as well be seventeen again, pining for his friend, Jake—the one who called him a "faggot" and never spoke to him again. Tom had walked by his house night after night, running different scenarios on a loop in his mind, trying to figure out how he could patch things up and restore the easy, close friendship that had fooled him into thinking Jake would understand. It was agony, and the only thing that had put an end to his suffering was Jake's father calling his house to tell Tom's parents to keep their faggot son from stalking his boy before he called the police.

Kevin was sitting at the counter when Tom walked in. For a second, he seemed too distracted by the waitress—not Tracy, but an older woman with absurdly large breasts and too much eye makeup—to notice Tom walking by. But at the last second, he turned his head and fixed his eyes on Tom. The best Tom could think of was to nod and then hurry over to one of the booths. It looked like Kevin was on his way out, anyway. He'd probably just leave.

But he didn't. He went to the cash register at the end of the counter to pay his bill, and then he wandered across the diner until he was standing beside Tom's table. This close, Tom could smell him—an earthy scent of cut grass mixed with sweat, as if Kevin had spent his afternoon mowing somebody's lawn.

Tom couldn't look at him. "Uh… hey."

"Mind if I sit down?"

"I guess not."

Kevin slid into the booth opposite him, and Tom risked glancing up at his face. He was pleased to see that Kevin looked as uncomfortable as Tom felt.

Kevin cleared his throat and said, "I guess I was kind of a jerk, Monday night." He paused for Tom to respond, but Tom really didn't know what to say to that, so Kevin continued. "I mean, it must have been hard for you to tell me that...."

"No," Tom corrected him. "It was awkward, I'll admit. And the timing seemed bad. But I've come out a dozen times by now—to family, friends, coworkers. It wasn't fun, but it wasn't some big, epic moment either." It pissed him off that Kevin seemed to think it was more than it really was—Tom being honest with him because he thought it was considerate. Perhaps it was because the way Kevin said it made it sound as if *he* was something special, as if Kevin was so important in Tom's life that Tom had agonized over telling him. Tom was prepared to admit that he had a crush on the guy, but he wasn't prepared to elevate Kevin to the same level as a family member or a close friend.

Kevin looked at him, his expression pained. "Well... I guess it was me that felt it was epic, then."

Tom didn't want to feel sympathy for Kevin. It wasn't his fault Kevin felt uncomfortable. Kevin needed to get over it.

But Tom never would have become a psychologist if he couldn't empathize with others, even if they were sometimes on the wrong side of political correctness. Kevin *did* need to get over being uncomfortable, but it was useless to insist he *couldn't* be uncomfortable. People couldn't always control the way they felt about things, even if it wasn't appropriate.

The waitress came over to the table with a couple of glasses of water and set them down. "I thought you were leaving, sugar," she said to Kevin. "Did you want something else?"

"That's okay, Ellen. I'm fine."

Ellen took Tom's order (steak tips again—why mess with a good thing?) and left. Silence descended on the two of them until Tom couldn't stand it anymore.

"Look, Kevin, if this is some kind of apology—"

"It is!"

"All right, fine. I accept your apology."

There was a long moment after that, during which neither could think of anything to say. Tom had almost expected Kevin to say "Cool" and then get up and leave. But Kevin just sat there, staring at the tabletop. Tom felt something under the table and for a weird moment, he thought Kevin was deliberately rubbing against his leg. Then he realized Kevin was tapping his foot in agitation, and the brush of his jeans against Tom's leg was unintentional.

"You want to come over to my place?" Kevin asked abruptly. "This weekend, I mean? We could throw some burgers on the hibachi. I'll buy the beer this time."

Jesus. This was starting to feel surreal. Tom could almost see Jake again, sitting just like Kevin was now, at the truck stop near their high school. They'd had another argument, one more tedious fight, this one about Jake flirting with the girl at the 7-Eleven and Tom being jealous—except neither of them really understood what the fights were about. They both fooled themselves into thinking they were fighting about something stupid like Jake wanting money for a soda, when he hadn't paid Tom back for the last time. Jake needed him with the intensity teenagers often had for their friendships, and he'd always been the one to patch things up. Until the last time, when Tom had laid everything bare and there had been nothing left to patch.

Tom could see something in Kevin's eyes now, something like the raw need he used to see in Jake's eyes. He really wasn't sure he wanted to deal with it. But still, he found himself answering, "All right, if you're buying."

"Great! How's tomorrow afternoon?"

"Fine."

Kevin had his receipt pad in his back pocket, so he pulled it out and tore off a blank receipt. "This has my address on it. It's just about a few miles south of your place, along Northside Road. You'll see the truck parked out in front of the trailer."

And then he left, obviously not comfortable enough to stick around any longer. If they could barely look each other in the eye now, Tom reflected, Saturday would probably be a hoot.

Six

As Kevin had promised, his trailer wasn't hard to find. In addition to the truck in his driveway, he had a wooden sign on the lawn with Derocher Repairs and a phone number on it. The sign wasn't fancy, and Tom suspected Kevin had made it himself, but it was a fairly professional job, demonstrating woodworking skill, if not necessarily artistic talent.

The trailer itself had a wooden porch with screened-in windows attached to it, and there was a separate garage off to one side. The yard was overgrown with weeds—if Kevin had been mowing a lawn yesterday, it hadn't been here—and car parts and miscellaneous bits of metal machinery were scattered about the yard and spilling out of the garage.

Kevin came out from the garage as soon as he heard Tom's car pull in, and he was grinning like an idiot, perhaps because Tom hadn't snubbed him after all. As Tom got out of the car, carrying a six-pack of Smuttynose Shoals Pale Ale, Kevin shifted the spool of cable he was carrying from his right hand to his left.

"You didn't have to bring that," he said, waving the cabling at the six-pack. "I said I'd have beer."

"Well, maybe I won't like the shit you drink."

"You'll like it."

Tom looked pointedly at the cable Kevin was carrying. "Are you planning on tying me up?"

"Only if we get really drunk," Kevin replied cheerfully. Then he added, "I turn in scrap metal for cash over at the Recycling Transfer Station. You can make a decent amount if you're willing to scavenge around for it. This stuff"—he held up the yellow cable—"has a copper core. It was left over from a housing project in Groveton. I can get two-fifty to two-seventy-five a pound if I strip the insulation off."

While he was talking, he led the way into the garage and up to a workbench with some kind of mechanical device bolted onto it. To illustrate his point, Kevin fed the end of the cable into a hole in the device and turned a crank. The copper center of the cable came out the other end, while the yellow plastic peeled away and fell to the floor. There were several coils of yellow cable on the floor, awaiting this same treatment.

"How much does it take to make a pound?" Tom asked.

"With this grade, about twenty-five feet—with the insulation stripped off."

Tom realized he must be a bit of a snob because he knew he wouldn't be willing to go through that much effort for two dollars and some change. It didn't look like the whole pile would net Kevin more than twenty bucks. But he smiled politely and listened to Kevin prattle on about it. He allowed his gaze to drift over the other odds and ends in the garage; all the tools mounted on the walls were well kept despite the clutter. Inevitably, he found himself looking up at the rafters. One of those beams, he recalled, was the one Kevin had tied himself to three years ago....

"It's that one over there."

Tom came back to himself and realized Kevin was looking at him with an amused expression on his face. When Kevin caught Tom's eye, he nodded toward the front of the garage. "Don't pretend you're not curious. That rafter's like crack cocaine to you. I knew you'd have to take a look when I invited you over."

"Sorry."

"It's cool." Kevin put a hand on his shoulder and pushed him forward. "Come on, I'll show it to you."

The rafter was near the front of the garage, and now that they were close to it, Tom could see the faint spot where Kevin's pant leg had worn away at the wood for a short time, leaving a patch that was slightly less weathered.

"I backed the truck up to the garage door," Kevin said casually, "so I could lower the tailgate and stand on it. Then when I had my pants off, I tied myself up and jumped off. The crotch of the jeans started ripping open, but it held."

Tom had grown used to Kevin oversharing. He also remembered the way he'd been three years ago in the therapy session, casually tossing out disturbing details like that. Tom was convinced it was a form of misdirection—keep people too shocked to ask the right questions. Maybe even make them so uncomfortable that they'd back off.

But it didn't work on Tom. Not anymore.

"Tracy told you she was pregnant the night before," he commented, "and you took the first chance you got when she left you alone in the house to kill yourself—or try to. But you insist you didn't do it because she was pregnant."

Kevin's smile faded, and now he was the one who looked uncomfortable. "I wanted the baby. Maybe not as much as she did, but I wanted it."

"I believe you. But that was the trigger, regardless."

Kevin's expression had turned to stone, though Tom could see something deep in those hazel eyes, something fearful. Kevin quickly turned away. "Enough of this bullshit. I need a beer."

ONCE he had a beer in hand, Kevin seemed to relax again. He took Tom on a short tour of the trailer—a cookie-cutter affair with a large bedroom at the front, followed by a living room and a kitchen, then a short hall with a small bedroom and a bathroom off to one side, and another bedroom at the far end. Tom had lived in one that looked nearly identical to this when he was a kid. Even the linoleum and the fake wood paneling was the same. Now that Kevin was living in it by himself, he'd spread his clutter into every room. The small bedroom in the hall was packed full of miscellaneous junk, and the bedroom at the far end had been turned into some kind of electronics workroom, full of old radios and TV sets and electronic toys that Kevin seemed to be fixing or soldering together into Frankenstein creations.

The back door of the trailer, coming off the hallway, opened out into a backyard, but it was so overgrown that small birch trees had taken root here and there among the high grass, and it probably wouldn't be long before the woods reclaimed it.

The hibachi was on the front porch, where Kevin also had a couple of folding lawn chairs. Tom settled into one while Kevin busied himself cooking the burgers. They'd been chatting about the trailer and Kevin's work and where Tracy was living now—at her mother's—during this entire time, but as Kevin settled himself into the other lawn chair, freshly opened beer in hand, he asked one of the questions Tom had been anticipating since he arrived: "So when did you first know you were gay?"

It was part of the song and dance Tom went through with nearly every straight man who found out he was gay—the curious prodding about things that were really none of their business, always the same questions, always the same answers. He'd grown used to it, and he didn't really mind—not even when the questions were offensive ("Do you have AIDS?") or far too personal ("Doesn't it hurt when some guy fucks you up the ass?").

"I've always known I was gay. Even before puberty, I had a crush on my best friend—a boy."

"So you never kissed a girl, then?"

"I was dared to kiss a girl in fourth grade. But not since then. And please don't ask me how I can possibly know I wouldn't like it. It will spare us both from me challenging you to kiss a man."

Kevin smiled at that and took another swig of beer. "So what am I allowed to ask about?"

"If we're going to be friends," Tom said, jabbing at him with the tip of his beer bottle, "you'll have to get used to treating me like a regular guy, not a sexual circus freak."

"Am I treating you like a freak?"

"I'm just saying if you want to ask me about being gay, go ahead and get it out of your system now. Anything you want to know: favorite position, penis size, do I swallow? But after today, I don't want to hear it."

"Penis size?"

"Six and a half inches."

Kevin laughed. "Dude, I beat you by a half inch."

"Good to know." Not quite as large as it had been in Tom's dream, but nice. And the less Tom was reminded of that dream, the better.

Kevin emptied his bottle and then sat there for a minute, blowing across the opening, trying to make it whistle. Once he managed a single, mournful note, he stopped and said, "I guess I don't really need to know any of that shit."

"My turn to ask you questions, then."

"No more psychoanalyzing."

"Fair enough. Did you grow up here?"

"Yeah." Kevin shifted in his chair and used the tip of his empty bottle to point up the road. "My parents had a house down that way until my mother went into a home."

"Your father has already passed away, I take it?"

Kevin gave Tom an odd sideways glance. "Oh, he didn't just 'pass away'. He was too *important* to leave quietly." His voice was dripping with sarcasm. "He offed himself when I was thirteen, just after I was sent to Hampstead. Something for you to chew on, counselor."

It was. But Tom gave him a wry smile and responded, "You made me promise not to psychoanalyze."

"You'll do it anyway. I just don't want to hear about it while we're trying to relax and shoot the shit."

"Is your mom still around?"

"Yeah. She's over at Riverview."

Riverview was an assisted living community a little down the road from Groveton, toward Lancaster. Tom had dated one of the nursing staff over there a few years ago. The gay community in the area was *small*.

"What about you?" Kevin asked, getting up to go poke at the burgers.

"Me? I grew up in Berlin, but my parents hated it as much as I did—still do. They're living out in New Mexico now. My older sister moved out there to be near them."

Kevin grunted—some kind of acknowledgement, perhaps—as he pulled one of the burgers off the hibachi and placed it on a bun. "I don't have any sisters or brothers. Probably for the best."

"You keep saying that," Tom pointed out.

Kevin snapped back, "Stop analyzing me, dickhead."

He didn't really sound angry. The insult was just more of Kevin's ribbing, so Tom didn't mind, but he took the not-so-subtle hint. He'd ruined friendships in the past by overanalyzing everything people did. There was no point in sabotaging this friendship before it even got off the ground.

TOM stayed there until after sunset, basking in the comfortable chat and good-natured teasing he'd come to expect from Kevin. Admittedly, he wasn't as comfortable surrounded by the clutter and debris of Kevin's lair as he would have been at his own house. The bathroom was particularly bad and could probably be classified as a biohazard. He'd been forced to venture in there once during the afternoon, and he felt emotionally scarred from the experience. Fortunately, the rest of his "business" for the day could be conducted standing in the bushes behind the garage. His host didn't seem to have a problem with that since that's what he did himself.

It was after he'd come back from the bushes a third or fourth time and leaned across Kevin to get another beer—they'd switched to Kevin's favorite brand, a local Vermont brew called Magic Hat #9— that Kevin said, "Hold up."

He reached up with both hands and placed one on the side of Tom's neck, while he picked something off Tom's collar with his other hand. The heat from Kevin's hand against Tom's bare skin and the gentle way his rough fingers cradled his neck caused Tom to freeze for a moment. He knew he had to be misinterpreting it, but he couldn't think clearly enough to figure out what else Kevin could be doing besides making a pass. Then Kevin released him and held up something brown and wriggling, pinched between his thumb and forefinger.

"Tick," he said.

Tom shuddered and stepped back so Kevin could get up and toss it into the hibachi. "Lovely."

"Welcome to the country. You planning on getting pets?"

"A dog."

"I can see you with a dog," Kevin said, smiling in a way Tom knew meant he was about to get jabbed. "A little yip thing with painted nails and a pink ribbon."

Tom opened his beer and flopped back into his chair, realizing he was pretty far gone already. "No, asshole. A big dog like a German shepherd or a Labrador. Not one that drools a lot," he amended.

"Well, you can expect ticks, then. And fleas."

"I can't remember what it's called, but there's stuff you can rub into their fur to kill all that."

"When are you going to get some furniture?"

"Jesus. It's not like I have to do this all at once, you know."

"You've been living there for weeks, and you don't even have a goddamned bed! I know a guy who sells antiques. I could get you a deal."

Tom leaned back and closed his eyes, his beer wedged in his crotch, cool against the underside of his balls, even through layers of denim and cotton. Now that the night had settled in, peepers were busy having noisy sex somewhere nearby, and mosquitos were setting off the bug zapper by the garage door. "Sure. When do you want to go?"

"He's open tomorrow, if you want."

"Okay." He really could use a bed. And maybe a few chairs. A table too.

How much beer had he had? He was no longer certain. He just knew he was floating, and he didn't want to get out of this chair for a very long time. Possibly never. Kevin let him sit quietly for a while until Tom became aware someone was snoring. He couldn't be certain, but he thought it might be himself.

"All right, counselor," Kevin said, sounding far, far away. "You're staying here tonight."

Tom was too fuzzy now to resist as Kevin put his arms around him to lift him up out of his chair. He drew one of Tom's arms around his shoulders to half lead, half drag him into the trailer. The heat of his body against Tom's felt good, but being vertical didn't—it just made everything spin. He worried for a moment that he was going to be dumped on the couch in the living room, where he'd seen Kevin's dirty laundry piled earlier, before he felt himself being lowered into a sitting position on what felt like a mattress.

He opened one eye to see Kevin kneeling and pulling one of Tom's sneakers off.

"Do you think you're gonna puke?" Kevin asked him.

"No, I just wanna lie here." He watched Kevin finish pulling his other sneaker off, wondering just how far he would go. Apparently the answer was "Not very far." Kevin laid him back onto the bed fully clothed and wedged a pillow under his head. Then he went back out onto the porch for several minutes, while Tom lay there, pissed off that the light was still on but too drunk to get up and turn it off.

Eventually, Kevin came back into the room. Tom's eyes were closed as he began to drift off, so he didn't see what Kevin was doing, but the light went off after a couple minutes, and he felt Kevin climb into the bed and under the covers. Tom was still lying on top of the blankets, but he was warm enough in his clothes, so he drifted off to sleep.

He woke later in the night, cold. Kevin was sound asleep, breathing slowly and evenly, so Tom fumbled around until he was underneath the top blanket. Then he fell asleep again.

THE first thing Tom was conscious of in the morning, besides the hateful sunlight coming in through a gap in the curtains, was the smell of dirty socks and stale charcoal smoke. The smoke smell, he quickly discovered, was coming from his own clothing. Unfortunately, the dirty sock smell was coming from everywhere else—the room seemed permeated with it.

He turned his head and found Kevin sleeping beside him. Tom was surprised by this, but though the exact sequence of events last night was a little fuzzy, he vaguely remembered Kevin putting him to bed and crawling into the bed with him. The fact that Tom was fully dressed told him nothing more exciting than that had happened, although he was curious what exactly Kevin had worn to bed. His shoulders were bare and so was one leg, jutting out from under the blanket. Did he sleep nude? Probably not, but it was nice to contemplate.

Tom slipped out of the bed as quietly as possible and went outside to take a leak. By the time he got back, Kevin was awake and sitting up.

"Hey," Kevin said sleepily. "I thought you'd taken off."

"Not yet. But I should head home. I need a shower and a change of clothes." Thank God he really did need a change of clothes, since his reeked of sweat and smoke. Otherwise, Kevin might offer to let him shower in that terrifying bathroom of his.

Kevin got up out of the bed, and Tom was disappointed—though hardly surprised—to discover he was wearing underwear. Even so, Kevin in tighty-whities was fucking hot. Tom had seen most of his body already, but not quite this much. And Kevin had a morning erection he didn't seem worried about hiding. Tom had to force himself to look up into the man's face.

"Did you still want to look at Mike's antiques this afternoon?" Kevin's sleepy "bedroom" eyes were, in fact, really sleepy bedroom eyes this morning, and Tom had a nearly overwhelming desire to kiss each of those heavy eyelids.

"Yeah, sure," he said, swallowing to moisten his dry throat.

"I'll stop by in a few hours to pick you up."

Seven

"HE PUT you in his *bed*?" Sue asked incredulously.

She was speaking on the other end of Tom's cell phone, but he could picture her shocked expression in his mind.

"It's not just me, then?" Tom asked. "It's weird?"

"That's hardly a professional assessment." Sue's voice was now tinged with humor. Tom could tell he'd be in for some teasing about this situation come Monday. "Considering the fact that he's straight and you barely know him, I would say it's... atypical. It's not like I've never heard of two straight men sharing a bed in a nonsexual context. You were both intoxicated and you claim there was no place else to sleep."

"No, the place was filthy. There wasn't even a chair inside that didn't have crap piled on it."

"I would say that he's either just a nice guy willing to put up with an awkward situation to keep you from driving home in that condition, or perhaps he's overcompensating a bit."

"Overcompensating? For what?" The first thing that popped into Tom's mind was "seven inches." But that was slightly above average.

"For being a homophobic ass on Monday," Sue said, her tone suggesting that he was being dense, which he probably was.

"Oh. I suppose he might be trying to prove how open-minded he can be."

Tom heard something outside and pulled his bedroom curtain aside to see Kevin's truck pulling into the driveway. *Shit*. Tom had showered a couple hours ago, but he hadn't dressed yet. He was getting into the habit of not wearing clothes in the house or around the backyard. Apparently, living in isolation was bringing out the nudist in him.

"Be careful, Tom. He might push it farther than he's really comfortable with, and then things could get ugly."

Tom had a hard time imagining Kevin getting "ugly," if by that Sue meant "violent." On the other hand, it was also hard to imagine Kevin hanging himself.

"I've got to go. He just pulled into the driveway."

"Christ, do you spend *any* time apart from him when you're not in the office?"

"I'll see you on Monday." Then Tom hung up.

IT DID feel rather… domestic, Tom had to admit, shopping for furniture with Kevin. Like they were a couple moving into their first home together. Kevin didn't just stand back and let Tom pick out what he liked. He acted as if it would be his furniture too and had to try out every chair and poke through all the dresser drawers. When Mike, the owner of the shop, led them to a beautiful old brass bed, Kevin immediately crawled onto it and stretched out full-length on the mattress.

"I don't know," he said. "It's kind of lumpy."

"Are you planning on sleeping in my bed very often?" Tom asked.

Kevin had the good grace to blush a little, but he was still grinning, which made him look all the more adorable.

His friend, Mike Davis, was an older man who still wore suspenders, like Tom's grandfather had, making Tom wonder just how old the cutoff for suspenders was. Seventy? Sixty-five? Sixty? Certainly, nobody under fifty wore them anymore. But Mike was charming, peering through round spectacles as they wove through stacks of bric-a-brac that threatened to topple down upon their heads. The antique shop was an enormous old barn, and it still had the original horse stalls and traces of hay embedded in the uneven wooden floor.

"You can get a new mattress," Mike pointed out to Kevin, as if he and Tom were shopping for a bed *together*, which Tom found both amusing and annoying. Also a little strange, since Mike should have known Kevin wasn't gay. "Sometimes these old ones have bedbugs or fleas in them."

"Especially with him rolling all over it," Tom said dryly. "Look, he's not the one looking to buy it. But yes, of course I'd buy a new mattress."

Tom shooed Kevin off the bed and leaned against the corners of it to see how stable the frame was. Rock solid. And the brass was in perfect condition. "I do like it," he admitted. "Do you deliver?"

Mike shook his head, but Kevin said, "We can fit it in the back of my truck, if we take it apart."

So that's what they did. It took a good twenty minutes or more to take the frame apart since it obviously hadn't been disassembled in years—perhaps not since the bed was first purchased by some family back in the early 1900s. Then they loaded it into the back of Kevin's truck, along with a kitchen table and a few kitchen chairs. Kevin had removed the covering over the flatbed before he picked Tom up, but even so, Tom was amazed they managed to fit everything in there.

When they got to his house, Kevin helped him assemble the bed, but of course without a mattress, it was nearly useless.

"Do you have any idea where I can get a mattress around here?" Tom asked.

Kevin finished tightening a massive screw and straightened up, mopping sweat from his brow with the back of his sleeve. "Not a clue. I've never bought one."

"What about that bed at your trailer?" Tom almost added, "that we slept in," but he thought better of it.

"Tracy's uncle brought that over for us."

Tom nodded. "I guess I'll go online and see what I can find. There's got to be something in Berlin." Not that Berlin was all that big a city, with just over ten thousand people. But a mattress store shouldn't be impossible to locate.

"Yeah." Kevin seemed to be debating something for a few moments before he finally said, "Guess I should get going. I've got to finish stripping those wires before Monday, and this guy down the road wanted me to do some yard work tomorrow."

Tom sensed he was reluctant to leave, and Tom didn't want him to go. But it would probably do him some good to have a couple of days or more away from Kevin. He was starting to feel too close to the man—closer than he should feel for a friend. He kept remembering what it had been like to wake up beside Kevin.

"Okay. Thanks for helping me find some furniture. If you want to hang out sometime soon, just give me a call."

"Yeah. If you find a mattress or any more furniture during the week and you need someone to haul it, you've got my number."

THAT evening, Tom decided it was silly to keep avoiding using the hot tub just because he was by himself. So he stripped down, removed the hot tub cover, and climbed in. It felt amazingly good. Muscles he didn't even realize were aching suddenly began to uncoil. He spent a little while playing with the settings on the console, turning on different water jets, and illuminating the underside of his ass and dick with an eerie blue light. When he finally found a setting he liked, he leaned back and closed his eyes, relaxing into it and wishing Kevin were there, naked in the water with him.

MONDAY was an uneventful day, apart from lunch with Sue, who kept lecturing him about letting his "infatuation" with Kevin get out of control. He nodded politely but mostly ignored her. That evening, he puttered around the house, having no idea what to do with himself. Arranging the table and chairs in the kitchen took all of five minutes, and finding the right spot for the bed upstairs took about the same. When he'd been in front of his computer in the office, Tom had looked online for mattress stores and found a couple. But oddly enough he didn't see anything in Berlin. The nearest one was in Littleton, about a half hour away, and he wasn't particularly motivated to go check it out.

What he did finally do was head over to Lee's Diner for dinner. He knew he was hoping he might run into Kevin there, though he hated to admit he was really that pathetic. But the black truck wasn't in the parking lot when he pulled in.

Tracy was there, though. In fact, she seemed oddly happy to see him.

"Hi, hon!" she bubbled at him when she brought the menu over to the table. "You're Kev's new friend, aren't you?"

"I guess so."

She leaned in confidentially and spoke in a low voice. "It's nice to see that he *has* a friend. He's such a loner." She seemed to realize this could be interpreted badly, so she quickly added, "Not that he's like a Unabomber or anything! He just spends too much time by himself. It's good to see someone drag him out of his shell a little."

If Tom hadn't already decided he liked Kevin—maybe a bit too much—this "recommendation" might have had him running for the hills. But he smiled and said, "He seems like a good guy."

Tracy took this as an invitation to sit down in the booth, which it hadn't been, but her conspiratorial air was making Tom curious. The woman glanced around to make sure none of the other waitresses were watching, and then leaned forward across the table. "I hope you don't mind, but Kev told me you were... you know...." She lowered her voice even further. "Gay."

That was disconcerting. But Tom didn't particularly want to be in the closet around here anyway. "Um... yes, I am."

She placed a hand over his, as if the fact that she knew his "secret" somehow made them close friends. "That's all good with me, hon. I think everybody has a right to live their life the way they want, long as they're not bothering nobody else."

"Thanks."

If Tom had hoped the embarrassing moment would end there, he was mistaken. Tracy merely leaned in closer and asked, "Are you two… together now?"

He found himself really wishing she'd brought a glass of water over to the table before starting this conversation. His mouth had gone completely dry. "You were married to him. Why would you think he's suddenly turned gay?"

"Oh, I *always* thought he was gay. I mean, after the first few times, he never laid a hand on me unless I got him drunk." Tom could sense an undercurrent of something in her voice, but not what he might have expected. She didn't seem hurt so much as… baffled. Tracy knew she was a beautiful woman. How any *straight* man could resist her was simply beyond her comprehension. Therefore, Kevin had to be gay.

Tom really didn't feel comfortable discussing Kevin's sexual dysfunction with a comparative stranger. Fortunately, he was rescued by Ellen walking by and giving Tracy the hairy eyeball. Tracy jumped up and said quickly, "I'll be right back with a glass of water. Take your time with the menu."

ON WEDNESDAY, Tom arranged to take the second half of the day off so he could go to Littleton and browse around the two mattress stores there. What he really wanted was a "memory foam" mattress because he'd slept on one at one of his old boyfriend's houses years ago and thought it was the most comfortable thing he'd ever slept on in his entire life. The first store didn't have any, but he lucked out at the second. They had one the right size for his bed, and it was in stock.

The problem was getting it to his house. The store would deliver, but the price they quoted him was obscene. Before agreeing to anything, Tom stepped out into the parking lot and dialed Kevin on his cell phone.

"What's up?" Kevin answered cheerfully.

"I know this is sudden, so if you're busy—"

"No, man, I'm fine."

"Would you be willing to take an hour or two of your time to transport a mattress from Littleton to my house? I'll pay you your hourly rate." Kevin charged twenty-five dollars an hour when he was on the clock, but it was still significantly cheaper than what the store wanted.

"Sure, man. Right now?"

"I'm at the store." He gave Kevin the address.

"I'll be there in an hour."

Tom told the salesman to hold the mattress, just in case of a sudden run on memory foam mattresses, and went down the street for a cup of coffee. When he returned, Kevin was pulling in. He'd brought an old sheet to prevent the mattress from getting covered with rust or grease, which Tom appreciated, and it didn't take long to load the thing into the truck bed along with a matching box spring.

They drove back to Tom's house and spent an entertaining half hour hauling both the mattress and the box spring out of the truck and then wrestling them through the front door and up the stairs into the master bedroom.

The moment everything was in place on the brass bed frame, Kevin yelled "Banzai!" and did a belly flop onto the mattress. Tom laughed and imitated him.

"Wow!" Kevin exclaimed. "This thing is awesome!"

"Most comfortable bed you'll ever sleep in, motherfucker!" Tom snapped back, only somewhat conscious of the implications of that statement. He leaned out over the side of the bed and grabbed his pillow off the mat and sleeping bag he'd been sleeping on. Then he fell back on the mattress, tucking the pillow behind his head.

Kevin did something weird then: he rolled over onto his back and casually shifted his body closer so his head could rest on the pillow alongside Tom's. Tom wasn't sure what to make of it. He felt Kevin's soft brown hair brushing his forehead and Kevin's left elbow lightly touching his, and he thought back to what Tracy had said in the diner. Was Kevin really gay? Had he felt trapped in his marriage, especially when Tracy got pregnant? If so, he seemed to be in denial about it, even now.

But that was a very dangerous line of reasoning. Tom was well aware that he *wanted* Kevin to be gay. It would be very easy for him to fool himself into thinking Kevin was a closet case, waiting for the right man—Tom, of course—to come along and rescue him. But some straight men were just affectionate; some just had sexual problems that had nothing to do with being gay.

"I heard you were talking to Tracy the other day," Kevin said, startling Tom out of his thoughts.

"What? We talked for about five seconds! How the hell could you hear about that?"

Kevin laughed. "How do you think?"

Tom thought about it for a second and replied, "Ellen."

"No shit. That place is Gossip Central."

"Okay. So, yes, I was talking to Tracy. If you're going to get jealous, I would remind you that I'm gay, and Lee is already sleeping with her."

Kevin whipped his left arm at him to give him a sharp jab in the upper thigh with his knuckle.

"Ow!"

"Way to be sensitive, asshole."

But Tom could tell Kevin wasn't angry, and it felt good to have a friend he could poke at like this, even if it resulted in a few bruises. When Kevin didn't pursue it, he said, "So? Don't pretend you brought it up just to be conversational. Aren't you going to ask me what we talked about?"

"I guess it's not really any of my business."

"No. It absolutely is not your business who I talk to or what we talk about."

"Okay. That's cool. I'm sorry I asked."

"But you want to know anyway."

Kevin hit him again. "For fuck's sake! Will you just tell me?"

Tom hesitated, but he knew Kevin wouldn't want him to sugarcoat it. "Well... she told me two things you probably won't be happy about."

"Shoot."

"She thinks you and I are fucking."

To his surprise, Kevin just laughed at that. "I'm sure she'd love to watch."

"And she told me...." Tom was reluctant to say it, but he forged ahead. "She said that you... didn't want to have sex with her, after the first few times."

Apparently, that was a bigger deal to Kevin than her thinking he was gay. He was silent for a very long time. Tom didn't prompt him to say anything. He just lay there quietly, listening to Kevin's breathing. At last Kevin said, "That's kind of personal. She shouldn't be spreading it around to people she barely knows."

"I agree."

Another long silence. Then Kevin took a deep breath and said, "It's not like I couldn't get hard when I touched her—"

"Stop!" Tom lifted himself up on one elbow so he could look down into Kevin's face. For the second time in a week, they were in bed together, and the desire to lean down and kiss those full, sensual lips was almost overwhelming. But Kevin was looking up at him with a pained expression, and Tom wrestled his desire into submission. Kevin didn't need Tom to make a pass at him. He needed Tom to understand. "I'm not your therapist. And I'm not your boyfriend. You don't need to tell me a goddamned thing about what you do or do not do when you're having sex. Tracy was looking for some kind of validation. She wanted me to tell her that it wasn't her fault you weren't... responsive to her. She wanted me to confirm that you were gay so she could convince herself that she was still appealing to straight men. But I *am* practically a stranger, at least to her, and she had no right to talk about this with me. Sometime, if you want to talk about this as friends, I'll be willing to listen. But you don't need to defend yourself to me."

Kevin looked up at him with those sleepy hazel eyes and asked, "Will you do something for me?"

"What?"

"Will you tell me something about yourself that embarrasses the fuck out of you?"

Tom had to think about that. For the most part, he didn't have much in his past, or in his life in general, that particularly embarrassed him. He'd wet the bed until he was nine, but that was ancient history. He wasn't particularly embarrassed by it. Still, one thing came to mind—something he'd never told anybody. "You swear you won't tell anyone?"

"I swear."

"When I was at Keene State College, about fifteen or more years ago… I used to hang around in the bathroom at the library."

Kevin raised one eyebrow quizzically. "The bathroom?"

"Yeah."

"You mean, for sex?"

Tom nodded.

"Dude! You were giving guys head in the bathroom?"

"Just a few times. I was in my early twenties," he added, as if that explained it. It didn't. It had been a stupid, risky thing to do. But he'd been isolated and desperate to connect with other men, even if it was just for a few sleazy moments. "Before you ask, yes, I've been tested since then. Several times. HIV, hepatitis, syphilis, the whole nine yards. I'm clean. I was lucky. But it was stupid."

Kevin looked at him for a long moment, and Tom began to wonder if he'd revealed too much. But then his friend raised his right hand and held it in a fist over his chest. Tom had no idea what it meant, at first, but then he smiled and bumped it with his own fist. "You're a weird guy," he said.

"You too, counselor."

Eight

THEY went out later, briefly, to buy some decent steaks. And more beer, of course. Tom worried that they might be overdoing it in that department, but at the moment he was too caught up in... well, everything about Kevin... to pay much attention to it.

Kevin did the grilling, and the steaks were some of the best Tom had ever tasted. While they ate, Tom said, "It's the Fourth of July two Sundays from now."

"Oh yeah," Kevin said past a mouthful of steak. "You do anything for that?"

"I usually hide eggs and sing carols."

"Cool."

Tom rolled his eyes. "What about you?"

"I know a guy who sells fireworks if you want some cheap."

Tom didn't particularly relish the idea of setting his house or his woods on fire. Maybe some sparklers might be fun. He set his empty plate down beside his chair, picked up his beer, and took a swig of it. Then he belched loudly before responding. "I guess what I was asking was, are you doing something with your family or something? Or did you want to hang out here?" He wasn't thrilled with the idea of hanging out at Kevin's place, truth be told.

Kevin laughed. "They don't allow fireworks at Riverview. It's not really a holiday my family ever gave a fuck about, anyway. I mean, Yay! We escaped religious persecution and killed off all the Indians."

"We didn't kill them all off."

Kevin finished his beer and got up to walk to the edge of the deck. "I'm actually part Indian, on my mom's side. Don't know what tribe, though. I should ask her sometime." He unzipped his fly and asked, "Is it okay if I go off the edge of the deck?"

Tom thought that was a bit crass, but he just said, "If you want."

While Kevin was pissing, Tom leaned back and closed his eyes. He was happy right now. Sitting on the deck of the house he owned, on a warm summer night, with a full stomach, the taste of good steak and beer still in his mouth, and Kevin nearby. If it weren't for that nitpicky little detail of Kevin being straight, everything would be perfect.

He heard the sound of the hot tub lid being lifted up and opened his eyes. Kevin was standing over it, engulfed in a cloud of steam. "Want to get in?" He folded the padded lid back on itself, and then lifted the entire thing off and set it against the deck railing.

It was tempting. "I only have one pair of swim trunks," Tom hedged.

"Don't be an ass. You don't wear a swimsuit in a hot tub."

And with that, Kevin stripped out of his T-shirt and shorts and climbed into the water. Tom was dumbstruck. Just like that, the guy he'd been fantasizing about was stark naked. As far as Tom could tell, Kevin wasn't even drunk.

Tom stood and walked over to the hot tub. The blue lights inside the tub illuminated the water and cast an eerie glow up into Kevin's grinning face.

"Don't tell me you're shy," Kevin teased.

"Fuck you." Tom stripped and climbed into the water. It felt wonderful, especially when Kevin fiddled with the control console and started the jets pumping.

Tom found one of the built-in seats and slid into it, where two of the jets could massage his lower back. He sighed in pleasure. He expected Kevin to stay on the other side of the tub, but the other man swam through the center of the tub and took a seat beside him.

They sat there in silence, eyes closed while the jets massaged them. Tom was intensely aware that Kevin was naked and within arm's reach. He couldn't touch, but Kevin didn't seem to mind if he looked.

Hot tubs were awesome.

KEVIN seemed to agree with him about the wonders of hot tubs because the man was over the next night and the night after that, ready to fire up the grill and jump in the hot tub after eating. It went on like that for the next few days. Not that Kevin was obnoxious about it. He didn't exactly invite himself over. He would just call to chat after Tom got home from work, or Tom would call him. And before either of them really knew what was happening, they were finding an excuse for Kevin to swing by.

Apparently they'd become friends, and that was just fine with Tom. He loved Kevin's company, and he loved Kevin's cheeseburgers, even though he was beginning to worry that nightly cheeseburgers and beer might not be so good for his waistline.

And he certainly didn't mind Kevin getting naked in front of him on a nightly basis. Especially since Kevin, once out of his clothes, tended to *stay* out of his clothes. He wasn't the least bit shy about bopping around the deck in the nude for the rest of the evening until he headed home and seemed to expect Tom to do the same. Whatever Kevin's issue had been the night Tom first came out to him, he seemed to have gotten over it.

Most of the time, their conversation was light and inconsequential. Every now and then, Kevin would talk about his work or his life with Tracy. Nothing particularly personal. Tom noticed that Kevin never volunteered any stories about his youth or his family, but although he was curious, Tom had no real reason to probe him about those subjects.

The exception to keeping it casual was talk about sex. Kevin seemed to delight in giving personal details about how many times he'd masturbated that day or describing techniques he'd tried that would make most men blush to admit to. And he had no qualms about asking for intimate details from Tom either, despite his professed lack of interest when the subject had come up the night they'd been hanging out at his trailer.

If Tom had felt his interest was at all homophobic—along the lines of "How can you let a guy fuck you up the ass?" accompanied by a look of disgust—then he would have been annoyed and put a stop to it. But Kevin's interest seemed genuine. He liked talking about sex. If anything, his interest in the details of Tom's masturbatory and sexual habits seemed prurient, as if hearing about Tom jerking off somehow turned Kevin on.

Maybe it did. Sexuality was complicated. Straight men often enjoyed masturbating with other men and couldn't always explain why.

Tom found he didn't really mind answering Kevin's questions. When Kevin was in this mood, it often lent a surreal eroticism to their time together that Tom enjoyed.

One evening, Kevin asked him, "Do you like the smell of come?"

Tom laughed. "Yes, I do. I like the taste, too, if I'm horny enough."

"I think it smells really gross," Kevin said. "I always have to wipe up right away and get that damned paper towel as far away from me as possible."

"I take it you're not one of those guys who has a favorite rag or sock, then," Tom said, amused.

"Hell no! Throw that shit away!"

Well, Tom mused, at least he wouldn't have to worry about finding any little "surprises" if Kevin stayed the night in his guest room someday.

But then Kevin surprised him by saying, "I'm not sure I really like sex."

"Says the man who talks almost constantly about jerking off."

"I like jerking off," Kevin amended. "But whenever a girl touches me, I feel kind of... cold inside. I don't like it."

Suddenly they were on dangerous ground again, and Tom squirmed in his chair. He got up to get himself another beer, using the action as an excuse to formulate his thoughts coherently. But when he turned around, he saw Kevin watching him with a broad grin on his face.

"I know what you're thinking," Kevin said.

"Do you?"

"You're thinking, 'Maybe the reason Kevin doesn't like making it with chicks is because he'd secretly like making it with a guy.'"

Tom fetched another beer for Kevin, too, and then went back to his deck chair. "I don't think I've ever used the word 'chick' in my life. And although I'll admit that the general thought did flash through my mind—it's kind of hard to *avoid* that thought—but.... Are you sure you really want to talk about this?"

Kevin took a swig of his new beer. "Fuck it. Yeah. Let's talk about it. Unless it makes you uncomfortable."

"It doesn't make me uncomfortable," Tom said, although that was only partially true. This was getting pretty personal, considering they'd only known each other a few weeks. "But... okay. So you have an issue having sex with women. But being gay isn't about aversion to women, no matter what you might have heard growing up. It's about being attracted to men. The two have nothing to do with each other."

"So the question is, am I attracted to men?"

"Yes. Are you?"

Kevin took another swig of beer, and this time Tom was aware the man was scrutinizing him intently while he did so, no doubt trying to gauge whether he had any kind of sexual reaction to Tom's body. It wasn't something Tom felt comfortable with, but he endured it patiently until Kevin spoke.

"I think you're attractive," Kevin said simply.

Tom felt a brief flutter of hope spring up in the back of his mind and quickly stomped it down. "Thanks. But it's possible to find people attractive without being turned on by them."

"Dude… I'm more comfortable with you than I ever was with Tracy."

"I'm glad to hear it," Tom said, "but a lot of straight guys are more comfortable hanging out with other men than being with their wives. It's one of the consequences of a culture that raises boys and girls to have very little in common."

Kevin was beginning to grow frustrated, as if he wanted Tom to just come out and slap a label of "gay" on him. "Hell, I don't know. There were times when I caught myself watching other guys in the locker room in school. And when I look at porn, I don't like the stuff that just has women. I like to see a woman and a guy going at it."

"Have you ever looked at gay porn?"

"No."

Tom smiled at him and shook his head. "Look, Kevin. Maybe you're a little bi-curious. More people are than want to admit it. And that's perfectly healthy. But that doesn't mean you really want to go as far as having sex with other men. There's a big difference between looking, or even fantasizing, and actually doing."

Kevin had his beer in his lap, contemplating it as he picked at the label with his thumb. After a long silence, he asked, "What if I asked you to kiss me?"

Tom's breath caught in his chest, and he had to force himself to let it out slowly, trying to appear relaxed. He'd be lying if he said he hadn't half expected it. Or perhaps "feared it" would be more accurate. "I'm not sure that would be a good idea," he said slowly.

"Not even just as an experiment?"

Tom couldn't answer. Part of him wanted to say "Yes!" and go for it, but another part of him pictured Kevin shoving him away, perhaps even deciding that he didn't want to hang out anymore.

"Look," Kevin said, lifting his eyes to Tom's, "I've been thinking about this for a long time now, ever since things fell apart between me and Tracy. I mean, if you couldn't get it on with your wife without feeling sick to your stomach, wouldn't you start to wonder if maybe you… weren't straight? That night you told me you were gay… well, that scared the shit out of me because I thought, 'Fuck! Maybe I'm about to find out if I really am that way.' Except I wasn't ready to deal with it."

Well that explained his reaction. "You think you're ready to deal with it now?"

Kevin shrugged. "I like you. It feels good to hang out naked with you. I don't know if it's sexual or not. But I know I can trust you."

The temptation to offer himself up to the experiment was strong for Tom. *Let's go upstairs and see if you like how it feels. No strings attached.* But of course there *would* be strings attached for Tom. That was the thing Kevin was overlooking. He was focusing on his own feelings and his own concerns: Would he like it? Would he want more? If he wanted to stop, would Tom let him?

Tom would let him stop, of course. But he wouldn't want to. And even if Kevin decided he wanted more, wanted to keep going until they both came, would he want to ever do it again after the first time? Tom didn't want a sleazy one-nighter—or even shorter—with Kevin. Even if Kevin didn't take off and never talk to him again afterward, it would still be hell for Tom if Kevin decided that was all he wanted. Every time they hung out together, Tom would wonder if there might be some magic combination of beer and relaxed conversation that might get the two of them in bed again.

On the other hand, some things might just be inevitable. Tom wasn't sure he really had it in him to resist giving Kevin what he wanted.

Kevin leaned forward in his chair, planting his feet on the ground to either side of it. "If I kissed you, would you be able to deal with it, if I didn't like it? If I decided I didn't want to do it again?"

Tom took a deep breath. *Fuck.* "If you decide you don't like it, are you going to leave? For good, I mean?" It was a lame question. Kevin probably didn't know the answer himself. Not really.

"You'll still be my best friend."

"We've known each other just over a month," Tom pointed out. But he knew it was true that they were best friends now, if for no better reason than neither of them had any other close friends. Well, Tom had Sue, but he honestly felt closer to Kevin, even after this short time.

"I won't do it if it will upset you," Kevin said.

Famous last words.

Tom looked deep into those beautiful eyes, the lids seemingly heavy with arousal. He really *didn't* want to do this, but he really *did* want to do it. This was a fucked-up situation, and he was annoyed at Kevin for putting both of them into it.

"I guess I can handle a kiss," Tom responded slowly, feeling as if he was making an enormous mistake. "But if you don't like it, you need to be honest with me. I had sex with a guy once who didn't tell me until *afterward* that he hated it. He said that he hadn't wanted to be rude. Well, fuck that! There's nothing worse than someone telling you an experience you thought was wonderful sucked for them."

"I wouldn't do that to you," Kevin said softly. "I'm not going to ask you for sex if I don't like the kiss."

"All right, then. I'll do it."

"Can we get in the hot tub?"

Tom rolled his eyes and gave him a smirk. But he went along with it. They climbed into the water and sat there for a long while, close together, looking into each other's eyes, both afraid to make the first move.

Then Kevin glided a bit closer until their faces were nearly touching. He hesitated just a moment before leaning in and kissing Tom on the mouth. It wasn't a half-assed quick peck on the lips. He gave it everything he had, joining their mouths together fully, even slipping Tom a little tongue. Tom felt his own excitement mounting, his cock stiffening. But even before the kiss ended, he could tell the experiment was a failure. Kevin pulled away, his expression downcast, as if he'd hoped this would solve everything for him. But both men knew it hadn't.

"No good?" Tom asked, trying to sound casual, but there was an enormous lump in the pit of his stomach. For an all-too-brief moment, it had been wonderful. Now, he wanted to run away and hide in shame. He tried to remind himself that he had no reason to be ashamed or embarrassed. Kevin's failure to get aroused wasn't a criticism of Tom's attractiveness. Kevin had said he thought Tom was attractive, but apparently that just wasn't enough to overcome whatever Kevin's issues were. Or perhaps Kevin was still basically straight—he just had a small amount of curiosity about men, like others who weren't absolute "tens" on the Kinsey scale.

In any event, Tom's sympathy for Tracy had just increased dramatically. Rejection sucked, no matter how you sliced it.

Wordlessly, Kevin climbed out of the hot tub and went to go stand by the deck railing, but not before Tom got a glimpse of his erect penis—all seven inches of it, at full mast. But Kevin didn't look turned on. He was hunched over the railing, hanging his head and rubbing one of his hands through his hair, as if he were about to be sick.

"Are you all right?" Tom tried again.

Kevin shook his head. Tom realized that he was gasping for air, as if he couldn't breathe, and his other hand was clutching the railing so hard that his knuckles were white. He was having a panic attack.

Tom climbed out of the tub and approached him but made no move to touch him.

"Kevin...."

"I can't breathe!"

"Yes, you can," Tom replied, soothingly. "I won't let you suffocate. The hospital is right down the road if we need it. But I want you to listen to the sound of my voice, okay? I want you to follow along with what I say."

Kevin was still breathing rapidly, but he nodded.

"I'm going to count now. Take a breath and hold it... three... two... one. Now, let it out... three... two... one. Hold it... three... two... one. Another breath... three... two... one...." He kept counting, pausing just a tiny bit longer between the counts as he went on, for several minutes.

Eventually, Kevin's grip eased on the railing, and his breathing calmed down to a normal rhythm. "I feel dizzy...."

"It's probably just too much oxygen," Tom said. "Let's go sit down. Can you take my hand?"

He was afraid the physical contact might cause Kevin to panic again, but Kevin took the hand he was offered and allowed Tom to lead him to one of the deck chairs. He fell into it, exhausted, his body dripping wet, though Tom couldn't tell if it was from the hot tub or from sweat.

"Christ...."

Tom sat down in the other chair and waited for Kevin to relax enough to talk.

When the silence had grown heavy between them, Kevin finally said, "What was that? Hypnosis?"

"Not specifically. I was just helping you slow your breathing down so you'd stop hyperventilating."

"I used to think I was going to die. My heart starts pounding and my chest hurts and my whole body feels numb and tingly."

Tom nodded. "I know. That's common. People often start hyperventilating during panic attacks. It can make your chest hurt, and the extra oxygen you're inhaling can make your body tingle."

"But people don't die from it?"

"No."

Kevin leaned back in his chair and wrapped his arms around himself. "Is it getting colder?"

Tom hadn't noticed that it was, but he went into the house and dug out a blanket he didn't mind getting wet and brought it out for Kevin. When he returned, he was disturbed to find Kevin hunched over in the chair, sobbing. Tom draped the blanket over him and took the chair near him, watching in distress while Kevin cried until he was too exhausted to continue.

When he'd calmed down at last, he lay back with his eyes closed and the blanket wrapped tightly around his body. "I'm sorry."

"There's nothing to be sorry about. It was an experiment, and we both knew it might not go well."

"I hurt your feelings."

He had, unintentionally, but Tom just said, "After I gave you that speech about you being honest with me, I'm not going to start whining because you *were*. You're not attracted to me. And that's fine. There's no reason for me to feel insulted and no reason for you to feel guilty."

"Except you do," Kevin replied. "And I do."

"Yeah. Maybe. But we're adults. We'll get over it."

After another silence, Kevin asked, "Did you see my dick?"

Tom had to laugh. "Yes, I saw your dick. I'm a gay man. What do you think?"

"I mean, when it got hard?"

"Yeah," Tom said, more seriously. "What was up with that?"

Kevin shook his head and took a long, tremulous breath. "I don't fucking know. It happened with her too. She'd kiss me, and I'd feel like puking, but my fucking dick always got hard as a rock. So she thought I wanted her—that I wanted *it*—when I just wanted to get the fuck away!"

Tom didn't know what to say in response to that. Hearing Kevin say he'd felt like puking after kissing him still hurt, even though he knew it wasn't personal.

"Christ, I'm tired," Kevin said.

"Do you want to stay here tonight? I can take the sleeping bag. I've been sleeping in that since I got here anyway."

Kevin laughed. "Dude. We can share a bed. I'm not *that* freaked out about you being near me."

TOM stayed downstairs to cover the hot tub and make sure there weren't any citronella candles left burning on the deck, while Kevin went inside. By the time he'd locked up and followed Kevin to the bedroom, Kevin was in bed, already dozing off. He'd found a folded towel in the hall closet and had that under his head for a pillow. The damp blanket had been discarded on the floor.

Tom lifted the blanket on the bed and saw that Kevin was still naked. Still, he wasn't sure of Kevin's mental state right now, so he didn't think it wise to crawl in there naked himself. He dug a pair of boxers out of the laundry basket and put them on before slipping into bed and turning off the light.

IN THE morning, Tom opened his eyes to see Kevin's face lying not far from his, Kevin's open eyes watching him intently.

"Hey," Tom said sleepily.

"Hey."

"How are you feeling?"

Kevin shrugged. "Okay, I guess. How about you?"

"I'm fine."

"You're not upset with me?"

"I don't see what I would have to be upset about," Tom said. "You wanted to try kissing, I agreed, and you discovered you didn't like it. So we file that under 'Things not to try again' and get on with our lives." He knew it wouldn't be quite that easy for either of them. For him, it still stung, even though his rational mind told him there was no reason for it to. And for Kevin…. Well, Tom suspected Kevin had almost wished he'd discover he was gay. It might have been easier for him to deal with than the idea that he just couldn't enjoy sex with *anyone*.

"Yeah," Kevin replied, sitting up and putting his legs out over the side of the bed. Then he stood up and stretched. "I gotta take a leak."

He walked out of the room and into the bathroom. Tom groaned in frustration. Kevin in the morning, disheveled and sleepy-eyed, was a beautiful sight. And it didn't help that he was not only naked, but also appeared to be oblivious to the fact he had a raging morning hard-on.

Fuck my life.

IT WAS Saturday, so neither of them had to go anywhere. Tom had no desire to kick Kevin out, and Kevin likewise didn't seem inclined to leave. So they scrounged up some breakfast and drove down to Ikea to pick out some more furniture. The only vehicle they had to carry it in was Kevin's truck, so Tom couldn't go completely nuts. But he managed to pick up a blocky (yet very comfortable) sofa with matching chairs—in black since he wasn't big on cleaning them every other day—and a coffee table. They also managed to wedge in a small bedroom nightstand to put the lamp on and some extra pillows.

Tom wasn't sure how he felt about the extra pillows. They were Kevin's idea. Was the guy planning on sleeping over a lot? And sharing the bed? Part of Tom hoped this was exactly what Kevin was planning. But the other part of him thought it was weird, especially after they'd just proven that Kevin wasn't sexually interested in him.

But the pillows were cheap, so Tom bought them.

The trip had taken about five hours, but it was still daylight while they unloaded the boxes from the truck.

"You want help putting this stuff together?" Kevin asked, surveying the assortment of waist-high boxes in the living room. All the furniture required assembly.

"Sure. I'll go find a knife to open the boxes with."

Tom went into the kitchen, retrieved a knife from one of the drawers, and then returned to the living room to find Kevin stark naked again. He stopped and stared for a moment, unable to hide his surprise.

"What?" Kevin asked. "I thought it was okay."

Tom raised his eyebrows. "Well, I guess it is. I just wasn't expecting you to strip down in the middle of the afternoon."

"We've been hanging out naked every night for almost two weeks. I feel comfortable like this when I'm around you now. Do you want me to get dressed again?"

"No," Tom said. He could think of a few things the sight of Kevin naked made him want, but Kevin putting his clothes back on was definitely not one of them. Tom added, "Maybe we should just get the rules out in the open. Is it always okay to be naked when we're hanging out together?"

Kevin shrugged. "As long as we're here and not like over at the diner or something, I'd say that's fine."

It was fine with Tom too. So he stripped down, and the two of them spent the afternoon in the buff, assembling the furniture. When they were finished and had cleared out the packaging materials, the living room looked like a living room for the first time since Tom had moved in. It was wonderful.

Tom couldn't explain why, considering how much time they'd already spent naked together, but for some reason he found the afternoon intensely erotic. Something about hanging out that way in broad daylight, rather than in the dimly lit deck at night. Fortunately, he managed not to get an erection, though he no longer thought Kevin would care if he did.

Kevin spent the night again. There was no real excuse this time. He wasn't exhausted; he wasn't drunk. But one o'clock in the morning rolled around, and they were both yawning, so Kevin mumbled, "I guess I better go."

And without a second thought, Tom said, "I don't mind if you crash again."

That was Sunday night. By Friday evening, Tom realized he and Kevin had managed to find excuses for sleeping together every night that week.

The relationship was definitely… different. And Tom wasn't all that sure it was healthy. No doubt Sue would have told him as much, which is why he had no intention of telling her about it. When they'd talked at lunch on that afternoon, Tom had told her about Kevin hanging out for the past several nights, which she disapproved of on the basis that Tom should be dating and finding a "real" relationship instead of crushing on someone unobtainable. If she'd known that the unobtainable object of Tom's desires was sleeping naked with him every night and tormented him in the mornings by walking around sporting "morning wood," he would never have heard the end of it.

But Tom had had so-called romantic relationships that were worse. Ones in which the sex was good, but the rest was shit. This relationship was weird, admittedly, but despite having no outlet for his sexual tension, apart from a hurried stroking in the shower some mornings, it felt good.

Until Kevin cut himself.

Nine

IT HAPPENED on Saturday night, the Fourth of July. Tom and Kevin went shopping during the afternoon and picked up burgers, beer—of course—chips, and other junk food. Kevin had managed to get a hold of some cheap fireworks—sparklers, firecrackers, bottle rockets. Nothing over-the-top, but some fun stuff to horse around with. Hopefully, they wouldn't get drunk and blow their fingers off.

It wasn't, in fact, a firework that did the damage. Kevin was wrestling with the packaging of some sliced American cheese that had decided it didn't want to come open. "Goddamn it! Can you hand me my pocketknife?"

"Where is it?"

"In my pocket," Kevin replied with amusement.

He wasn't wearing his jeans, of course. They were in a heap by the deck railing. So Tom went over and rummaged through the front pockets, finding a small pocketknife tangled up with Kevin's ring of keys. He extricated it and tossed it to Kevin.

But when Kevin stuck the knife in the packaging and sliced it open, he exclaimed, "Fuck!"

The cheese package fell on the deck, and Kevin clutched his hand against his leg as a couple of drops of blood fell against the bare skin of his knee and onto the wooden deck. "All right, that fucking cheese is getting tossed over the railing! Let the goddamned raccoons eat it!"

"Hold on," Tom said, trying not to laugh, "I'll get some bandages."

He'd bought a first aid kit when he moved in, figuring he might need it now that he was a rough and rugged he-man living in Coyote Country. So far, he'd used it to remove a splinter. But now he grabbed a large Band-Aid and some antibiotic ointment. On his way out of the bathroom, he grabbed a bottle of rubbing alcohol for good measure.

When he got back to the deck, he set the bandage and the ointment down on the arm of one of the deck chairs and opened up the bottle of rubbing alcohol. It was a new bottle, and he sloshed a little on his hand when he opened it, which made him flinch away from the strong fumes. But that was nothing compared to Kevin's reaction.

"Get that shit away from me!" He was hunched over his hand as if guarding it, gritting his teeth in pain.

Tom stepped toward him, giving him a wry smile. "Don't be a baby. It'll help kill any germs that were on the knife."

"I said get it *away* from me!"

Before Tom could react, Kevin swung his fist around in an arc and connected with the side of Tom's head. Tom hadn't been hit since high school, and the shock was almost as severe as the physical pain—though not quite. He staggered backward, tripped over the deck chair, and went sprawling. The rubbing alcohol sprayed across the deck. His head was throbbing, and his left eye was blurry, but he staggered to his feet just as Kevin ran by him.

"What the fuck?" Tom shouted after him, but Kevin kept going.

A moment later, he heard Kevin's truck start up and pull out of the yard.

Tom became aware of a stinging on his hip and looked down to discover that he'd scraped skin away on the wooden arm of the deck chair. *Fucking awesome.*

He hobbled inside and looked at his face in the bathroom mirror. He had a welt the size of a baseball on the left side of his head, and his eye was looking puffy. He didn't have to be back at work until Wednesday, thanks to the holiday, but he would probably still have a bruise by then. There was a small amount of blood, but that turned out not to be his. It must have come from Kevin's hand. Tom washed it off in the sink.

This was bullshit. Fuck Kevin Derocher and whatever the fuck his problem was. Tom had had enough. He was fairly convinced Kevin had just had another panic attack. Why, Tom had no idea. The alcohol? Perhaps. But it was one thing to talk Kevin down from hyperventilating, and quite another to get punched in the head.

It wasn't until he went back out onto the deck to assess the damage—there was rubbing alcohol splashed all over the place, but the deck chair didn't appear to be broken—that Tom realized Kevin's jeans were still there in a heap where Tom had last dropped them. He picked them up and found Kevin's key ring still in the pocket. How the hell had Kevin managed to drive away in the truck without his keys? And what was he *wearing*?

He picked up the bottle of alcohol. There was still a small amount left in the bottle, and he used that to wash the scrape on his side. It stung like a motherfucker, but unlike *some* people, he could handle it. The cap had rolled into the crevasse between two floorboards, so he retrieved it and put it back on the bottle.

A couple of minutes later, his cell phone rang. His first thought was that it was Kevin, but Kevin's cell phone was still in his jeans pocket. Was he calling from his trailer? But Tom's caller ID wasn't displaying Kevin's name or home number—it was displaying Groveton Police Dept.

Shit.

"Hello?"

"Is this Tom Langois?"

"Yes."

"Mr. Langois, this is Chief Burbank, from the Groveton Police Department. Do you know someone by the name of Kevin Derocher?"

Oh God. Was Kevin hurt? Or *dead*? Had he been so out of control he'd gotten into a car accident? Tom realized Kevin couldn't be dead, or the police would never have known to call him.

"Yes, I know him. Is he okay?"

"He's fine," the chief said. "We pulled him over on Northside Road and… the thing is, we can't let him go like this. He says you can bring his clothes to him. Otherwise, we're going to have to take him to the station."

Tom had to refrain from sounding too amused. "Oh. Yeah, we were in the hot tub when he took off," he lied. Not that that really sounded better.

"That's fine," Chief Burbank said, sounding amused himself. "Do you know where Recycle Road is?"

Tom had seen it, on his way to Kevin's trailer the other day. Apparently, they were pulled over near that intersection, so Tom promised he'd be there in just a few minutes. He hung up, dressed, and gathered up Kevin's things.

Well, at least nobody was asking him for bail money.

TOM found two police cruisers with Groveton insignias on the side—Stark was too small for a full-time police force—and blue lights flashing, pulled over at the entrance to Recycle Road. As far as Tom knew, the road just led to the recycling station, so nobody was likely to be going in or out at this time of night. Kevin's truck was pulled over about thirty feet away from the cruisers, and Tom could see Kevin sitting in the cab, looking miserable. He also looked shirtless. No doubt Chief Burbank had found it very entertaining when he'd approached to ask for license and registration.

Tom parked beside the truck. When he climbed out of his car, he glanced over at Kevin, who gave him a pleading look. But one of the two officers standing by the cruisers was already walking over to him, so Tom couldn't immediately hand over the bundle of clothes in his hands.

"Mr. Langois?"

"Yes."

The officer smiled and flashed him a badge. "I'm Chief Burbank. Do you have an ID?"

Tom showed him both his license and his business card.

"A psychologist?" Burbank asked.

"Yes."

"Is he a patient of yours?"

Tom glanced over at Kevin, knowing he could hear everything they were saying, but Kevin refused to look at him. "No."

He knew the circumstances could make it look as if he and Kevin were a couple—why else would they be hanging out naked together? But that wasn't Tom's concern. On the other hand, he'd forgotten about the bruise on the side of his face. Chief Burbank noticed it, and his expression turned to one of concern. "Did he hit you?"

Apparently, Burbank didn't care if Tom and Kevin were gay. Spouse abuse was spouse abuse. That was actually nice to know.

Tom knew if he admitted it, Kevin could be in even more trouble than he already was. For the first time, he wondered if Kevin had ever assaulted Tracy during one of his panic attacks. What if this was a pattern with him? "He has panic attacks. This is the first time I've seen him lash out."

"Do you want to file charges?"

"It's the first time it's happened," Tom repeated. "I haven't seen him like this before, so... I guess I'd like to give him the benefit of the doubt."

Chief Burbank didn't look convinced, but he nodded. "May I take a look at the clothes, please?"

Tom handed him the bundle of clothes: Kevin's pants, T-shirt, and sneakers. Tom hadn't found any socks, and he wasn't sure if Kevin had been wearing any. The chief was about Tom's age and had a pleasant, ruddy face, like a man who spent most of his time outdoors. He was smiling now as he examined the clothes—checking for a gun, perhaps—then handed them back to Tom. "No underwear?"

"He doesn't wear any."

Burbank smiled and rolled his eyes. Then he called out to Kevin, "Climb out the passenger side, please, so you can get dressed without people driving by and seeing you."

Kevin looked surly and uncooperative, but he did what he was told. Tom went around to meet him and hand his clothes over. In the few moments they had out of Burbank's hearing, Kevin asked him, "Did I hurt you?"

"You punched me in the head and sent me tumbling backward over a wooden chair," Tom replied calmly. "Of course you hurt me."

Kevin looked pained when he saw the bruise on his face. "God, Tom. I'm sorry."

He looked a mess. His hair was plastered against his forehead, dripping with sweat despite the fact that it wasn't a very hot evening. This confirmed Tom's theory of a panic attack. But Tom wasn't in the mood to give him much leeway right now.

"Did you ever hit Tracy like this?"

The expression on Kevin's face turned to one of pure horror. "No! Jesus! No! Never!" When Tom didn't look convinced, he added, "Go talk to her if you want."

"You're serious? You really want me to do that?"

"Go ahead. Call her. She won't lie to you."

"I will, then," Tom said coldly. "Because if you're the type of man who beats up his wife, I won't have anything more to do with you." If it had truly been a panic attack, Kevin might not have had any control over himself. But Tom needed to know if this was a one-time incident, or if Kevin routinely lashed out and hit people during these attacks.

Kevin nodded, unable to look him in the eye. "Do it," he said quietly. "And I'm sorry again."

Tom watched Kevin dress, and then the two of them walked around the back of the truck to where Chief Burbank was talking to the officer from the second cruiser.

"All right," Burbank said to Kevin. "Are you going back with Mr. Langois?"

Kevin shook his head. "My place is just down the road. I think I should just go home."

The chief looked back and forth between them before saying, "That might be wise. Do I have your word that you're going to go straight home?"

"Yes, sir."

"Okay, you can go, then."

Kevin glanced at Tom, but Tom was still angry with him, and his face probably showed it, so Kevin didn't say anything. He just climbed into his truck, started it up, and drove off down Northside Road.

Ten

SUNDAY was as dreary as Tom felt, overcast and threatening rain. He woke up alone in his bed for the first time in over a week, and he hated it. The desire to call Kevin and ask him over was so strong that Tom called Lee's Diner instead, wanting to get the whole thing over with. If Tracy would just tell him that Kevin had never raised a hand to her, then maybe he and Kevin could go back to the easy friendship they'd had. He could forgive Kevin a moment of lashing out in panic. Things like that happened. Or at least, they happened to some people. But the last thing Tom needed was someone in his life who was going to land him in the hospital periodically.

Tracy was at the diner, thankfully—Tom would have gone crazy if he'd found out she had the day off. But he couldn't bring himself to talk about something like this over the phone. "When's your lunch break?" he asked. "I'd really like to talk to you."

There was a long pause at the other end of the phone. Then Tracy responded, "What's this about, hon? Something to do with Kevin?"

"Yes. But I'd really rather talk to you in person about it."

She sighed. "Well, all right. I take a break around two when the lunch rush settles down."

Tom showered and went out on the deck to see if the rubbing alcohol had damaged the deck at all. But it had evaporated and hadn't left a stain that he could see.

He showed up at Lee's just after one o'clock and was relieved to see that Kevin's truck wasn't there. The place was packed, and for the first time since he'd started coming there, Tom was forced to wait a couple of minutes for a table to open up. The waitresses were running from table to counter and back again, looking harried, but all smiles and chitchat and attitude, with a healthy dose of flirtation thrown in. Tom had to admire that kind of energy level. There were days when he could barely manage the calmly attentive attitude required of his own job.

When he did finally get a small table with two chairs against the far wall, his waitress was a cheerful young woman named Kelly, whom he'd never met before. But it was unreasonable to assume that Tracy would have time for him during all this chaos. He caught her eye at one point as she hurried past, and she smiled at him, but she didn't have time to stop. Tom ordered some blueberry pancakes, bacon, orange juice, and coffee, and did his best not to make Kelly's job difficult as he ate his late breakfast.

It was getting closer to three by the time Tracy had a moment to come over to his table. "I'm sorry to keep you waiting, hon. It's been hell today."

"So I saw. That's all right. But do you have a second to talk in private?"

"I've told the other girls I'm taking a few minutes."

"Do you mind if we go out to the parking lot?" Tom asked. "I really don't want people overhearing this."

She didn't seem thrilled by the idea—perhaps she was used to male customers trying to get her alone for a few moments—but she gave a reluctant nod. Outside, the sky was even more ominous than it had been a couple of hours ago, and the wind was picking up, but the rain wasn't coming down yet. They leaned against Tom's black Nissan Sentra, and Tracy asked him, "Is this about that bruise on your face, hon?"

"Kevin and I had an argument last night."

"Oh my God!" Tracy's jaw dropped in the overtheatrical manner Tom was beginning to associate with her. "Did Kevin do that to you?"

"Yes."

"I can't believe he would ever do something like that."

"That's what I wanted to talk to you about," Tom said. "Kevin already knows I'm here. You seem to still be fond of him—"

Tracy waved a hand dismissively. "Well, of course I am. Sure, things went south right after we were married, and I still want to kill him whenever I think about that stupid stunt he pulled—"

"The suicide attempt?"

"That was when I knew he really was crazy. The screaming in his sleep and smashing the radio… I tried to overlook all that, but coming home to find him like that…."

But Tom's ears had perked up about the radio. "Why did he smash the radio?"

"Darned if I know. Some song came on, and he just took one of the kitchen chairs and beat on that thing 'til it was dead."

That was intriguing, but it was off the subject. "Tracy… did Kevin ever hit *you*?"

"God, no! I would have walked out that door faster than you can blink. And that's what you should do, hon. I admit, I was a little… surprised… to find out that Kevin… you know… that you're his type. Though it sure explains a lot. But if he's getting crazy enough to start hitting on people, you need to get the hell away from him and find a nice guy who's sane."

Tom wasn't actually convinced that Kevin was any "crazier" than he'd ever been. "I don't think he did this on purpose."

"He just accidentally clubbed you in the face?" Tracy asked skeptically.

"During a panic attack, when he wasn't really in control of himself," Tom tried to explain, though he wasn't sure if Tracy even knew he was a psychologist. She probably thought he was talking out of his ass. "Look, Tracy, I think something traumatic happened to him when he was younger. Certain things cause him to have panic attacks because they force him to remember."

"Remember what?"

"I don't know. It's possible he doesn't even know himself."

Tracy was just looking at him blankly, so Tom asked, "Do you know of anything that might have happened to him, maybe when he was a kid? Something particularly bad?"

She shook her head. "I don't know anything about that, hon. He never talks about his childhood; he doesn't even keep in touch with his mother. I never saw him send her a card for Mother's Day or anything. If he has any brothers and sisters, he never told me about them."

KEVIN'S truck was in the driveway when Tom got home, and Kevin himself was sitting on the front steps. He didn't grin the way he usually did as Tom got out of his car. Instead, he sat hunched over, staring at his hands, while that foot tapped frantically, reminding Tom of a jackrabbit from a cartoon. He was probably expecting Tom to tell him to get the fuck off his property.

On the step beside him was a new bottle of rubbing alcohol and, to Tom's surprise, one of the single red roses with cellophane wrapped around the base sold in supermarkets and convenience stores.

"You bought me flowers?" he asked incredulously as he walked up to Kevin.

Kevin tilted his head to look down at the rose as if he wasn't sure how it got there. "Just one. I guess it was a stupid idea."

Not exactly stupid, Tom thought. But weird. Male friends didn't generally give each other roses after they'd had a fight. Still, Tom couldn't help but be touched by it.

Kevin picked the rose up and was about to throw it off into the bushes, but Tom sprang forward and grabbed his wrist. He half expected the touch to trigger another panic attack, but Kevin just looked up at him, his soft hazel eyes full of pain.

"I like flowers," Tom said, taking the rose out of his hand. "Thank you."

He released Kevin's wrist and picked up the bottle of alcohol, as well. "Why don't we go inside? Are the windows on your truck rolled up? I think it's going to rain soon."

IT WAS Kevin's idea to talk in bed. Tom had given up being surprised by his contradictory needs for intimacy and distance. They stripped naked and lay close together, not quite touching, sharing a pillow so their faces were near enough that Tom could feel Kevin's breath on his lips.

Like lovers, but not. This friendship was going to drive Tom insane.

"I tried to stay away," Kevin told him, "but I couldn't."

"Why did you want to stay away?"

"I didn't want to. But you were mad at me, and you had a right to be."

That was certainly true. "I spoke with Tracy today." When Kevin didn't say anything, Tom continued. "She seems to think you're crazy."

"I *am* crazy. You should know that better than anybody."

Tom snorted. "You're sane enough. You know who you are and where you are, and except for some occasional episodes, I don't think you're a danger to anyone."

"What about when I'm having one of my 'episodes'?"

"I'm not sure yet, but Tracy says you've never hit her."

"I haven't. I can't remember ever hitting anybody before. Well, except for when I was thirteen, the year I went to Hampstead. I took a swing at a male nurse."

"Why?"

"He touched me."

Tom frowned and raised himself up on one elbow. "Do you mean sexually?"

"No." Kevin shook his head adamantly. "He was just doing his job. But I was upset about something—I don't even remember what—and he tried to put his arms around me to restrain me. He wasn't really mad that I hit him because it was hardly the first time a patient hit him in a situation like that."

Tom looked at him intently and said slowly, "Well, *I'm* mad about you hitting *me*. You got it? I can forgive you—and basically I have—but if you ever do that again, we're going to have a big problem."

"Good," Kevin said, looking him straight in the eye. "I don't want you to take that shit from me."

Tom sighed, feeling a weight lift from him. He wasn't completely convinced—he'd heard of too many wife abusers swearing they would never raise a hand in anger again, only to fall right back into the same pattern when they lost their tempers again. True, there was an enormous difference between an abuser and someone with PTSD who didn't exhibit a pattern of abusive behavior apart from some isolated incidents during flashbacks or panic attacks. But Kevin was still out of control at those times, and that was reason for concern.

I need to talk to Sue about this, Tom thought. *I'm out of my depth here.*

"Kevin, you really might want to think about getting treatment for these panic attacks. Tracy told me about the radio you destroyed. Maybe you're not out of control all of the time, or even very often, but it's often enough. Aren't you concerned that you might actually hurt someone someday?"

"I don't want to go to another psychologist," Kevin said.

"I have a colleague, Sue Cross, who's excellent with cases like this. She's done a lot of counseling for veterans suffering from PTSD."

"I'm not a veteran."

"All kinds of things can cause PTSD. It's post-traumatic stress disorder. It can be brought on by a lot of types of traumatic stress—not just combat. Rape, childhood physical or sexual abuse, car accidents...."

"You can help me," Kevin insisted. "You know how to see past my bullshit. And I trust you."

Tom sighed and laid his head back down on the pillow, gazing into those beautiful sleepy eyes, wanting to reach out and touch Kevin, kiss his full mouth....

"Kevin... I think I'm starting to fall for you."

Instead of looking shocked or uncomfortable, Kevin smiled and said, "It was the bottle of rubbing alcohol, wasn't it? Nobody can resist a bottle of rubbing alcohol."

"Stop joking for a minute, please. I need to know what this is. We have this fucked-up relationship that feels almost romantic one moment and like we're just friends the next. You don't want to have sex with me, but you like being naked with me and sleeping in the same bed with me. I don't know what to make of it."

Kevin's smile faded, and he shifted his head on the pillow, as if he were trying to get a better view of Tom's face. "It's fucked up because *I'm* fucked up. Especially about sex. But I thought a lot about it last night when I was alone at my place. And I realized that I was terrified that you'd tell me to fuck off. It scared me more than when Tracy asked me for a divorce. I'm happier with you than I ever was with Tracy."

That threw Tom for a loop. He'd hoped for clarification, but he'd expected something along the lines of a delineation of what Kevin's boundaries were. Now he felt even more confused. Was it possible Kevin might be falling for him, too, even if he wasn't sexually attracted to him? Or was this just some kind of intense need for a friend?

"There are plenty of straight men who prefer hanging out with their male best friends to spending time with their wives."

"I've been thinking about you when I jerk off."

Christ. "What do you mean?"

"I don't know. It's kind of vague. Mostly just thinking about you without your clothes on."

Tom let out a long sigh and tried to find something in Kevin's eyes that would give him a clue what all this meant. What he found there was longing. But longing for what exactly?

"What do you want?" Tom asked. "If it was entirely up to you, what would you want our relationship to be like?"

"I guess I'd pretty much want to keep it the way it is. I just want to be with you as much as possible."

"Until you find a girlfriend."

"I don't want a girlfriend," Kevin said adamantly. "I don't want to be with anyone but you."

That sounded a bit too much like Jake passionately declaring they would be friends forever and nothing—*nothing*!—would ever separate them. Teenagers were prone to that kind of hyperbole. But he and Kevin weren't teenagers.

"I can't think of any way to ask this," Tom said, "without sounding like I think you're five years old. So forgive me. But... you *can* tell the difference between platonic love and romantic love, can't you?"

Kevin gave him that shy smile, and Tom knew he wouldn't be able to keep up his resistance much longer. "It feels romantic to me, counselor."

"Really?"

"Yeah."

"Then are you saying you want to be my boyfriend?"

"If you can handle a boyfriend who can't kiss or have sex...."

It did seem like a tall order. But Tom knew he couldn't push Kevin away for that reason alone. "Well... for now, I think I can. But I certainly can't be your boyfriend and your therapist at the same time. A therapist needs to maintain some professional distance, or he won't be able to see clearly."

Kevin was silent for a long time. At some point, the rain had started, and it was coming down in a torrent outside, making Tom feel as if they were isolated from the world, buried together beneath the warm blankets. He liked the feeling. And he liked the feeling that had welled up in his chest as they had toyed with the word "boyfriend."

At last Kevin said, "Way back when I first came to see you, you said I could have Tracy come in with me. If I agree to see your friend, will you come in with me?"

"That's usually only done for couples counseling."

"So now we're a couple, right?"

"It's for couples who are having trouble with their relationship," Tom amended.

"You'll dump me if I don't get my head together, right? That sounds like relationship trouble to me."

"You're being melodramatic. I'm still trying to wrap my head around the idea of you being interested in me romantically. I'm nowhere near thinking about dumping you."

"It's the only way I'll do it," Kevin said emphatically. "You're the only one I trust enough to let you fuck around in there." He raised a hand to tap the top of his head.

Tom sighed. "I'll talk to her. Maybe she'll be willing to do it."

Kevin smiled at him and pulled the covers up over his shoulders, snuggling down into the blankets like a little kid. Tom found it ridiculously adorable. "Can we sleep now? My stomach has been in knots since last night, 'cause I thought you were going to tell me you didn't want me around anymore. Now that you've decided I'm not completely hopeless, I'm just feeling warm and sleepy, and I feel like I could sleep for a week."

Tom shook his head in amusement. "God, I wish there was a way I could kiss you."

Kevin stuck his hand out of the blankets and gently pressed his palm against Tom's lips. Tom kissed the palm and the tip of each finger in turn. Then, to his surprise, Kevin took Tom's hand and brought it to his own lips. They felt warm and silky against Tom's skin.

The rain pouring down around the house made it seem late in the day, though it was only about five in the afternoon, and Tom found himself feeling tired too. Resolving a major point of stress could do that to a person. So they slept.

Eleven

TOM woke to Kevin screaming.

He was wrenched out of a deep sleep to find Kevin sitting up in the dark, panting heavily. At first Tom couldn't be certain he'd heard the scream. Perhaps he'd dreamt it? But then, why would Kevin be awake?

"Kevin?"

Kevin started at the sound of his voice. "It's okay!" He didn't sound okay. He sounded terrified.

"What's okay?"

"Everything's good. Everything's fine."

Tom reached over and fumbled with the reading lamp until he found the switch to turn it on. Kevin flinched when the light came on, even though it was fairly dim. His naked torso was completely covered in a fine sheen of sweat, and the sheets where he'd been sleeping were drenched with it.

"Are you all right, Kevin?"

Kevin was beginning to shiver, so Tom took the quilt that had been lying over them and draped it around Kevin's shoulders, careful not to touch him directly, in case he was having an episode. The quilt was dry, at least. "Were you having a nightmare?"

"I don't know," Kevin said vaguely, as if still half-asleep.

"Do you remember what you were dreaming about?"

"Keeraylayzah."

"What?" It sounded like gibberish, but maybe Kevin was just slurring it.

"No."

"What did you just say, Kevin?"

"I wanna lie down."

"Do you remember screaming?"

"I wanna lie down...."

Tom gave up and let him lie back on the mattress, still wrapped in the quilt. He would have liked to change the sheets, but Kevin was asleep almost as soon as his head hit the pillow. Tom got up and found another quilt in the closet. He spread it out across the bed to cover both of them, and then he climbed back in.

Frustrated that he couldn't hold Kevin or even reach out to caress his back to reassure him that Tom would be there if he needed him, Tom lay there in the dark for almost half an hour, unable to sleep. When he was certain Kevin was sleeping peacefully, he got out of bed, found his bathrobe, and went down to the kitchen to make himself something to eat.

He made himself a cheese and mustard sandwich and sat down at his new kitchen table, listening to the rain outside while he ate. It was only about midnight. Normally, Tom wouldn't even have gone to bed yet, but they'd fallen asleep so ridiculously early. He wasn't sure he could sleep if he went back upstairs now.

Instead, he dug a notepad and pen out of his briefcase and sat at the table, trying to make some kind of sense out of the man he'd just agreed to be in a romantic relationship with. He wrote down the header: *Things That Trigger Panic Attacks*.

Then under that, he wrote:

Being kissed
Being touched (in a sexual way)
Rubbing alcohol (the smell?)
A song on the radio?
Finding out his wife was pregnant?
Keeraylayzah?

Underneath that short and not terribly informative list, Tom wrote: "Despite an intense aversion to being touched sexually or kissed, he seems hypersexual. He enjoys being naked, looking at other naked men (or at least, me), masturbating and talking about masturbation, and he seemed to get an erotic charge out of describing the erection he had when he hung himself (naked). When he had a panic attack induced by kissing, he grew erect, and I'm pretty sure he had an erection when he panicked about the rubbing alcohol."

Tom wasn't very experienced with people who had suffered from sexual abuse as children, but all this seemed to point in that direction, including the fact that Kevin claimed to have very little memory of his childhood. Tom wished he could sit down and have a chat with Kevin's mother, but obviously that couldn't happen without Kevin's permission. According to what Tracy had said, that seemed unlikely. It was also possible the woman didn't know anything, or had blocked it from her mind just as Kevin had.

In cases of child sexual abuse, Tom knew, the abusers could be women, of course, but were most often male—on the order of 60 percent or more. Most victims knew their abusers. They were often members of the family or family friends. Combine that with the odd circumstance that Mr. Derocher committed suicide *after* his son had been sent to Hampton—not before—and Tom was beginning to have suspicions about just who that abuser might have been.

Kevin's father.

IN THE morning, Kevin claimed to have little memory of what had happened the night before. "I'm sorry I woke you up" was all he said when Tom asked him about it.

"That's not a big deal. But you seemed terrified. You don't remember anything about what you were dreaming?"

"No. I never do."

Tom shooed him out of the bed so he could strip the sheets off it. They were still slightly damp on Kevin's side, and there was no way Tom was going to leave them on the bed another night. "You said something when you were half-awake. I couldn't quite make it out."

The expression on Kevin's face was guarded as he stood there naked, hugging himself in the cool morning air. "What?"

"It sounded like 'keeraylayzah'."

If Tom had turned away a split second earlier to toss the sheets on the floor, he might not have caught the way Kevin's face blanched. As it was, he just caught it out of the corner of his eye. By the time he'd checked himself and turned back, Kevin had put up a mask of complete cluelessness again. "You recognize it, don't you?" Tom said.

Kevin started to shake his head in denial, but Tom pressed, "I saw your face when I said it. You recognized it."

"I don't know what it means."

"But you've heard it before."

Kevin shifted uncomfortably from one foot to another and grabbed the quilt off the floor to wrap it around himself, but Tom waited through this little dance until Kevin finally answered him. "I hear it every time the radio plays."

Tom went to the closet to retrieve some clean sheets. "A song?"

"No," Kevin said. "I don't mean I really hear it on the radio. I just hear it in my head whenever the radio's playing, like I'm trying to remember something I heard once. It's why I never listen to the radio."

"Can you sing the melody?"

Kevin shook his head. "It's just like two notes. Over and over. There's no music—no musical instruments, I mean. It's just some voices singing nonsense."

It was clearly distressing him to talk about this, so Tom let it drop. He tossed the fitted sheet on the bed and started to spread it out. "Can you help me put this on the mattress?"

IT WAS a Monday morning, but Tom had the day off, thanks to the holiday. He also had Tuesday off, for the same reason. What Kevin's schedule was like, he had no idea, but the man hadn't shown any sign of wanting to leave yet. Neither of them had showered, and it was already going on ten. The weather outside was still miserable—cold and drizzling—so going out wasn't terribly appealing.

Tom decided omelets might be a good idea, if he had enough eggs and cheese, so he rummaged around in his refrigerator for a few minutes. Cheese wasn't a problem. Kevin's favorite food in the entire world being cheeseburgers, Tom had stocked up on sliced cheese, beef patties, and buns. Eggs were less of a given, but he found a half-full carton of them.

When he surfaced again, he realized he'd just made a big mistake: he'd left his notepad open on the kitchen table.

Kevin was sitting at the table, looking at the notes Tom had taken at midnight. Tom couldn't even be annoyed with him for looking at them because there had been nothing covering up what he'd written. It had just been sitting there in plain sight.

Kevin sensed Tom was looking at him, and he glanced up. He didn't seem angry at first—more embarrassed. He gave a little half laugh and said, "Boy, whoever you're writing about sure sounds fucked up."

"No—"

"That shit's just totally fucking crazy, isn't it? I mean, he sounds like a real loser."

"Nothing there—"

"I thought you didn't want to be my therapist?" Kevin's anger was beginning to surface now. "But you're keeping *notes* on me?"

Tom didn't have a response for that. It hadn't seemed like there was anything wrong with it at the time, but how would he feel if he discovered his boyfriend was keeping those kinds of notes on *him*?

"I thought you were okay with…." Kevin broke off, anger warring with hurt on his face. "But this sounds like you think I'm some kind of pervert, getting off on fucked-up shit like suicide, when you can't even get a good fuck out of me!" His volume began to increase, and Tom knew they were in for a fight. Kevin shoved the notepad away from him so that it flew across the table and fell off onto the tile floor.

"Calm down, Kevin…."

"Oh, sorry. I keep forgetting you're going to leave me unless I stop acting crazy."

Tom tugged at his beard nervously. "I didn't say that."

"Maybe I should take some notes about you," Kevin interrupted. He stormed around the table and snatched the notepad up off the floor. "Let's see," he said, flipping to a blank page, "'Crazy Shit Tom Does.' We can start with the way you tug at that goddamned beard every time someone calls you on your bullshit. That's some kind of OCD behavior, isn't it? And how about this obsessive note-taking habit?"

"Look, Kevin, I'm sorry—"

"Or the way you think other people are too helpless to solve their own problems without you?"

"I just want to help you."

"No!" Kevin practically shouted back at him. "No! You aren't trying to help me. You're trying to *fix* me so you can have a normal boyfriend. One who likes to suck your cock and take your dick up his ass! And if I can't be *fixed*, then fuck me! You'll go find somebody else."

He threw the notepad on the table and stormed out of the kitchen through the back door. He was naked, as usual, and the weather outside on the deck was miserable, but Tom let him go. There was nothing he could do to stop him.

On one level, he knew exactly what all this was about. Kevin was projecting his fears onto Tom—the fear that Tom wouldn't be satisfied with a nonsexual relationship, the fear that Tom really did think he was crazy. Neither was true, of course. But lecturing Kevin about "projection" clearly wasn't going to fix things.

Tom fumed about it for a few minutes, convinced Kevin had acted childish, and it was up to him to get his ass back inside if he wanted to warm up. But when he looked out onto the deck, Kevin was just leaning against the railing, looking out into the acres of forest behind the house, not moving. Eventually, Tom gave up feeling self-righteous. He removed the bathrobe he'd been wearing, since he knew he was about to get soaked to the skin, and went outside.

The drizzle was just as cold and wretched as he'd thought it would be, and the wind was picking up, so he went over to the hot tub and dragged the lid off it. Kevin turned to glare at him as he climbed into the water, but when Tom said "If you get in here with me so we can both warm up, I might consider apologizing" he sighed and joined Tom in the tub.

"First of all," Tom said, having to raise his voice against the wind, "there's only one thing that'll get me to just straight-up leave you, and that's if you keep hitting me. I know you were out of your mind when it happened, and I should have listened when you told me to get the alcohol away from you. But I won't keep giving you a free pass on that if I start to feel threatened."

"I know."

"The rest of it... well, I guess you're right." The anger in Kevin's eyes seemed to be dying down to a smolder, so Tom risked moving a bit closer. "I do want to fix everybody. That's why I became a therapist. Most of the time, I'd argue that's a good thing, but... well, I guess you're right about me trying to fix you so you can be my boyfriend. Part of me was probably thinking that if I helped you figure out why you had such an aversion to sex, then we could *have* sex."

Kevin looked away, embarrassed. "Sounds logical."

"But selfish," Tom admitted. "It was more about what I wanted than what you wanted. And I can see where you might get the idea that, if you don't eventually satisfy whatever criteria I have for a good relationship, I might give up on you and move on to someone else. But that's not going to happen. I'm not that fucking shallow, okay?"

For a moment it looked as if Kevin might relent, but then his face hardened again. "You said I was a pervert."

"I said you were hypersexual," Tom corrected, "which isn't really a legitimate diagnosis. I simply meant that I found it odd that someone so averse to sexual contact was, in other ways, raunchier than many people I know."

"You don't like me because I'm not sexual enough, and you don't like me because I'm *too* sexual...."

"I like you quite a lot, Kevin. I like it when you're cute and shy, and I like it when you're running around naked with your morning wood waving around. God, I *love* that! I find your raunchy sense of humor kind of sexy, even when you're being crass. You're full of contradictions, and I find you puzzling, but that doesn't mean I don't want to be with you."

The rain had begun to pick up, and as sexy as Kevin looked with the drops beginning to form rivulets of water down his face, Tom had just seen a flash high up in the clouds. He was beginning to worry they'd be struck by lightning if they stayed out there much longer.

Kevin wiped the water out of his eyes and said, "I know where you're going with all this. You think it means I was molested or something, as a kid."

"Maybe. I've read that those experiences can make people averse to sex later in life, or just the opposite—extremely sexual. But it's not really my specialty. You're the only one who knows if it applies to you."

"No." Kevin shook his head. "I don't know. I don't remember."

Twelve

"Didn't Tom already tell you all this?"

Kevin was sitting on the couch in Sue's office on Friday afternoon, fidgeting as he always did when he felt he was on the spot. But despite the argument he and Tom had had that weekend, he hadn't backed out on the idea of going to therapy again. Sue had agreed to see him and to allow Tom to sit in on the session, though she hadn't been happy about the latter.

"No, Kevin," Sue replied calmly. "Tom told me that he was seeing someone he'd counseled three years ago, which I have to confess I wasn't thrilled to hear, but he never told me what you'd been counseled for. That would have been a breach of his professional ethics."

"Why didn't you want him to see me?"

Sue glanced at Tom, who was sitting on the couch beside Kevin, feeling extremely uncomfortable. "Because it isn't uncommon for someone who's been through therapy to develop feelings of attachment to or even affection for his therapist. It can be a natural reaction to somebody who has guided you through a rough time in your life. A therapist needs to be aware of this and not take advantage of the situation."

Kevin seemed to find that funny. He laughed and looked over at Tom. "Did you take advantage of my fragile psyche, counselor?"

"I saw you once, three years ago," Tom said defensively.

Kevin snorted and turned back to Sue. "I know what I'm doing. I don't need to be protected from the big, bad doctor."

"I don't have a doctorate," Tom muttered, but the other two ignored him.

Sue took a sip of her coffee and said, "It's all rather a moot point now, I think. What interests me more is your history."

"Tom can tell you about it."

"Tom is here to support you," Sue replied, "but he isn't the one being counseled. If you'd like help, you'll have to do the work."

Kevin grunted and said in the surly tone of voice Tom suspected Sue heard a lot from her clients, "Yes, ma'am."

"Would you care to tell me why you came to Tom in the first place?"

And so the story slowly unraveled, with Kevin dragging his feet in places, but Sue nudging him forward relentlessly. Her no-nonsense approach appeared to work with him, and Tom found himself a little jealous of her ability to extract details he hadn't yet managed to uncover.

Such as the specific reason Kevin was sent to Hampstead.

"I burned down the toolshed," he said. "That was kind of the last straw, I think."

"Which toolshed?"

"The one in the backyard. It was actually my mom's gardening shed. It was this flimsy old wooden thing that she kept her pots and tools and shit in."

Sue shifted in her chair and regarded him thoughtfully. "Why did you burn it down?"

Kevin shrugged. "Probably just to piss people off."

Sue wasn't able to get more out of him on that subject, but a short while later, when they were going over the nature of Kevin's panic attacks and what triggered them, the mysterious "keeraylayzah" came up.

Sue's response startled Tom. "Do you mean 'Kyrie Eleison'?"

"What?" Kevin looked just as shocked as Tom. More so, in fact. He'd turned pale, and that leg was going a mile a minute. "You know what it is?"

Sue stood and walked across the room to where she kept a stack of CDs near a CD player. "I'm not sure. It just reminded me of a section of the standard mass liturgy. *Kyrie eleison*. It's a Greek phrase meaning Lord, have mercy', and it's usually followed by *Christe eleison*—'Christ, have mercy'." She removed one of the CDs from the stack and placed it into the player. "There have been thousands of musical settings for the phrase, so I don't know how we would isolate a particular one you might have heard. Was your family Catholic?"

"No," Kevin said, "Baptist."

"Then you probably didn't hear it in church. Although choral masses are performed all the time outside of Catholic mass—they're very popular at Christmas, of course, and you might have heard it in a movie. Would you like to hear one from Mozart? It's a popular one."

Kevin nodded, but Tom could see he was already starting to sweat. Tom wanted to reach out to him, but how could he do that when his touch only made things worse? He tried to catch Kevin's eye, but the man was staring intently at the CD player, as if it were about to fire a bullet at him.

Sue forwarded to the correct track and then pressed Play. Tom didn't listen to Mozart very often, but the piece sounded familiar. Perhaps it had been used in the film *Amadeus*, which he'd seen years ago. But Kevin immediately shook his head.

"No," he said quickly, sounding relieved. "That's not it."

Sue turned it off and went back to her seat. "I would have been surprised if it was. As I said, there are thousands of musical settings for the *Kyrie*. And perhaps I'm wrong about the phrase you keep hearing in your dreams. It might not be *Kyrie eleison*."

Tom could practically see the gears turning in Kevin's mind as he tried the phrase on for size.

"I think it might be," Kevin said slowly. "I'm not sure, though."

"Well, perhaps it will come to you before our next session. You do plan on coming back?"

"Yeah, I guess so."

Sue went to her desk and reached for her appointment book. "Perhaps we could do without Tom next time?"

Kevin looked distressed at this suggestion, so Tom immediately jumped in with, "I didn't really contribute anything."

But Kevin gave him a dark look. "I need you here. Or I won't do it."

"All right," Tom said, seeing no reason to fight over it. To be honest, he wanted to be there anyway. "No problem."

TOM had about forty-five minutes after the session to grab a quick lunch before he had a client of his own due, so he and Kevin walked down to Tony's Pizza & Sub Shop on Main Street and bought some Italian grinders.

"How do you feel?" Tom asked Kevin on their way back to his office.

Kevin shrugged. "Okay."

"You were looking a little freaked out by that *Kyrie eleison* thing."

"No shit," Kevin said, giving Tom one of his cute little smiles. "I feel like it's crawling around in my brain now, worse than before. I thought I was going to hurl when she turned the CD player on."

"But that wasn't the right music."

"No."

Tom took a bite of his grinder, chewed, and swallowed before he asked, "Do you mind if I do a little digging to see if I can come up with a more likely possibility?"

"I guess not," Kevin answered carefully, "but how will you know if something is more likely than Mozart?"

"I don't know. Maybe I can search through old news articles for the area, from the time you were, say, five, up 'til you were about fifteen. Look for anything with *Kyrie eleison* in it—concerts, performances of masses, stuff like that."

Kevin gave a loud, short laugh. "Good luck with that."

Tom had to admit, it didn't sound like a great plan. This wasn't a big city, with decades of news archives available in searchable databases. He'd have to go to local libraries and see if they had newspapers on microfiche or something. "Well, I'll start on the Internet and see what turns up. I might not find anything, but I just wanted to check with you that it was okay for me to research it."

Kevin reached over with his hand and brushed a finger along the side of Tom's face, tracing a path through his beard. It was a gesture he'd adopted a couple of days ago, and it was Tom's new crack cocaine. That simple gesture seemed to validate their relationship, to prove that Kevin really did feel something more than friendship. Tom craved and reveled in it. "Go right ahead, counselor."

When they reached the door to Tom's clinic, Kevin said, "I have to get over to Lee's. He asked me to put up some chain link fence in his yard to expand his dog pen. You want me to come over tonight?"

"Of course."

Kevin had been over every night that week, but he'd called every day to ask if it was okay. And every day Tom had said, "yes." It would probably take a few weeks of this for them to decide that it was always okay for Kevin to come over.

Kevin brushed a finger lightly against Tom's cheek again. "I'll see you."

TOM'S appointment was late. So he sat down at his desk to finish his sandwich and brought up a web browser. He typed "Kyrie eleison" into Google, figuring it would bring up thousands of useless links, a hopeless rat's maze to get lost in.

But he was wrong.

The first few links were to Wikipedia articles, but the first video link that came up wasn't to some orchestra playing Mozart or Brahms. It was a rock video from 1985, when Kevin would have been nine years old: "Kyrie" by a band called Mr. Mister.

A chill came over Tom as he listened to the song. It was vaguely familiar. He assumed he must have heard it on the radio a lot the year it came out, as Kevin probably had—they were the same age. But it wasn't until he got about two and a half minutes into the song that his breath caught in his throat and he brought a trembling hand up to tug at the dark hair on his chin. For just a couple of lines, all the instruments stopped abruptly, while the lead singer and the other members of the band—all men—sang:

> *Kyrie eleison down the road that I must travel,*
> *Kyrie eleison through the darkness of the night.*

Without music.

Thirteen

"You can't know if that's it until Kevin listens to it," Sue said reasonably.

Tom was in her office during a brief respite between clients. He'd downloaded a bootleg copy of the song onto his laptop and played it for her.

"What if he freaks out?" he asked. "I can't tell him he needs to get control of himself and then deliberately start pushing his buttons to see what might make him have another flashback."

"For all you know, the two of you could be cuddling in bed watching a movie one night, and that song could start playing on the soundtrack," Sue said. "If it *is* a potential trigger for him, he needs to learn how to handle it in a controlled situation—not just stumble blindly along until he bumps into it by chance. If he's aware that what he's about to listen to may trigger unpleasant memories and feelings, and he understands that he's in a safe environment, and those memories no longer have the ability to harm him, he can begin to desensitize himself to the trigger.

"But having said that," she added, "I really don't recommend you tackling this on your own, Tom. You haven't had much experience with PTSD and, as all three of us keep pointing out, you're not his therapist—you're his lover. Wait until we're back in my office next Friday afternoon."

Tom had to admit that was probably the best way to handle it. Unfortunately, things didn't quite work out that way when he and Kevin were alone in the hot tub later that night.

"So have you found my song yet, counselor?" Kevin asked bluntly. He was grinning, clearly assuming the answer was "no." There hadn't been any time, after all. The idea that a simple Google search could solve the riddle in less than five minutes seemed preposterous.

Tom could have evaded the question, but he was terrible at that. And he was even worse at outright lying. So he said, "I don't know. I might have found some possibilities…."

Kevin gave him a quizzical look with one eyebrow raised, which Tom couldn't recall ever having seen someone do in real life before. "What did you find?"

Tom hesitated but realized it was too late to backpedal. "There was a song that was popular on the radio… it came out in 1985. You would have been nine."

Tom stopped talking because Kevin's demeanor had changed suddenly. All the humor had faded from his expression, and he was holding up one hand partly in front of his face, as if to ward off a blow. He'd obviously been bluffing when he'd asked if Tom had found anything. He hadn't expected Tom to call his bluff.

"Are you okay?" Tom asked.

"I'm fine." Kevin climbed out of the hot tub and reached for his towel. "I've just got to use the bathroom. I'll be back in a minute."

He was gone a lot longer than a minute. When he did finally return, Kevin had a couple of beers in his hands and handed one to Tom. He climbed back into the water and took a big swig from his bottle. "Hey!" he said with a grin, "Are you still looking for a dog?"

"A dog?" Tom hadn't really given it much serious thought yet. "Well, I want one, yes. But I'm still furniture hunting."

"Lee has a black Lab pup, about a year old, that he's looking for a home for. He had two others, but they've been taken."

Tom knew this was largely an attempt to derail the conversation about the song, and he had no doubt Kevin knew he wasn't fooled by it. But that was fine. Tom didn't want to deal with another panic attack right now anyway. So he went along with the change of topic. "I don't know if I'm really ready for a dog yet."

"He's awful cute," Kevin said, his eyes twinkling. "And Lee can't keep him forever. He already has four other dogs."

"I don't have time for a dog," Tom protested. "I have to work during the days."

"Everybody has to work. Nobody has stay-at-home wives—or husbands—anymore. They still get dogs. You just crate him while you're at work."

"Isn't that cruel?"

Kevin couldn't answer right away because he had his beer tilted to his lips, but he shook his head. Then he swallowed and said, "Dogs are den animals. They like being in caves and holes in the ground. For a short time anyway—sure it's cruel if you leave him in there all the time. But as long as he's in a cool spot with a comfortable mat, a bowl of water, and a chew toy, he'll be fine in there while you're working. Once he settles in, and you can trust him not to piss in the house or chew shit, you won't have to crate him anymore. For now, I can stop by in the middle of the day and walk him."

That would, of course, mean Kevin would have his own key. Things were probably heading that way, but... it seemed awfully fast. "Why don't *you* adopt him?"

Kevin looked uncomfortable at that. He glanced away before replying, "He needs someone responsible to look after him. I can barely take care of myself."

"So you're admitting you're irresponsible," Tom said, "but you want me to trust you to come walk my dog every day?"

Kevin turned back to him and flashed him a smile. "I can be responsible for an hour or two out of the day, counselor. But all the time? That's a tall order."

They went back and forth like that for a bit longer until Tom finally agreed to go with Kevin to see the dog the next day, if that was okay with Lee. Tom had a bad feeling that, if he had a hard time saying "no" to Kevin right now, he'd find it impossible to say "no" to Kevin and an adorable black Lab puppy when they were teamed up against him.

THE dog was named Shadow, and he was beautiful. He hadn't quite grown into his big head and paws, though Lee said he was already over seventy pounds. His big ears and nose gave him an adorably goofy look, but he had a sleek, jet-black coat, and he promised to grow into a handsome pooch. As soon as Lee let Tom and Kevin into the large dog pen in his backyard, the four adult dogs—all purebred black Labradors—mobbed them for attention, but Shadow sat off to one side, knowing he couldn't compete with the other dogs. Still, he wagged his tail frantically, hoping the humans would come over to pet him. When Lee lured the other dogs away to another part of the pen, Kevin crouched down and started rubbing behind Shadow's floppy ears. The pup succumbed to full-blown puppy ecstasy, and the two ended up wrestling in the dirt for a couple of minutes. The two of them were already old friends since Kevin had visited several times after Shadow was born.

Tom's introduction to the pup was a bit more sedate, but Shadow wasn't at all shy and responded to Tom's pets and scratches by lapping at Tom's face with enthusiasm. *God knows where that tongue has been*, Tom thought. But he knew it was a lost cause. He was no match for an affectionate puppy tongue.

"He's a good boy," Lee commented when they had Shadow out of the pen on a leash, pulling a bit to sniff around at exciting clumps of grass and dandelions. "But it costs a fortune to feed these guys."

Lee was a big man, over six feet tall and getting a bit broad in the middle. His features were coarse, with a heavy brow over a large nose. Kevin had mentioned that Lee had been in the Marines, way back, and he still kept his hair in a buzz cut. Not someone Tom would want to run into in a dark alley. But he was friendly enough, and Tom was pleased to see no trace of animosity between him and Kevin over Tracy's defection.

"Normally, I sell the pups," Lee went on, "but since you're a friend of Kevin's, I'll let you have this little guy for nothing. Just so long as you treat him right."

Tom sighed, resigned, as he watched Shadow and Kevin going at it again, wrestling affectionately in the lush green grass. They were both adorable, and the combination was deadly.

"Thanks," he said.

THERE was an Agway in Lancaster, about fifteen minutes down the road, so Tom drove there with Kevin riding in the backseat, keeping Shadow calm on his First Ever Car Ride. The puppy handled it well, with only a bit of whimpering, which Kevin soothed away. By the time they pulled into the Agway parking lot, Shadow was an old pro, sniffing excitedly at the top of the window Kevin had rolled down a couple inches.

They were allowed to take the dog into the store, and Tom insisted on holding the leash this time. If Shadow was going to be his dog, then they'd have to bond. It was great seeing the bond the puppy already had with Kevin, but Kevin's role in Tom's future was even more uncertain than Shadow's at the moment. Although he didn't like to think about it, a year from now, Tom and Shadow might be on their own.

Still, there was a wonderful feeling of family as the three of them walked through the store, picking out the largest dog crate they could find and three dog beds—one for the crate, one for the bedroom, and one for the living room—along with food, bowls, and an assortment of chew toys.

Tom picked up a stuffed mallard and squeezed it. The toy gave out a low *honk!* and Shadow's ears immediately perked up. "Do you like this one?" Tom asked, amused by the dog's intently focused expression.

Shadow raised himself up until he was balancing on just his hind legs, sniffing at the duck as if it were the most fascinating thing he'd ever come across. When Tom playfully bumped the dog's nose with it, Shadow immediately snapped it up in his jaws.

Honk!

Tom laughed. "You like that one?"

Honk! Honk!

"Okay, you can have it."

Honk! Honk! Honk!

And so they walked to the counter, Shadow cantering in front of the two men, honking at everybody they came across along the way to make sure they fully appreciated his prize. He was Shadow, the Mighty Duck Hunter, and he'd just made his first kill!

The pup refused to be parted with the stuffed mallard, even long enough for Tom to pay for it, so Tom had to snap the tag off in order for the price to be scanned. The three of them returned to the car with Shadow carrying the duck in his mouth, and the men had to listen to him joyfully honking all the way home.

"I think you've created a monster." Kevin laughed, sitting in the front seat this time since Shadow was entirely preoccupied with his new toy.

Honk!

"As long as it makes him happy," Tom said. "But I may have to take it away from him at night, or we'll never get any sleep."

Honk! Honk!

APART from his newfound duck obsession, Tom discovered Shadow had a couple of other eccentricities. His entire life, thus far, had been outdoors in a large pen. Therefore, he wasn't housebroken. The moment they brought Shadow into the house, the dog lifted his leg on one of the boxes in the dining room. Kevin handled it by interrupting what Shadow was doing and quickly bustling him outside. Since he seemed to have a handle on the training part of it, Tom stayed behind to clean up the mess.

What have I gotten myself into?

The other eccentricity was discovered later that evening. They'd all been hanging around in the lower part of the house—setting up Shadow's crate in the dining room and allowing the dog to familiarize himself with his new surroundings—and walking Shadow around the yard. When it grew late and Tom decided he'd like to hang out in bed for a while to read before going to sleep, he and Kevin went upstairs and called to Shadow.

He didn't follow.

Tom went to the top of the stairs and called down, "Come on, boy!"

Shadow paced back and forth at the bottom of the stairs, whimpering. Beginning to grow concerned, Tom called to Kevin, who joined him at the top of the stairs for a moment before descending to the bottom. Once he was downstairs, Shadow stopped whining and panted happily.

"I think he's fine," Kevin observed. "He just doesn't want to go upstairs."

"Is he trying to tell us there's a vengeful dead Japanese girl in my bedroom?" Tom was only half joking. It always spooked him when animals acted as though they saw things humans couldn't see.

"He's probably just afraid of stairs."

"Stairs?"

Kevin crouched down and scratched behind Shadow's big floppy ears, letting the pup lick all over his face—something that made Tom incredibly envious of the dog. "Stairs are scary, aren't they, boy?" Kevin asked in a singsong voice. "Especially for a puppy who's never been in a house before. Yes, they are!"

Tom came down the stairs to pet Shadow on the head and was rewarded by an affectionate licking of his fingers. "He didn't have trouble going up and down the front steps to the porch today."

"There's only four or five of those," Kevin replied. "Here, we've got—" He counted. "—twelve. That's huge! And God knows where they go. It could be the Scariest Place in the World up there!"

Tom laughed, touched by Kevin's ability to empathize with the dog. *Yeah*, he thought, *you'd make a good father, if you can ever get past your own baggage.* "So what should we do? I hate to leave him alone down here in his crate, especially on his first night in the house."

"Hold on," Kevin said. Then he scooped the seventy-pound puppy up in his strong arms and carried him up the stairs.

Once at the top, Kevin set Shadow down, and the dog appeared to be fine. He sniffed around the small upper landing and nosed his way into the library and the spare bedrooms.

"Problem solved," Kevin announced.

"I hope we don't have to do that every night," Tom said, climbing the stairs to join them in the upper hall. "And it will be interesting to see if he pees all over us when we carry him down in the morning."

Kevin smiled at him and reached out to scratch his beard. *Progress*, Tom thought. A full scratch, instead of the light, tentative brushes with Kevin's finger he'd been getting during the week. Baby steps, but each one touched him.

He met Kevin's sleepy hazel eyes and smiled back at him. "Where did you learn to be so good with dogs?"

"I don't know." Kevin shrugged. "We had a couple big dogs when I was a kid. My father liked yellow Labs. And I play with the mutts at Lee's whenever I do work at his place."

"You're wonderful," Tom said. "Shadow and I are lucky to have you."

He was rewarded with that shy smile he adored as Kevin came damned close to blushing.

Fourteen

"I DON'T hate my mother, if that's what you mean."

Sue shifted in her chair and picked up her cup of coffee. "I merely asked why you haven't seen her in four years," she replied coolly.

Kevin had immediately made it clear that the subject of The Song was off-limits for this session. He wasn't ready to deal with it, and he'd forbidden Tom to even tell him the title during the intervening week. Sue had been willing to put that off for another time, but in exchange, she'd begun to delve into the details of Kevin's childhood.

Tom felt Kevin's hand squeezing his fingers. The delicate touches and caresses Kevin gave him—always on the face, arms, or legs, never directly on his body—had progressed to Kevin occasionally taking his fingers in his hand and holding them for a time. Now, Kevin's grip had grown uncomfortably tight, almost painful, but Tom let him hold on.

"We don't get along," Kevin said, his leg twitching.

"Have you had a falling out?"

"No."

Sue took a slow sip of her coffee. "When did she move to Riverview?"

"Five years ago."

There was a long silence, during which Sue seemed content to simply sip her coffee and watch Kevin fidget. At last Kevin gave a frustrated sigh and said, "Look. She'd almost hit retirement age, and she wasn't in great health. She never took care of her diabetes properly. She wanted me to move back into the house and look after her and take care of the repairs it needed, but there was no fucking way."

"You didn't want to look after your mother?"

Kevin frowned. "I didn't say that. I can't say I *wanted* to do that, but I would have."

"Then why didn't you?"

"Because I hated that place. I'd rather cut off my balls than move back into that house."

He noticed he was crushing Tom's fingers and let them slip from his grasp, muttering, "Sorry." Then he leaned forward and rubbed his face with his hands. "Tracy would've moved into the house, but I couldn't. And Mom wouldn't move into the trailer. So we arranged for her to go to Riverview. She wasn't real happy about it. But it's a nice place."

"Yes, it is," Sue agreed, "but why couldn't you move back into your house?"

"Because I get sick just thinking about it!" Kevin snapped. He stood up and started pacing. "I know everyone's supposed to be all nostalgic and shit about their childhood and where they grew up, but there's nothing in that place I want to remember."

"What happened to the house?" Sue asked. "Did your mother sell it?"

"She tried. It's still on the market."

"So you could still go visit it."

Kevin stopped pacing and glared at her. "Why the hell would I want to do that?"

There was something dangerous in the way he was standing, looming over Sue with his hands balled into fists, his mouth set in a grim line, and one of the muscles in his jaw twitching with suppressed anger. But Sue didn't even adjust her position in her chair. She looked back at him calmly, meeting his eyes without any sign of being intimidated. Tom could see why she did so well with veterans suffering from PTSD.

"You said it yourself, Kevin," Sue replied calmly. "Although indirectly. You said, 'There's nothing in that place I want to remember.' But we both know that not remembering is part of the problem, don't we?"

Kevin didn't answer. He went back to the couch and plopped down on it beside Tom, but this time he made no move to take Tom's hand. He was withdrawing into himself like a petulant child, not wanting to admit Sue might be right.

Sue seemed to sense this and gave him a couple of minutes, while she went to the coffeemaker and poured herself a new cup. "Would anybody like some?" she asked, holding the carafe up.

"Yes, please," Tom said. Kevin just shook his head.

When they were all situated again, Sue said, "Sometimes in cases of suppressed memories, we bring in family members to help us reconstruct the period in a client's life that has gaps. You don't have any siblings. Do you have any grandparents or aunts or uncles still in the area? Any cousins? People who knew you as a child?"

"No," Kevin said. "My grandparents are all dead. I haven't seen my mother's sister since she went into a retirement home in Maine, and she was never around when I was a kid anyway. If I have any cousins, I've never heard of them."

"Any childhood friends you're still in touch with?"

Something seemed to flicker briefly in Kevin's features—something Tom couldn't identify—but it vanished just as quickly. Kevin simply said, "Not really. I didn't have many friends when I was young, and I was away through a lot of junior high school. I sort of knew some kids, like Lee and Tracy, but I never hung out with them."

"Then that leaves your mother. Is there any way we could bring her in for a group session?"

Kevin shook his head adamantly. "No. That's not going to happen."

"Because you don't think she'll come, or because you don't want her here?"

"Both."

Sue sat back in her chair and gave Kevin a long, evaluating look. Tom could see she was beginning to find Kevin exasperating. The list of things Kevin considered off-limits was growing: his father's suicide, his mother, the song he might or might not be dreaming about.... Tom began to fear Sue would tell Kevin she couldn't help him after all. But Kevin needed her more than he realized.

Tom spoke up. "Do you still have a key to your house?"

Kevin gave him a sharp look. "The real estate agent that's been trying to sell it off—he made me take a key, in case of... God knows...." He looked away, down at his fidgeting knee. "I might be able to find it."

"Then why don't we take a look at the house this weekend? Just a quick walkthrough to see if it jogs any memories for you."

"I'll be there with you," Sue commented. "And we'll leave if you feel you can't handle it."

"I *already* don't feel like I can handle it," Kevin said testily.

Sue smiled at him, unperturbed. "I understand. But we can't stay completely safe. We'll do what we can to make sure you don't feel threatened."

"Like what? How are you going to protect me from what's in my own head?"

Sue said gently, "One possibility is to give you a mild sedative."

Kevin did not look pleased with the idea. His entire face looked closed off, his eyes narrowed, his mouth flat and tense. Even his nostrils seemed to be constricted. "It was falling apart four years ago. The roof will probably collapse on us the moment we open the front door."

"We'll take the chance."

Tom could see Kevin was beginning to sweat again. Kevin looked over at Sue, but she was the last person he could expect to bail him out of this. He looked down at his knee again. At last, he said, "Fine."

THE house certainly didn't *look* as if it was about to collapse. It was a large, white colonial with a small screened-in front porch and an attached two-car garage. There was a "For Sale" sign on the front lawn, and the real estate agency had apparently sent somebody around recently to mow the grass. If it was in need of repairs, that wasn't obvious from the outside. Overall, Tom thought it was a lovely house—one he wouldn't have minded living in.

But Kevin's face wore an expression of utter disgust as he got out of the passenger side of Tom's car. He opened the back door and had to body-block Shadow from bolting out of the car until Kevin had a hold of his leash. It was a hot day, and the sun was beating down on them from a nearly cloudless sky. There was no way the dog could stay in the car without the air conditioner running.

"He might lift his leg on something if we bring him inside," Tom observed. Shadow had gotten a little better about that, in the past week, but still didn't have the whole not-peeing-in-the-house thing quite down yet.

Kevin let the dog jump down from the seat, and then he slammed the back door. "So what? I hope he does."

Tom rolled his eyes at him, but Shadow was nuzzling his hand for attention, so he leaned down to scratch the pup on the head. Shadow was so excited to be in this new place that he couldn't stop wagging his tail, which had the effect of making his entire body wag in the opposite direction as a counterweight. His tail, Tom and Kevin had discovered by now, was incredibly strong and heavy. It frequently knocked objects off low surfaces, such as glasses of coffee foolishly left sitting on boxes in the living room while Tom rushed around getting ready for work. And both men had been struck in the testicles so often that it was probably a good thing they didn't plan on having children.

"Here, take him," Kevin said, handing the leash to Tom.

Tom escorted Shadow onto the lawn to pee, while Kevin fished the house key out of his pocket. Shadow strained against the leash, fascinated by every rock and blade of grass in this new yard.

Sue's car was nowhere to be seen, which worried Tom. She'd promised to arrive before the scheduled time, and it wasn't like her to be late for anything. Tom pulled out his cell phone to call her, but it rang the moment it was out of his pocket.

"Tom!" Sue exclaimed when he answered. "I'm sorry I didn't call sooner, but things have been crazy here at the hospital—"

"The hospital! Why are you at the hospital?"

"One of my clients attempted suicide this morning," Sue replied. "I can't really go into much detail. But please pass my apology along to Kevin and tell him we'll have to reschedule for another time."

"We're already at the house," Tom protested, though he knew it was pointless. Sue couldn't simply walk out on her other client.

"I'm sorry, Tom. Just ask Kevin if we can reschedule. But don't go in there without me. I think that might be… risky." Before Tom could respond, she added, "Here's her doctor. I've got to go. I'll see you on Monday!"

When he relayed her message to Kevin, Tom was surprised by the man's almost hostile reaction. "Fuck it. We're going in now."

"This isn't her fault, Kevin."

"I know that," Kevin replied darkly. "Do you think I'm a total asshole?"

"No."

"Other people have problems. It's not all about Kevin Derocher. I get that. I hope her patient's okay. But I'm not coming out here again."

"We can come tomorrow—"

"Tom!" Kevin's voice was so sharp that Tom staggered back from it, as if he expected the man to hit him. Apparently, Kevin noticed because when he spoke again, he was calmer, but his voice still had an edge to it. "Tom, you have no idea how much I had to psyche myself up to come here. You're the one who wanted to see this place. So fine! Let's see it! We'll tell Dr. Cross all about it later. But I am not coming here again. This is it."

With that, he strode across the lawn, ignoring the walkway, and unlocked the front door. Tom had little choice but to follow him.

He caught up with Kevin standing in the empty front hall, eerily still, as if listening for something. But there wasn't a sound. The bare walls had ghostly rectangular shadows in places, where decades of sunlight had faded the paint around picture frames, now absent, and the carpeting exuded a smell of cleaning chemicals.

When Shadow nosed his hand, Kevin rubbed the top of the dog's head absently and said, "This is the first time I've seen it since everything was taken out."

"Where did all the furnishings go?" Tom asked. "Your mother couldn't have brought them to Riverview with her."

Kevin shook his head. "No, we put whatever she wanted to keep into storage. God knows why. I'll never touch any of it. When she's gone, I'll have to either sell it or trash it."

Tom found that incredibly sad, but he said nothing. He and Shadow simply trailed behind Kevin as he drifted from room to room. Not all the furnishings were gone. Some things Mrs. Derocher hadn't wanted were still in the rooms, covered with protective sheets, in case a new owner might want them, but they merely enhanced the barren atmosphere of the house.

The downstairs had a large living room with a fireplace and window seats Tom coveted, a dining room, a half bath, and a beautiful kitchen with a stainless steel gas stove and refrigerator, granite countertops, and tiled walls with a country motif of apples and pears on them. Everything about the house screamed "affluence" to Tom, even devoid of most of its original furnishings.

"What did your parents do for work?" Tom asked.

"My father was a lawyer," Kevin replied, still seeming lost in thought as he brushed his fingers along the natural wood top of the kitchen island. "My mother was a receptionist at his firm, but she quit working when she married him. I think being forced to go back to work, after he killed himself, upset her more than losing her husband."

"I thought you said this place was falling apart."

"I lied," Kevin said curtly. "I just didn't want to come out here."

That was irritating, but Tom didn't see much point in making a big deal about it. "You said your mother wanted you to move in so you could keep up with repairs."

"That part was true," Kevin said. "The roof needs some repair, and there were other things my mother needed done around the place—electrical work, some plumbing—so she wanted me to move in and take care of things. At least, that was her excuse. Really, she just wanted me to come home. As if I ever would."

He turned and strode out of the kitchen back to the hall, calling over his shoulder, "Nothing more exciting than dinner and Saturday morning cartoons ever happened down here. The real excitement in the Derocher family was upstairs!"

Tom had to carry Shadow up the broad staircase, so it took a minute for them to catch up to him at the far end of the hall. Kevin had stopped in one of the upper hall doorways. He flipped the light on, and Tom looked past him to see a bathroom, tiled in blue and white, in a geometric pattern that seemed vaguely Roman. The room was large enough to accommodate both a shower and a square tub not much smaller than Tom's hot tub, in addition to the toilet and sink.

"Here's where the real family drama took place," Kevin said, sounding like a tour guide. "He did it in the tub."

"Your father? His suicide, you mean?"

Kevin walked up to the tub and waited until Tom was standing beside him, peering down into the basin, before continuing. "Most men might have been happy to just slash their wrists open but not my father. He never did anything by halves."

He raised his right hand and spread his index and ring fingers apart into a V. "After I burned down the gardening shed, my mother went out and bought all new tools for her garden. She had a kick-ass garden back then. So Dad filled up the tub with hot water one night when Mom was asleep. Then he sat down and took her brand new pruning shears—" Kevin slid his open fingers down along his front until they were framing where his penis would have been sticking out if he hadn't been wearing jeans. "—and clipped it off." He snapped his fingers shut.

Tom's stomach churned at the thought. "That's... revolting."

"Then he just sat there until he bled out. Mom found him sitting in a tub full of bloody water in the morning."

"Nice." Clearly, Kevin's father had had some issues himself. "I'm beginning to sense a theme here."

Kevin looked at him uncertainly for a moment. Then he gave Tom a sad smile. "Yeah, well... I may have shown it to everyone on Northside Road, but I didn't cut it off."

"That's good. I'm rather fond of your penis."

"Even if you can't touch it?"

"I can admire it from afar," Tom replied and then immediately regretted the semiflirtatious tone it lent to the conversation. It hardly seemed appropriate, given the context.

What would possess a man to mutilate himself that way? But Tom thought he might already know the answer to that: guilt. In particular, guilt over inappropriate sexual behavior with his son. Tom had no proof of that yet, but he strongly suspected it.

"Where were you when this happened?" Tom asked.

"I was still at Hampstead." Kevin took a deep breath and walked out of the room, scratching Shadow behind the ear on his way out. "I'll show you the bedrooms, not that there's anything there."

He was right about that. The room Kevin's parents had shared contained a bed and a couple of dressers, but of course all the personal effects had been taken away. Kevin's bedroom was the same.

Kevin pulled the sheet off the twin bed in his room to expose the bare mattress. "I had the same bed from the time I was about three until I left home at eighteen." He stretched out on the mattress, and he had to bend his knees to keep his feet from hanging over the bottom. "By the time I was seventeen, I was too tall for this damned thing. Mom wanted to buy me a new one, but I wasn't planning on sticking around much longer, so I kept telling her it was fine."

"How does it feel to lie there again?" Tom asked. He had hoped being in his old room might trigger something in Kevin's memory.

But Kevin just shrugged. "It's not a very comfortable mattress. I'm glad I don't have to sleep on this thing anymore."

He got up to look out one of the two double-hung windows. Tom went to stand beside him. The window looked out upon a fair-sized backyard with a rust-colored picnic table and small patio coming off the kitchen. Across the yard was a small stand of birch trees, and beyond that, more of the ubiquitous pine and birch forest that blanketed this part of the state.

"Where was the shed?" Tom asked.

Kevin nodded in the direction of a small patch of overgrown grass in one corner of the yard. "My mother wanted to replace it, but after my father killed himself, she never got around to it."

"Let's go take a look."

But Kevin shook his head. There was an odd look in his eyes—a troubled look. But he wasn't staring at the grass where the shed had been. He was looking at the forest, as he often did when they were hanging out on Tom's deck. For the first time, Tom found himself wondering if there was something significant behind that look. He always just assumed Kevin was lost in thought, and where he was looking was irrelevant. But perhaps he was wrong. Was there something about the forest itself that drew Kevin's attention?

"I'd like to stay up here a minute," Kevin said quietly. "You go ahead. I think Shadow needs to go out again anyway."

That was probably true. The pup had gotten better at letting Tom and Kevin know when he needed to relieve himself by pacing back and forth in a frantic manner, and now he was doing so by the door of the bedroom, straining against his leash. They'd learned the hard way not to ignore this behavior. So Tom left Kevin alone with his thoughts, hoping it would be good for him. He had to carry the pooch downstairs, but fortunately he managed to get him outside without Shadow having an accident.

After Shadow had finished his business, Tom led him around to the back of the house. Along the way, they passed what had once been a flower bed, now overgrown with weeds, and Tom found himself smiling as he remembered Kevin talking about kicking down the urinating boy lawn ornament.

He took Shadow across the empty yard, past the patio and the picnic table, until they came to the overgrown patch Kevin had pointed out from the window. To Tom's surprise, there were still blackened, burnt boards underneath the vegetation. Someone had cleaned the area up a bit and stacked the few intact boards off to one side, where they had lain untouched for twenty-five years, as grass and weeds grew around and through them, almost obscuring them. But not quite. There was something eerie and unsettling about it. But the question in Tom's mind was whether there was anything *significant* about it. Had it just been a random act of rebellion—something relatively harmless, yet still dramatic and destructive? Or had there been some reason Kevin wanted to destroy the shed?

Shadow was nosing curiously through the weeds and the wreckage, but Tom pulled him back, fearful of old nails that might still be in the boards. He glanced up at the forest no more than thirty feet away and wondered again if anything lay out there that might provide another piece of this puzzle.

As he and Shadow walked back to the house, Tom looked up to see if Kevin was still watching from his bedroom, but the window was empty. *It's probably time to leave*, he thought. They'd been through the place, he'd learned a bit more about Kevin's family, and he'd seen the infamous gardening shed. But there was probably nothing more to be learned here.

"Kevin!" Tom called when he stepped into the front hall once more. "I'm ready to go if you are."

There was no answer. Tom listened, but the house was disturbingly silent, apart from Shadow's heavy panting. "Kevin?"

Still no answer.

Tom left Shadow to wander around by himself downstairs while he walked slowly up the stairs. He was unable to shake the feeling he was stepping into a Hitchcock film, and Mr. Derocher's mummified corpse was about to fall out of a broom closet, clutching its withered, severed penis in one hand.

"Kevin?" Still no answer. Growing fearful, Tom quickly searched the rooms until he came to the large upstairs bathroom.

That's where he found him.

Kevin lay in the tub, despite the fact that there wasn't any water, curled up in a fetal position with his arms holding his knees close to his chest. From what Tom could see, he was naked. Kevin's face was resting against the rim of the tub, and he was staring blankly into space, so motionless that Tom felt a chill prick up the hair on his scalp.

"Kevin?" he asked quietly, afraid to draw near—afraid he might find Kevin sitting in a pool of blood.

But Kevin wasn't dead. His eyes remained glassy and seemingly sightless as he said, in a voice barely above a whisper, "The water's cold...."

"There isn't any water, Kevin."

Kevin didn't seem to be listening. He was silent for a long time before he said, "I don't wanna take a bath. I had one this morning." His voice sounded odd, as though he were talking in his sleep, and there was a childlike quality to it. "Okay...." He laughed faintly. "Daddy...," he said, his voice scolding, "I'm big now... I can do it myself...." His expression grew uncertain, and his voice more docile. "Okay... no, I won't tell... yeah, I promise...."

But after a long silence, during which his face wore an expression halfway between bewilderment and anxiety, Kevin suddenly screwed his face up in disgust. "No, don't—that's gross. I don't wanna...." Then his anxiety appeared to ease a bit. "Okay... yeah, that feels okay...."

This unsettling monologue went on for quite some time. Tom had heard of PTSD sufferers having flashbacks, but he had little experience with it. *Damn you for barreling in here without Sue, Kevin!*

Tom sat down on the floor near Kevin and let him ramble on in this vague way. He was tempted to call Sue, but she had her own mess to deal with right now, and Tom didn't want to do anything that might disrupt what Kevin was going through. Whatever Kevin was experiencing, Tom felt reasonably certain he needed to let it happen. At least he hoped that was the right way to handle this.

At some point, tears began to leak out of Kevin's eyes and trickle down around his nose and lips, but his expression wasn't that of someone crying. He still looked vaguely anxious, but not really frightened or upset. And the fragments of dialog Tom overheard seemed mostly confused. The boy Kevin had been had trusted his father and not felt threatened by him. It was apparent some of the experience had even been pleasant, a sort of bonding between a boy and his father, but the whole thing seemed to have left him uneasy and baffled by this new way of looking at the man. His father had suddenly become a different person—one who liked to do things Kevin found gross and embarrassing, one who forced a closeness Kevin wasn't comfortable with, and one who had effectively cut Kevin from his mother by a solemn oath never to reveal their "secret."

Tom wasn't certain when he himself began to cry. He simply became aware that his face was wet as he watched this replay of parental betrayal. He was sickened and enraged. If Kevin's father had still been alive, Tom wasn't sure he'd be able to restrain himself from seeking the man out and punching him in the face—just before calling the police on the bastard.

Downstairs, Shadow had begun to grow distraught at being left alone. He began to bark and whine piteously, and that finally brought Kevin back to the present. His face an emotionless mask, as if all feeling had been drained from his body, Kevin's eyes focused on Tom's anxious face.

"Kevin?"

"Why did you do this to me?"

Tom wasn't certain if the question was directed at him or at Kevin's father. But Kevin stood up in the tub, a little unsteadily, and said, "I want to go home."

Fifteen

IT WAS a challenge getting Kevin dressed again and into the car. His face was still blank and expressionless and he was behaving like a zombie—the old-fashioned kind of undead robot from pre-George Romero horror films that would just stand motionless and stare into space until its master issued a command. But Kevin wasn't a particularly good zombie, and he had to be told two or three times to put on each article of clothing, one at a time.

Despite his reluctance to touch him, Tom was finally forced to take Kevin's wrist and guide him down the stairs and into the car. He went back inside to fetch Shadow and lock up with Kevin's key, and then he drove to his house.

As they pulled into the long driveway, Kevin appeared to become aware of his surroundings for a moment, and his face darkened. "I said I wanted to go *home*. Not here."

"I'm sorry, but I don't want you to be alone right now. You can go upstairs and be by yourself, but I want you here."

As soon as the car stopped, Kevin got out and slammed the door angrily. But he walked up onto the porch under his own power and let himself in with his key, while Tom retrieved the dog. By the time Tom was inside the house, Kevin had closed himself in the bedroom.

"You were right to bring him back to your place, Tom," Sue said on the other end of his cell phone. "It could be very dangerous to leave him alone right now."

"He *is* alone," Tom replied, pacing in his kitchen. "Well, except for the dog. Shadow was pacing at the foot of the stairs and whimpering, so I brought up him up to the landing. When he scratched at the bedroom door, Kevin let him in. But then he closed the door again."

"That's good. Shadow will make him feel less alone, without intruding on his privacy."

"So you're saying I should just leave him alone? I thought you said that was dangerous."

"You have to give him some privacy, if he wants it," Sue said, "but at least if you're both there, you can be available if you're needed."

None of this was sitting well with Tom. He wanted to be up there in the room—not downstairs feeling helpless. "I can't watch over him while we're in separate parts of the house," he complained. "What if he hangs himself? It could be hours before I figured out there was something wrong."

There wasn't much furniture in the bedroom yet—really just the bed and the lamp. But people had managed to hang themselves from bed frames before.

"I don't have an answer to that," Sue said, utterly failing to reassure him. "Just go by your instincts. One thing, though: if Kevin comes out of the bedroom, don't push him to talk about what he remembered. If he wants to talk about it, then fine. That can be good for him. But pressuring him to talk about it could trigger another flashback or an anxiety attack."

Tom wasn't overly reassured, but he finally pulled himself together enough to ask about the crisis Sue had been dealing with all day.

She sighed. "She's out of the woods physically," she said. "They got the pills out of her system before there was any serious damage. But I spent most of the day counseling her family while she was unconscious. This is an enormous setback."

"Two steps forward, one step back," Tom said, but his eye was on the stairs leading up to his bedroom.

TOM fretted downstairs for a couple more hours. After the first hour, the bedroom door opened just long enough to let Shadow out and then closed again. Tom took the dog outside to pee and then brought him back upstairs. He saw the bedroom door open just enough to admit the pup. Then it closed yet again.

It was after dark before Kevin finally came out of the bedroom. Tom listened anxiously as Kevin used the bathroom and came downstairs, bringing the dog with him. He was naked, having removed his clothing in the bedroom.

"I'm hungry," Kevin said, walking past the living room into the kitchen.

Tom put down the book he'd been struggling to read and scrambled after him. "There are some cans of soup in the cupboard, or I can make you a ham sandwich...."

"Do you have any peanut butter?"

"Sure."

Kevin moved to get the peanut butter from the cupboard, but Tom gently shooed him away and made the sandwich for him, while Kevin sat at the kitchen table with Shadow under his feet. Tom started to ask how he was feeling and then bit his tongue. Kevin would talk when he felt like talking.

So Tom moved on to a more innocuous topic. "I really need to get more furniture." Kevin didn't respond, so Tom plowed ahead on his own. "Maybe another trip to Ikea this weekend would be a good idea."

Kevin didn't respond until Tom had set the plate down in front of him. Then he said, "Thank you," and proceeded to wolf the sandwich down as if he'd been starving. Of course, he hadn't eaten anything since early that morning.

When he was finished, he got up to put the plate in the sink and then went outside onto the deck. Tom could see him climb into the hot tub, and after agonizing over it for a few minutes, he followed him outside, Shadow trailing after him. They'd put up a gate at the end of the deck that led to the front porch—a flimsy thing Shadow could probably have broken through if he'd wanted. But while they were out on the deck with him, the gate proved enough of a deterrent to keep him from wandering off.

"Is it okay if I join you?" Tom asked as he approached the hot tub.

"Okay," Kevin said, "but I don't know if I feel like talking."

Tom was still dressed, so he stripped out of his things and laid them on one of the deck chairs. Then he climbed into the water and settled into the tub, careful not to let his feet bump into Kevin's. He was afraid any contact would spook him and send him back into the bedroom.

Shadow settled down beside the tub, and the three of them lay back for a long time, watching the stars in the clear night sky. The hot tub lights illuminated the water so that it glowed a pale cyan, gradually fading to pink, and then to green. Some modern tubs, Tom had learned when he'd been considering replacing this one, had little waterfalls—which he could do without—and music players built in. A music player might be nice. He'd have to see about rigging some speakers someplace on the deck that would be safe from rainstorms. There must be some way of doing that....

"Isn't it supposed to feel better," Kevin asked, breaking the silence at last, "when you remember something that was blocked?"

"No, not necessarily. You've been hiding the memories from yourself all this time for a reason. They aren't pleasant and remembering them isn't going to make you feel good. Sue is the expert on PTSD, but from what I know of it, remembering is just the beginning. The memories themselves can trigger flashbacks, so you may need to be deconditioned to them over time."

"How do I do that?"

"Basically, you make yourself remember, but in a controlled environment—one in which you feel safe and apart from the memories. You need to be continually reminded that the memories happened somewhere else, in some other time, and they can't hurt you anymore."

"They didn't... hurt...," Kevin said slowly. "They just... I don't know... they just didn't feel right...."

Tom didn't want him to be delving into this so soon, so he tried to curtail it. "You don't need to talk about it if you don't want."

"You're afraid to hear it, aren't you?" Kevin snapped. "You don't want to know all the disgusting details... what I let him do to me...." He seemed to be growing angry again.

Tom tried to soothe him. "I'll listen to anything you want to tell me. And nothing you tell me will make me disgusted with you. Whatever happened—even if you went along with it—it was forced on you. You were just a kid, doing what your father told you to do."

"I didn't... I never told him to stop or anything...."

"But you did," Tom said emphatically. "I heard you. You told him it was 'gross'. You told him you didn't want to do it. You may not have known how to say 'no' to him, but you tried to tell him you didn't want what was happening, and he ignored you. You're not the guilty one."

Kevin wiped his eyes with his hand, as if they were threatening tears again. "You don't fucking get it. There were times when... times when I fucking *liked* it!" He shook his head angrily, his face screwed up in a mask of revulsion. "Not everything. Not the... *mess* when he was done. God! I still... the smell still sickens me... but the massages... the cuddling... touching... some of it felt *good*, goddamn it!"

"Kevin, everybody likes being caressed and touched and massaged. It's the way our bodies are built. These things feel good to us, even when we go to a total stranger who might be the opposite of what we're sexually attracted to and pay him sixty dollars to give us a body rub. But there's a thin line between that and sex. Even a little kid can sense when that line is being crossed, and it can be confusing or terrifying when that happens. And," Tom added, enunciating very slowly and carefully, "it is never... the child's... fault."

Kevin was silent for a long time. When he spoke again, at last, he said, very quietly, "I don't think I can do this anymore, Tom."

It was the first time he'd used Tom's name in a very long time, and for that reason, Tom found it unsettling.

"I wanted you to be happy with me," Kevin went on, "but this is killing me. I'm sorry."

"You don't have anything to be sorry about."

"I'm sorry, but I just can't do it." Kevin didn't seem to be listening anymore. "I don't want to think about this shit anymore, okay? I can't keep going to therapy. I know you need somebody you can have sex with; I know you're afraid of me snapping and hurting you. And I thought I could make you happy. But I just can't. I'm sorry."

"Make *me* happy?" Tom asked in confusion. "This is about making *you* happy!"

Kevin snorted and shook his head.

"I thought you wanted this."

"Why would *I* want it?" Kevin asked. "I had everything I wanted: someone I felt completely comfortable with, someone who looks great naked and doesn't mind me ogling him. A great place to hang out with a hot tub, and all the burgers I can eat, and a great dog to play with. It was Kevin Heaven." He smiled at that, but it was a sad, bittersweet smile.

Before Tom could think of anything to say, Kevin climbed out of the hot tub.

"I like you," he said, unable to look Tom in the eye. "I really... *really* like you. But I'm not what you need."

The words struck Tom like a slap in the face.

"You're not...?" He gasped, struggling to scramble to his feet against the water jets. How the hell did things start spiraling out of control like this? "What are you talking about, Kevin? You aren't breaking up with me…?"

Kevin picked up his towel and dried off, taking his time as if he were thinking about it. Then he shrugged. "You can't fuck me. You can't kiss me. You can't even touch me. What's there to break up?"

He draped the towel over the hot tub railing, turned, and walked into the house. Tom scrambled out of the hot tub and ran after him. He spent the next few minutes while Kevin dressed pleading with him to stay until he'd had a chance to sleep on it.

But it was already too late.

Sixteen

"HE'S not right for you," Sue said for the thousandth time that week.

They were having lunch at Tea Bird's Café. It was Friday again, and there had been no word from Kevin all week. Tom was going out of his mind. He'd tried calling, but Kevin either wasn't home or he was screening his calls. None of Tom's messages were returned.

Trying to focus on his client's issues instead of his own had been pure hell.

"I liked him," Tom said. It was a gross understatement. By now, Tom was head over heels for Kevin. But Sue was unsympathetic, to say the least.

"He had issues, Tom. Serious issues. I feel for him, and I hope he gets the help he needs." Kevin had missed his therapy appointment, and both Sue and Tom suspected he wouldn't be back. "But as your friend, I have to say, you don't want to be in a relationship with someone you feel you have to take care of all the time."

Trying to take care of Kevin had been Tom's big mistake. He'd fucked up. He, better than anyone, should have known someone like

Kevin would hate being looked after like a child. Tom's behavior had been well meaning but insulting.

"The hot tub smells funny," Tom said.

"The hot tub?" Sue clearly had no idea what the connection was.

"Kevin always took care of balancing the chemicals in the hot tub. I have no idea how to do it. Now it smells kind of swampy, and I'm not sure it's safe to get in it."

Sue gave him a disgusted look. "So pick up a manual or find a website that tells you how to take care of the hot tub. You're a big boy. I'm sure you can manage."

"And Shadow won't eat," Tom went on. "He just ignores his food."

She was a bit more sympathetic about that, owning a dog herself. "I'm sure he's missing Kevin too. Animals are very sensitive to people coming and going in their environment. He'll probably eat when he's hungry, but it might not hurt to take him to the vet, just to be on the safe side."

Tom nodded. He looked at the plate of fried squash and root vegetables in front of him and decided maybe he could use a trip to the vet too.

ON HIS way home that evening, he passed by Kevin's trailer. He didn't really have much choice, unless he wanted to go several miles out of his way. As always, he couldn't avoid searching for Kevin, hoping he'd be out in the yard or sitting out on his porch. He wasn't. Tom hadn't so much as glimpsed him all week.

Sometimes Kevin's truck was in the driveway, but today it wasn't. The garage door was closed and clearly nobody was home. But this time Tom saw something that alarmed him: a "For Sale" sign on the lawn.

He slowed down and pulled over on the side of the road. It wasn't any of his business. Kevin was making it very clear that any relationship they'd had was over. But Tom also knew he had to take a closer look, to make sure he'd really seen what he thought he had.

Feeling like a stalker, he slowly backed his car up along the breakdown lane and into the end of Kevin's driveway. Then he put his car in park, got out, and walked across the front lawn to get a closer look at the sign.

It was a "For Sale" sign all right. And even more disconcerting, Kevin's business sign had been taken down. Tom didn't feel right trespassing any further than he already was, but he could see from the driveway that Kevin had been doing some work around the place. The unruly backyard had been mowed, at least as far as the birch saplings would allow. Kevin had refrained from cutting those down. The porch had been cleaned up, from what Tom could see. He could only assume the inside of the trailer and garage were being straightened up, or had been already.

Is he even still living here? The thought that Kevin might have already left chilled Tom to the core. If he was already gone, there would be no chance of ever reconciling. And Tom was still desperately clinging to that possibility.

He heard something behind him and turned to see Kevin's truck pulling into the driveway. For a second, Tom's heart danced. *He's still here!*

But as soon as he glimpsed the irritated look on Kevin's face as he was forced to drive his truck over the grass to get around Tom's car, Tom realized Kevin was a long way from being happy to see *him*. Kevin stopped the truck and got out, slamming the door behind him.

"Why are you here?" he asked curtly as he strode across the grass, his expression anything but friendly.

"I… saw the sign…." Tom was having difficulty forming a coherent sentence. Even angry, Kevin was strikingly handsome, and the desire to reach out to him was overwhelming.

"Yeah. What about it?"

"You're moving?"

"I'm moving."

When he didn't volunteer anything further, Tom asked, "Where are you going?"

Kevin sighed and shook his head. "I don't know. Away from this shithole."

"That's awfully sudden, isn't it?"

"Yeah? Well, I do shit like that. I'm psychologically unstable." He started walking past Tom toward the door, his expression making it clear the conversation was over as far as he was concerned.

"I don't think you're—"

Kevin silenced him by groaning loudly in frustration. "Maybe I haven't made it clear that I don't like you being here. I know you mean well, and… really, I don't hate you or anything. But I can't deal with you in my life anymore. Okay?"

Tom stared at him, a piteous look on his face, struggling to think of anything he could say that would get Kevin to sit down and talk things out. He was a psychologist, damn it! He was supposed to know how to deal with people's anger and pain.

As if he knew what was going through Tom's head, Kevin said, "You fucked it all up for me. I mean, yeah, I had some issues. But I was doing all right. Now, I've got this constant—" He fluttered the fingers of one hand near the side of his head. "—*noise* in my head! It's like you fucking opened Pandora's box in there, and now I can't stop remembering things. I can't even jerk off without feeling my dad's hands on me, smelling his breath…."

He had to stop a moment, disgust written on his face as he shook his head. "Everything in this fucking town reminds me of stuff I don't want to think about. You really did a job on me, counselor. And I'd really like it if you'd just let me be."

He turned away, and this time Tom let him go. There was nothing he could say that would fix things. He knew that now.

Tom walked back to his car and left Kevin's trailer behind him.

SHADOW didn't eat again that night, turning away from his bowl and going to plop down on his dog pillow with a depressed sigh. When he did the same thing in the morning, Tom panicked and called the veterinary hospital in Lancaster—the closest one he could find.

"We're open," the woman on the other end of the line said dubiously, "but we close at noon, and we're booked solid until then."

"Can't somebody just look at him?" Tom pleaded. "He's barely eaten a thing in a week!"

"Did he get into something that you're aware of?"

Tom explained the situation, and the woman said sympathetically, "Your puppy's probably still grieving. It can take a couple weeks or more for a dog or cat to regain their appetite when someone they love leaves. They're very sensitive to changes in their environment. I'm sure he'll be okay, but we do have a slot open on Monday morning, if you'd like to bring him in."

Tom made the appointment. He had to reschedule one of his own Monday morning appointments, but fortunately his client was a dog lover and when he called her, she was more than willing to come in later in the week if it would help his ailing pup.

After making the phone calls, Tom went online and tried to find instructions for balancing the chemicals in his hot tub. He found plenty. But it seemed too complicated for his weary brain to sort out right now, so he just bookmarked a couple of pages and decided to deal with it later.

He took Shadow for a walk in the woods behind the house instead. The puppy perked up a bit for the first time since Kevin had walked out, and Tom was relieved to see it. Shadow was still likely to run off if he wasn't on a leash, so Tom held his lead and followed along after the dog, letting him sniff around to his heart's content.

Tom's property extended a good distance into the forest, though he hadn't yet taken the time to find the property markers. The real estate agent had said they were small stone posts sticking up out of the ground and showed him the property lines on a map. As he wandered through the forest, he toyed with the idea of searching the markers out, but he began to grow nervous about being this far out in the woods. He was no outdoorsman. He could barely tell east from west on a sunny day. And according to the map he'd seen, there were miles of forest to get lost in before he might stumble across a highway in the middle of nowhere.

"Let's go back to the house, Pup," he said.

Shadow had no idea what he meant, of course, but he'd learned by now that "Pup" was one of his names. He came trotting back to Tom and didn't strain too much against his harness when Tom started to lead him back to the house.

Tom had to rely on his memory of landmarks, like streams and fallen trees, to find his way back, and more than once he got turned around. But eventually he spotted the back of the house through the trees.

Thank God.

Before they'd actually come out of the forest, Shadow started pulling hard at his lead, dragging Tom off to his right. Since they were within sight of the house, he allowed the dog to investigate whatever had caught his interest.

It turned out to be a cylindrical pipe made out of cement, jutting up out of the forest floor. It was about three feet wide and a couple of feet high, and it was capped by a five-inch-thick cement disk with metal handles on it.

"That's bizarre," Tom said to no one in particular—maybe to the dog. "Is that the artesian well?" He knew the house had one, but he'd never looked at it. He'd just arranged for people to come test the water during the house sale.

Shadow didn't answer. He sniffed around the base of it for a minute, before losing interest and wandering off again, this time in the general direction of the house. Tom forgot about the well, or whatever it was, and followed after him.

BY MIDAFTERNOON, Tom was fairly certain Shadow wasn't dying, though the dog still turned his nose up at the food in his dish. He decided he could use a little time away from the house, and maybe Shadow would be interested in steak tips if Tom brought some home from the diner in a doggy bag. So he put the dog in his crate, along with a bowl of fresh water and the dish of kibble, and drove into Groveton.

Part of him had hoped to see Kevin's truck in the parking lot, but it wasn't there.

God, I'm starting to stalk him!

Tom parked his car and went inside. Fortunately, the diner wasn't too busy for a Saturday. The last thing he wanted to deal with was a noisy crowd of people. Tom found a table and waited for a waitress to notice him.

The cheerful young woman who'd waited on him the last time he was there—Kelly, if he remembered correctly—saw him and flashed him a welcoming smile. He smiled back as she headed over to him, hoping his disappointment didn't show on his face. He'd really wanted to talk to Tracy. Though perhaps it was better that he not.

But apparently Tracy wanted to talk to him as well. She intercepted Kelly and said something in her ear. Kelly nodded and then flashed Tom another quick smile as she waved to him and wandered off in a different direction. Tracy hurried over and immediately slipped into the seat across from him.

"Tom! I've been hoping you'd stop by. It's been days."

"I've been busy," he said lamely. The real reason, of course, had been that he felt this was *Kevin's* diner—the waitresses were all friends with him anyway—and Tom might not be welcome here anymore.

Tracy gave him a shrewd look. "Something's wrong between you and Kevin, isn't there? That's why I wanted to talk to you. He's been acting really weird… talking about leaving town. Did you two have a fight?"

"I guess you could say that." It hadn't really been much of a fight, Tom thought. But that was beside the point. "He said he can't be around me anymore because I keep fucking with his head."

And then without really meaning to, he found himself spilling the whole mess. Not about Kevin's past sexual abuse—Tom still felt bound by client confidentiality, even though Kevin hadn't been his client, and he knew Kevin wouldn't want that information being gossiped about. But he told Tracy he was a psychologist, and he'd been trying to help Kevin cope with his panic attacks, that he'd pushed too hard and too fast, and now Kevin wouldn't talk to him and his life was shit….

She let him blather on until he was finished and then gave him a sympathetic smile. She put her hand over his. "You tried, hon. Bless you for that."

"I tried too hard," Tom said miserably.

"Maybe. But I'll tell you something: he was happier in that short time he had with you than I *ever* saw him in the time we were married. And the few times he was in here this week, he was looking like he just lost his best friend. I don't care what he says—he still needs you, hon."

She glanced up as another customer entered the diner. "I should get back to work. You want your usual?"

"Sure."

Tracy gave him another smile and a quick pat on the hand before jumping up and running off. Tom wasn't sure he believed her about Kevin still needing him, but it had been nice to hear. And he couldn't help but smile at the thought that he now had a favorite diner he could go to, and the waitress would know what he meant if he ordered the "usual."

Seventeen

SHADOW hadn't touched his kibble by the time Tom got home and let the dog out of his crate. But Tom was pleased to see that even depression couldn't outweigh a dog's love of good, tender steak tips. Shadow ate them, if reluctantly. He was a Labrador, after all—he had a reputation to uphold. But then he went back to his dog bed and stayed there throughout most of the evening, only getting up when Tom coaxed him into going outside to pee.

By the time it got dark, around ten, Tom was outside on the deck—alone, since Shadow refused to be coaxed away from his dog bed—drinking a six-pack and glaring at the smelly hot tub. He couldn't motivate himself to do anything. None of the books on his Kindle seemed interesting to him; nothing he could watch on the Internet seemed worth the effort of finding it. He'd tried distracting himself with porn but had given up when his dick refused to cooperate.

So he just drank until the buzz seemed to help soothe his frayed emotions. And then he kept drinking, which he should have known would be a mistake. The beer stopped soothing him and started to make him maudlin until he was swimming in a sea of dark, depressing thoughts.

How could Kevin do this to him? He'd only been trying to help. Sure, he'd fucked it all up, biting off more than he could handle.... Was that a mixed metaphor? Shouldn't it be chewing... something?

Anyway, it was all Sue's fault. She'd made him do it! Hadn't she? What a bitch....

Why doesn't my dog love me?

Somehow—he couldn't even remember going into the house to find his cell phone—he was dialing Kevin's number. Kevin didn't answer. Of course. The answering machine picked up, and Tom wanted to hang up on it. But instead he found himself talking into the stupid thing. Worse, he was crying.

"All I ever wanted to do was love you. That's all. But you don't give second chances, do you? One shot and if somebody screws up, well, fuck 'em! It's over! Now Shadow won't eat anything, and I think he might be sick, but the vet won't see him, and the hot tub is all swampy, and it'll probably rot my skin off if I try to get in there. Where I come from, people are supposed to get second chances, man! Love is supposed to be.... If somebody loves you, they deserve a second chance! That's all I'm sayin'...."

It went on and on, even though part of him knew he was making a fool of himself and he was just repeating everything. It was hopeless.

Until Kevin picked up the phone and interrupted him. "Jesus Christ! It's almost one in the morning, you dumb shit! If talking to you is the only way to get you to shut the fuck up, then fine! I'll talk to you. You're drunk, aren't you? You sound totally shitfaced."

Tom was so shocked by the sound of Kevin's voice, he was stunned into silence. He just sat there sniffling for a moment until Kevin asked, "Are you still there?"

"Yeah." Tom's voice sounded small and vulnerable.

"What's wrong with Shadow?"

"I don't know. I think he's depressed. Everything sucks now that you're not here."

There was a long silence on the other end of the phone, until Kevin sighed and said, "Christ. Don't do anything until I get there. Give me a few minutes."

And then he hung up.

Tom sat in the deck chair, staring at the phone as comprehension slowly dawned on him. *He's coming over.*

Shit. Tom's head was swimming with the alcohol, so he wasn't sure if he was happy about that or not. Kevin might just take one look at how pathetic he was and tell him to give Shadow back to Lee if he was too useless to care for a dog properly. Although Kevin could have told him that over the phone. Tom was too confused to think clearly about what this might mean.

The only thing he knew for certain was that he wanted to throw up.

He was still leaning over the railing when the kitchen door opened and Kevin came out onto the deck, Shadow scampering around his legs in puppy ecstasy. "Well, isn't that a pretty sight."

Kevin bent down to pick up the empty six-pack carton and held it up. "Did you drink all of this by yourself?"

"Unh" was all Tom was able to get out. His mouth was full of acid.

"Jesus. I'll be right back." Kevin disappeared into the house again and returned a moment later with a glass of water and a hand towel. He set the water on the deck railing for a minute while he wiped vomit off Tom's mouth and chin. Then he held up the glass. "Here. Rinse and spit. Over the railing, please."

Tom did what he was told.

"You feel better?"

"I guess." Tom's head was still spinning, but he no longer felt quite so nauseous.

"Do you need to throw up some more?"

"I don't think so."

"Come on, then." Kevin put an arm around his naked waist and pulled Tom's left arm over his shoulder.

"I shouldn't touch you," Tom said, slurring his words.

"I'll tell you when you can and can't touch me, counselor. I'm taking you up to bed, so don't give me any more shit."

Tom let Kevin lead him into the house and upstairs. He could hear Shadow whimpering as they climbed the stairs because the dog was still afraid to follow them up, but Kevin told him, "I'll be right back, Pup. Good boy!" Then he dragged Tom into the bedroom and lowered him onto the bed.

"Are you sure you're not going to puke again?" Kevin asked.

The room was spinning, but Tom felt if he could just manage to lie still for a while, maybe it would stop. "I don't think so."

"All right." Kevin pulled the blankets out from under Tom and drew them over his naked body. "I'm gonna take Shadow outside for a minute and then see if I can get him to eat something. But I'll be back."

"Thanks."

And then, though he couldn't really be sure of it with his eyes closed and his head swimming, Tom felt something warm and soft brush his forehead. It felt like Kevin had kissed him.

WHEN he woke in the morning, Tom immediately became aware of three things: his mouth tasted like vomit, his head ached, and Kevin was sleeping beside him. It was only gradually that he began to remember making a total ass of himself the night before.

He sat up gingerly, feeling as if his body might shatter if he moved too quickly. When he lifted the covers, he couldn't resist peeking at Kevin's body. Yep. Naked, all right. And still amazing.

Is he back? Tom didn't dare believe it was true. Probably, Kevin had just taken pity on him and stayed to make sure he'd be okay. As soon as he woke up, he'd be gone.

Tom slipped out of the bed quietly. Shadow was lying on his dog bed, but for once he didn't get up when Tom did. He glanced at Tom, but then he sighed, and his eyes went back to Kevin's sleeping form. The dog seemed to be just as cautious of Kevin's return as Tom was.

Don't let him out of your sight, Pup! Tom thought. Then he quietly opened the door and went into the bathroom.

He brushed his teeth, wishing he'd done it before sleeping, and gargled with mouthwash to get the taste out of his mouth and the smell off his breath. Then he used the toilet and washed his hands and face before returning to the bedroom. He would have liked to take some ibuprofen but not on an empty stomach. And he had no intention of going downstairs until he'd had a chance to talk to Kevin. He didn't want the man blowing by him with a quick "See you" as he headed out the door.

Tom lay there a long time, watching Kevin and reveling in how adorable he looked with his hair tousled like a sleeping child. When Kevin opened his soft hazel eyes at last, he gave Tom a sweet smile that made Tom's heart flutter in his chest.

"Mornin', counselor."

"Good morning." Tom reached out to touch those full lips but stopped himself. His hand settled on Kevin's pillow, rubbing a finger on the cotton pillowcase instead. "I'm sorry I was such a jackass last night."

Kevin's smile didn't dim. He shook his head and said, "I'm not."

"No?"

Kevin hesitated before saying, "I thought I was done with you. Even when you came to my trailer, somehow I was strong enough to tell you to go away. And I was damned proud of myself for doing it. I told myself nothing you could say or do would ever get me to come back. Then you call in the middle of the night, blubbering like an idiot about how much you and Shadow need me... and my heart melts."

"Did you really hate me that much?"

"I never hated you, counselor. If I hadn't loved you, I never would have let you fuck with my head like that. But that's why I had to get away from you."

Tom's brain seemed to be stuttering. It couldn't process everything Kevin was saying because it was stuck on one word. "You... loved me?"

Kevin sighed and reached up to slide his fingers through Tom's beard. "Still do."

"I... love you too."

"But I need you to promise me something," Kevin continued. "If you want me back—"

"I do!"

"—then I need you to stop helping me. I know all of this has been because you want to help. But you need to stop. Okay?"

Tom lifted his own hand to clasp Kevin's and hold it tightly. Then he brought it to his lips and kissed it. "I never wanted to hurt you. I'm sorry. You do what you have to do. I won't interfere anymore."

Kevin looked into his eyes for a long time, as if he wanted to say something more. At last, he said, "Lie back."

Tom did as he was told, rolling onto his back and laying his head against his pillow. Kevin lifted himself up on one arm and leaned over him, hesitating just a second before lowering his face and kissing Tom gently on the mouth. Tom felt the warmth of the kiss shoot down through his body, straight to his crotch, and he exhaled a shuddering breath into Kevin's mouth. But he didn't dare move for fear he would make Kevin panic. Kevin didn't seem to be panicking, though. He lingered with the kiss, exploring Tom's lips with his own and licking them with his tongue. When he pulled away, he looked down at Tom with eyes full of desire.

"That was nice," Tom said, though it was an enormous understatement. He was hard as a rock now and wanted nothing more than to pull Kevin down on top of him. But he held back, knowing Kevin wasn't ready for that.

"It was... good," Kevin agreed.

"Did it make you feel anxious?"

Kevin nodded and let out a long breath, as if he'd been holding something in. "Yeah. But it feels different now. I have all kinds of shit going on in my head that I really don't want to think about when I'm kissing you. But it's not as... terrifying... as it was before."

That was good. And it was the entire point of digging into past memories—to decrease their power over us. But Tom didn't say that. He'd promised to let Kevin do this on his own, and he meant to stick by that promise.

"I loved it," he said.

"That's good. I was afraid I'd suck at it."

Tom pulled the blankets aside to flash his erection at him. "Does that look like it was a bad kiss?"

Kevin laughed. "Now who's being crass?"

"I learned it from you."

Kevin made a rude noise and then glanced over at Shadow. "I think someone's trying to get our attention."

The dog had been whimpering and thumping his tail on his pillow for a while, stuffed ducks having long been banned from the bedroom. But Tom had been too caught up in what was going on between him and Kevin to acknowledge it. *I'm a bad parent.*

"He ignored me when I first got up," Tom said. "I think he wants *you* to take him out. He's missed you a lot."

Kevin gave Shadow a warm smile. "I've missed you, too, Pup. Almost as much as your daddy."

Eighteen

"YOU just need to shock it," Kevin said, looking at the somewhat murky water of the hot tub.

"What?" Tom asked. "You mean with electricity?"

Kevin laughed. "No. You just put an extra-large dose of chlorine in to kill everything. The tub will be unusable for a day, but we can have it running again by tomorrow afternoon."

"That'll be nice."

Tom leaned over the side of his deck chair to put his plate down for Shadow to lick. The maple syrup on what was left of his pancakes probably wasn't good for the dog, but it wasn't like Tom fed him maple syrup on a daily basis. And it was nice to see the pooch scarfing down anything put in front of him. Kevin had said Shadow ate a bowl of kibble before bed last night, and the dog had certainly been enthusiastic about breakfast.

Tom lifted his head to see a magnificent view of bare ass as Kevin leaned over the hot tub console to remove the filter. Things were definitely looking up.

"Are you still going to sell your trailer," Tom asked, "now that you're no longer bent on escaping my clutches?"

Kevin straightened up and turned to grin at him. "I don't know. Can't say I'm particularly attached to it. But it's a run-down piece of shit. Probably nobody will want it anyway."

They both knew, of course, that Kevin was likely to spend all his time here at the house now that they'd patched things up. Moving in permanently might not be far behind. But neither mentioned it. There was no point in rushing things.

"Do you have any hamburger?" Kevin asked, eyeing the grill.

"In the fridge. But I wouldn't recommend eating it. It's been sitting there since you left."

"Well," Kevin said cheerfully, "it looks like it's time to go shopping."

THE hot tub water turned a disconcerting piss-yellow when Kevin added the chlorine, but he assured Tom it would all settle out. They just needed to leave the cover off and let the sun evaporate the extra chlorine for the rest of the day.

In the meantime, they picked up groceries, grilled cheeseburgers—much to Shadow's delight, as well as Kevin's, because he always got a burger for himself—and generally spent a relaxing Sunday hanging out on the deck.

ON MONDAY, Tom had the daunting task of informing Sue that he and Kevin were back together again. He waited until they were walking down Main Street on the way to Wang's to break the news.

"I knew it," she responded with a sour expression. "Whenever I tell someone that he's better off without his ex, he always manages to patch things up."

"Does that technique work well in your couples counseling?" Tom asked.

She ignored the question. "Don't get me wrong. I don't dislike Kevin. I just have reservations about someone with such severe emotional issues—completely *understandable* issues, mind you, under the circumstances—dating someone who is, let's be blunt, a bit of a mother hen."

Tom bristled a bit at that, even though he knew it was true, but Sue held up a hand to stave him off before he could interrupt her. "Yes, yes, I know. It's none of my concern. I'm not your therapist."

"But you are my best friend," Tom said, "and it would be nice if you didn't hate my boyfriend."

Sue offered him a conciliatory smile. "I don't hate your boyfriend. He seems like a nice enough man, he's gainfully employed, and I think he does genuinely care for you."

"Then be happy for me!"

She didn't respond to that, and Tom felt sure she was remembering the black eye Kevin had given him weeks ago. Instead, Sue asked, "I don't suppose he'll be coming back for therapy?"

Tom shook his head. "I don't think so. I think he needs time to integrate the memories that are flooding back to him now. The last thing he wants is for you or me to keep 'poking at him', as he puts it."

They arrived at the restaurant, and the conversation broke off long enough for them to find a table and order from the waiter. Then Sue said, "Normally, I refuse to see a client who stops attending sessions without having the courtesy to call me about it. But as a favor to you, I'd be willing to work with Kevin again if he decides he needs my help."

Tom was tempted to make a snide comment about that being big of her, but he actually thought Kevin might need Sue on his side again in the future. It was probably best not to piss her off about it. Abrasive as she could be, she was a good therapist, and Tom wasn't sure he'd be able to handle things on his own if Kevin's PTSD started spiraling out of control.

HE CAME home to find Shadow at the top of the basement stairs—the normal ones, as opposed to the spiral staircase—his stuffed duck in his mouth, whimpering as he looked down into the basement.

"What are you looking at?" he asked, but he'd already seen Kevin's truck in the driveway. He called down the stairs, "Are you down there?"

"Yeah," Kevin's voice called back, so Tom gave Shadow a quick scratch on the head and left the dog at the top of the stairs as he descended into the basement. Shadow whimpered even louder, but there didn't seem much point in hauling the pooch down the stairs until he found out what Kevin was up to.

Apparently, he was setting up a TV room. He'd brought in a beat-up old couch, a short table, and a small flat-screen television to set on top of it—from his own trailer, Tom was certain, because he recognized that ratty couch, even without its piles of dirty clothing. Kevin was arranging them in one corner of the finished basement and hooking it all up.

Tom hated television. He found it noisy and distracting, and he was much happier curling up with a good book. For this reason, he'd fought with his local service provider to just give him Internet and phone, *without* television, thank you very much. He didn't care what kind of stupendous—and temporary—savings he could get by bundling them together. So what Kevin was going to hook a television up to, Tom couldn't imagine.

"You do realize I don't have cable?" Tom asked, having a difficult time disguising his annoyance. "Television, I mean."

"I figured that out," Kevin replied. "Who the fuck doesn't have cable in this century?"

"Me."

Kevin was searching through the channels, but it was hopeless. Everything was static.

"You might have asked me before bringing all this stuff over," Tom said.

"I thought I'd surprise you."

And just like that, all Tom's annoyance vaporized, and he felt like a prime asshole. It still seemed inappropriate for Kevin to move a bunch of his furniture into Tom's house—Thank God he put it in the cellar!—but if Kevin had been thinking Tom really wanted a TV but hadn't gotten around to picking one up… well, that made this a gift. Didn't it? "Oh. Thanks. I'm sorry, but I never had the television cable hooked up. I don't generally watch it."

"Can we get it hooked up?"

Tom raised his eyebrows at him. "We? Are you moving in?"

Kevin gave him a cute, embarrassed smile and actually blushed a bit, which Tom found adorable. That was something they'd need to work out soon. Kevin had practically moved in already, but he still had his own place. He still had someplace else to go if they got into a fight or broke up.

Before Kevin could think of a response, they both heard a tentative *honk?* coming from the direction of the stairs. They turned and saw Shadow about halfway down the stairs, looking at them nervously. Apparently, he'd gotten lonely enough to venture down but not quite all the way.

"Hey, Pup!" Kevin exclaimed. "You want to come down here with us?"

Shadow whimpered again and wagged his tailed at them.

"Come on, boy," Tom said in the singsong voice he'd picked up from watching Kevin with the dog, "You can do it! You're already halfway there."

Shadow wagged his tail harder, but he clearly had no intention of going any farther. Both men walked to the bottom of the stairs and started clapping their hands and calling to him.

"Come on, Pup!"

"Good boy!"

"You can do it!"

"You're almost there!"

"It's one small step for a dog—"

"—one giant leap for dogkind!"

Clearly Shadow was a fan of Neil Armstrong because that did it. In one epic, heroic moment that was somewhat less than graceful, the

Lab pup came barreling down the stairs at full speed, as if the lower stairs were made out of hot coals and a moment's hesitation might prove disastrous.

Honk! Honk! Honk! Honk!

Tom and Kevin showered the pup with pets and kisses and let him bump his saliva-covered duck against their faces in paroxysms of puppy ecstasy. He'd done it! He was The Best Dog in the World! Poets would sing his praises, and the President would probably give him an award!

He was so excited, he peed a little on the tile floor, but that hardly detracted from his stupendous victory.

Honk! Honk! Honk!

Unfortunately, it soon became clear that going *down* the stairs was completely different from going *up* the stairs. When Tom and Kevin went up to the main floor, Shadow went back to whimpering and pacing at the bottom of the stairs, and no amount of coaxing would get him to come up. Finally, Tom fetched the dog's leash and went down to the cellar.

While Kevin cleaned up the spatters of excited puppy pee on the tile, Tom took Shadow outside through the cellar door. Thanks to the fact the house was built into a low hill, the back wall of the cellar was actually above ground, so the door didn't have any stairs. Tom let Shadow do his business and brought him around to the front of the house, up the low porch steps, and into the front hall.

Kevin passed them to go into the hall half bath and wash his hands. He came out just as Tom finished removing Shadow's harness, and the two men watched in surprise as Shadow immediately bolted for the cellar door and scampered down the stairs again.

"What the fuck?" Tom asked irritably.

Kevin laughed. "It's *fun* to go down stairs!"

"Just not back up them."

"Let me have the leash. I'll get him this time."

From the depths of the cellar came a distant *Honk?* as if to ask, *Are you coming or not?*

"Fine," Tom said, "but I'm blocking the cellar door, for now. We don't need to keep playing this game all night."

Making a mental note to pick up a "baby gate" the next time he got a chance, Tom pushed a box of books into the doorway to block it and stacked another one on top to make it harder to move. When Kevin brought Shadow in the front door, the dog headed for the stairs again and was disappointed to find his way blocked, but it was dinnertime anyway. A bowl of dog kibble was enough to distract him from his new game.

THAT night, Shadow had to be carried upstairs as usual, but in the morning, he gleefully barreled down them like a child on a waterslide. Tom took him out to do his business and came back inside to find Kevin whipping up some pancakes. It was an idyllic scene to Tom: an adorable pup scampering around the legs of a gorgeous naked man who was cooking Tom breakfast. He grabbed a cup of coffee from the carafe Kevin had set to brew and sat at the kitchen table to watch.

I've never been happier, he realized. It was everything he'd ever wanted.

There were still things that worried him, though. Shadow's inability to go *up* stairs would probably sort itself out eventually. But Kevin's issues were much more deep-seated and couldn't be overcome by a sheer act of will, despite the fact Kevin seemed to think so. Tom had promised he wouldn't try to "fix" Kevin anymore, and he intended to stick by that promise, at least until Kevin asked for help. But it wasn't going to be easy.

Over the next several nights, Kevin awoke screaming only once, but it was still upsetting. Poor Shadow was terrified. And again Kevin claimed to have no idea what he'd been dreaming about.

On the other hand, there were signs Kevin was coming to terms with things he was remembering. He seemed to take as much delight in kissing Tom as Shadow did in running down stairs. He was clearly still anxious about it, but proud of himself whenever he managed it without panicking. Tom was proud of him, too, and never pressed for fear of undoing Kevin's progress. He just let it happen when Kevin was in the mood for it.

Then there was the evening Tom found Kevin in the bathroom, taking tentative sniffs of the open rubbing alcohol bottle. Kevin noticed him and gave him an embarrassed smile as he recapped the bottle.

"Have you figured out why it made you panic last time?" Tom asked.

"Um… yeah," Kevin replied. He seemed reluctant to say anything further, and Tom thought that would be the end of it, but Kevin cleared his throat and said, "My dad… used to like giving me massages with it."

So that was it. Tom had never known anyone to use rubbing alcohol for massages, but he supposed it had been common at one time, or it wouldn't be called "rubbing" alcohol. And apparently Mr. Derocher had liked to use it on his son, which meant Kevin hadn't been able to smell it without memories of those inappropriately sexual massages struggling to surface in his mind—memories he was terrified to recall. But now they were being recalled, and the panic had lessened as a result.

"Are you all right?" was all Tom asked.

"Yeah. I'm fine."

But was he? It seemed unlikely. People didn't go from the kind of breakdown Kevin had experienced to "fine" in a matter of a couple of weeks, Tom knew. It could take years of work to integrate the repressed memories in such a way they no longer had power over him. And judging from the continued nightmares and the fact Kevin could never remember what they were about, it seemed likely he was still unable to recall some of the abuse.

Could Kevin work all this out on his own? Perhaps. Tom was skeptical, but then he would be. He'd made a career out of helping people who couldn't do it on their own, so of course he would be convinced most people needed help. He might be wrong where Kevin was concerned. On the other hand, Kevin could be headed for another crisis.

It was worrisome, to put it mildly, but Tom had promised to let Kevin do things his way. And Kevin was definitely right about one thing: they couldn't be in a romantic relationship if Tom couldn't treat Kevin like an adult. Only Kevin could decide if he needed help. And so far it looked as if he was making progress.

Then came the night of the storm.

Nineteen

IT STARTED as mostly wind. The sky was dark at an unusually early hour, with heavy, black storm clouds gliding ominously overhead like a troubled sea and the leaves of the trees showing their pale undersides as the wind blew low and fast along the ground. Tom loved days like this. He loved being warm and cozy inside, snuggled up in front of a fire with a cup of coffee and a good book as the world raged around him. It wasn't really cool enough to start up the pellet stove, though he was tempted.

Shadow, he quickly learned, did not share his assessment of storms as "cozy." He was pacing around the house, tail and ears down, panting with anxiety. That wasn't really surprising. Tom knew a lot of dogs were afraid of storms, just as children were.

What was more surprising was that Kevin was acting the same way. He couldn't put his ears down, and he didn't have a tail, but he was clearly anxious and walking from room to room as if searching for something.

"Are you okay?" Tom asked.

"I'm fine."

"I'm getting the impression you don't like storms much."

"I'm fine, counselor," Kevin replied curtly. He turned and headed for the kitchen. "Do we have any beer left?"

Tom recalled that Kevin had tried to head off a panic attack with beer before his suicide attempt years ago. Was it a good idea for him to be drinking now? Not that Tom could really stop him. Kevin was an adult, and he had a right to drink a beer to relax.

Nevertheless, when Shadow followed Kevin into the kitchen, hovering close to him as if for protection, Tom trailed along after them.

Kevin found one last beer in the fridge. "You mind if I snag this?"

"No, go ahead."

He found the bottle opener and popped the cap, while Tom set up the coffee machine to brew a pot. But even while Kevin was drinking the beer, he was moving about the kitchen, unable to stay still. Tom had never seen him this agitated during storms before. But then this one felt different, even to Tom: the air was oppressively heavy, and the sudden darkness the storm had brought with it gave everything a surreal quality. Tom had checked the weather forecast earlier. There was nothing to worry about. It wasn't a hurricane or anything like that—just a bad thunderstorm. But something about it was bothering Kevin.

"Have you had panic attacks during storms before?" Tom asked and then immediately regretted it.

Kevin practically snarled at him. "This isn't a panic attack! I'm fine. Stop analyzing me, goddamn it!"

"Sorry."

"And stop tugging at your goddamned beard! Are you trying to pull it off your face?"

Tom yanked his hand away from his chin as if Kevin had slapped it down. He nearly snapped back at Kevin, but something in Kevin's eyes looked pained, as if he knew he'd gone too far but hadn't been able to stop himself. So Tom just looked back at him calmly until Kevin looked away.

Shadow whimpered at seeing his two dads fighting, but Kevin misinterpreted it.

"When's the last time he was out?" he asked, his tone somewhat quieter.

"I don't know. A couple hours ago, I think."

Kevin set his beer down on the sideboard and called to the dog, "Come on, Pup! I'll take you out to pee."

He led the way into the front hall.

With Shadow already nervous about the storm, Tom wasn't sure if it was such a good idea to take him out into it. He supposed it made some sense to take him out to do his business now, before the really bad weather kicked in, but Kevin himself was starting to behave strangely. Tom knew he could be trusted with the dog, of course, but something was clearly wrong. He decided to follow them outside.

Kevin had tossed his clothing over the arm of the sofa when he came in the night before.

Now he slipped back into them, while Shadow paced around by the front door, sensing that they were going out. Tom was wearing nothing but his bathrobe, but he found his sneakers by the door and put them on.

"What are you doing?" Kevin asked him.

"I thought I'd join you and get some fresh air before the rain hits."

Tom caught the slight frown that passed over his face before Kevin turned to put Shadow's harness on. "What the hell do you think is gonna happen? I'm just taking him out to pee, for Christ's sake!"

"I can't go out for some air?"

"Fine." Kevin opened the door, and Shadow ran out.

It wasn't enthusiasm that propelled the dog forward. As Kevin and Tom followed him, they could see how agitated the poor pup was. He didn't seem to know which way to go as he darted this way and that, straining at the end of his lead. If he had to pee, he didn't show any sign of it. He was just panicking.

"Come on, Pup!" Kevin called above the wind. "Let's go around back."

Shadow had enough presence of mind left to obey, but he was still straining at the lead.

The rain started as they walked around to the back of the house, and Tom began to consider going back inside. But when he looked at Kevin, he thought better of it. The man's eyes were wide and his jaw clenched. He was staring into the forest behind the house as if he was expecting some ferocious beast to come charging out of it, and when Tom said his name, Kevin didn't seem to hear him.

There was a flash of lightning, followed a few seconds later by a low rumble of thunder, which terrified Shadow. The dog was running back and forth at the end of his lead, clearly not thinking about going to the bathroom. He needed to get inside where he could warm up and calm down. From the look of it, Kevin needed that too.

"I think we should go back in," Tom shouted.

Kevin turned slowly toward him, and Tom realized it was too late. There was no comprehension in those hazel eyes. Kevin looked at him but didn't see him, his focus on something far away and, Tom suspected, long ago.

Before Tom could react, there was another flash of lightning, almost immediately followed by a loud thunderclap. Shadow yanked his leash from Kevin's hand and bolted into the forest, the heavy handle on the retractable leash dragging along after him.

"Shadow!"

The dog was too frightened to come when he was called. Tom was torn for about two seconds between running after Shadow and staying behind to help Kevin with whatever the hell was happening in his head, but Kevin was an adult. Shadow was a frightened puppy. So Tom ran into the woods after the dog, his bathrobe fluttering awkwardly around his naked legs.

He'd expected the heavy handle of the retractable lead would slow the dog down, but to his horror, Tom quickly stumbled across it tangled in the brush. The lead was there, but Shadow was nowhere to be seen. Tom reeled the lead in and found the harness Shadow had been wearing, empty. It had plastic buckles designed to give way if the dog pulled hard enough, in case he got trapped somewhere. Apparently he'd been terrified enough to pull free.

"Shadow!"

There was no response. No barking, no sound of anything moving through the underbrush. Just the hissing of the wind and rain through the trees.

Tom started half walking, half running through the forest, where a foot-high blanket of ferns obscured the ground and made his footing treacherous. It began to pour, making his bathrobe hang heavy and sodden on his body, and his sneakers grew caked with damp earth and pine needles. "Shadow! Come here, boy!"

There was an answering cry—not a bark, but almost a human cry of anguish.

Kevin? Tom stopped running to listen, straining to hear over the wind and the rain.

He was turned around again, no longer certain which direction he'd come from. He spun around in place, searching the darkening forest. There weren't any footprints or crushed vegetation—the ferns covered everything in an undulating sea of feathery green fronds. Terror began to grip him. Even if he found Shadow, how would he find his way out again?

"Shadow!"

Then from far away came the cry, "He's in the well!"

Tom ran toward the sound, although he couldn't make any sense out of it. The well? The only well he knew of was sealed under a heavy cement lid. Shadow couldn't have fallen into it. Unless... was it possible something had collapsed? Or was there an old well somewhere on the property?

"Where are you?" Tom called in a tremulous voice.

This time, the answer was a *yipe*, like the sound of a dog in pain.

"Shadow!"

Tom ran, hoping desperately he'd judged the direction of the sound correctly. His foot suddenly punched down into a small crevasse or animal hole he couldn't see. There was a jarring sense of falling for an extra two or three inches beyond where the ground should have been, and then his foot thudded hard against the earth. His entire body sprawled forward into wet leaves, branches, and mud.

Tom lifted himself up with his arms, feeling the sting of scraped skin on his palms, as he craned his neck to see over the groundcover of ferns.

A dog! He could hear a dog whimpering! It had to be Shadow. And something else…. Kevin's voice. But Kevin wasn't calling Shadow or even Tom. He was wailing something that sounded like *Jesus Christ! Jesus Christ!*

"Kevin! Where are you?"

He scrambled to his feet and stumbled forward, trying to follow the sounds, terrified of what he might find. Was Shadow injured? *Dying?* Tom could no longer imagine his house without the cheerful pup he'd grown to adore. *Oh God! Please let him be okay!*

Another yelp from the dog helped him get his bearings again and soon the roof of the house appeared through the tall white pine trees that surrounded him. He found them by the cement well he and Shadow had stumbled upon almost two weeks ago. Shadow was pacing back and forth in a panic, whimpering, and now Tom could see why. It wasn't the dog who was hurt—it was Kevin.

Tom had witnessed breakdowns before, and he knew that's what he was seeing now. Kevin was beating his hands against the thick cement cap of the well and scraping at it with his fingernails. His hands were bleeding, leaving streaks of blood all over the cement, blurring in the water that poured down upon it. His forehead was gashed where he'd apparently struck it against the well cover. He was sobbing hysterically and wailing, "He's in the well! Jesus Christ! He's in the fucking well!"

Tom called his name, but Kevin was beyond hearing him. When he extended a tentative hand to touch Kevin's shoulder, braced for the possibility of Kevin lashing out at him, Kevin acted as if he couldn't feel it at all.

"Kevin! Who's in the well?"

"My God!" Kevin sobbed, "My God! My God!"

"Kevin, I promise—"

"Jesus Christ!"

"You need to stop scraping your hands up, Kevin. Listen to the sound of my—"

"He's in the well!"

It was hopeless. Nothing Tom could say was getting through. Even though Tom was reluctant to leave him like this, poor Shadow was completely terrified by Kevin's screaming. Tom put the dog back into his harness and ran with him to the house.

There, Tom let Shadow seek out his crate to hide in, and he grabbed his cell phone. He dialed 911 and gave them his location. Then he rushed out on the deck. From there, he could see Kevin draped over the cement well enclosure through the trees and at least make sure he didn't suddenly run off.

THE police arrived before the ambulance since they had come from Groveton and the ambulance was coming from Berlin. Tom heard them pull into the driveway and ran to a spot at the side of the house where he could flag them down while still keeping Kevin in sight. He felt ridiculous, standing there in his sopping wet bathrobe, praying the wind wouldn't whip it open and cause him to flash the police. But there hadn't been time to go inside and dress.

Part of him was worried Kevin would bolt into the forest the moment the police came into view. Fortunately, he didn't. He showed no sign he knew others were there at all.

"What's happening?" Chief Burbank asked Tom as he approached, trailed by the officer who'd been with him the last time Tom had seen him.

Tom gave him a quick rundown of the situation, while the chief stared in disbelief at Kevin, who was continuing to bloody his hands on the well cover.

"Well, I can't just let him do that to himself," the man snarled. "Mr. Derocher! This is Chief Burbank of the Groveton Police. Kevin!

You need to calm down, or I'm going to have to restrain you. Do you understand?"

That got no response. Tom was worried about how Kevin might react to being restrained, but he didn't have any more time to think about it. Burbank walked up to Kevin, and in an instant he had him on the ground, face down in the soft, wet leaves, with his arms pinned behind his back. Kevin didn't seem aware of what had happened. He just kept sobbing and screaming himself hoarse, struggling but not really fighting.

Burbank ordered Tom to go around to the front of the house and direct the EMTs when the ambulance arrived. Tom did as he was told. The ambulance pulled in just a few minutes later, and he directed the two EMTs, carrying a stretcher between them, around to the back of the house. Kevin still seemed oblivious to what was going on as they strapped him into the stretcher and carried him to the ambulance.

Once they'd established Tom was Kevin's boyfriend, one of the EMTs told Tom, "You can ride in the front of the ambulance, if you want to go with us to the hospital."

Tom was grateful to be given the option, but he didn't relish having to take a cab back to the house later. He also needed to make sure Shadow wasn't completely panicked. "No, thank you. I'll get dressed and drive myself over."

"We won't be going to the hospital," Chief Burbank told him as the ambulance pulled out of Tom's long driveway, and the two policemen followed Tom up onto the porch to get out of the rain. "It's out of our jurisdiction, and I'm sure they'll take good care of him there. But I'm curious...." He glanced back in the direction of the artesian well. "*Who* is in the well?"

Tom was wondering that, too, but he said, "There's nobody in that well."

"Who did he *think* was in the well?"

"I don't know yet what was going on in his head," Tom replied. He didn't like where his own thoughts were going, and he didn't like the fact that Chief Burbank's thoughts seemed to be going in the same direction. "He was delusional. Something was upsetting him earlier—I think it had something to do with the storm. Then the dog ran off, and I guess Kevin stumbled across the well when he was searching for Shadow."

"And he thought there was a body in it?"

Tom shrugged. "I don't know."

But he was more disturbed than he was letting on. He couldn't escape the possibility that the storm—and the sight of the well—had triggered a flashback, another repressed memory. And the implications were chilling.

Twenty

BY THE time Tom made it to Androscoggin Valley Hospital, Kevin had been taken to a room and sedated. Tom was known to the staff there, and they were relieved to see him when he walked in, if for no other reason than he could provide some kind of explanation about Kevin's condition. Normally, there would have been an interview with the doctor on call—in this case, Mark Belanger—but Kevin had been too hysterical for Mark to get anything coherent out of him. The EMTs had passed along the information that Tom was on his way, so the doctor had waited to talk to Tom about it.

"Is he your patient?" Mark asked him.

Tom shook his head. "No." He glanced at the nurses chatting nearby at the reception desk and asked, "Do you mind if we go somewhere private?" He wasn't really "out" to the hospital staff.

Mark led him into his office and closed the door behind them.

"He's my boyfriend," Tom said, taking a seat on Mark's small sofa.

Mark smiled as he leaned back to sit on the edge of his desk. He was older than Tom, though not by much, and had a 1950s-TV-father aura about him that just lacked a cardigan and a pipe. Now he turned his full fatherly demeanor on Tom. "So the EMTs mentioned. I admit I was surprised. I had no idea you were gay."

At least he doesn't seem freaked out by it, Tom thought. "No, not many people in this area do. And I'd just as soon it didn't get around."

"I understand," Mark said, "but didn't I send him to you for counseling?" Tom sensed thinly veiled disapproval behind the question, and he couldn't blame Mark for that. Tom wouldn't think much of a therapist who dated someone he was treating either.

"I saw him once when you sent him to me three years ago," he explained. "That was the last I saw of him professionally. We just happened to bump into each other this spring when I needed some work done at my house."

Mark nodded thoughtfully, though he didn't look convinced. "Well, I won't gossip about it." He thought for a minute. "You're not married?"

Tom shook his head. "No, of course not. We've only been dating a few weeks."

"And he's not your client. So you really don't have any legal right to commit him."

Tom sighed and buried his head in his hands for a moment before lifting it again and replying, "I think I'm in love with this guy, Mark. I don't want him committed. I just want him to get through this intact. I called the ambulance because he was out of control and hurting himself. If he's stable in the morning, then I want *him* to make the decision about whether he stays here or not."

"Is he being treated by anyone else?"

"He saw Sue Cross for a short time, but he hasn't seen her for a while."

Mark raised his eyebrows, as if he couldn't believe someone with Kevin's history wouldn't be in therapy. Tom had to admit he would think the same thing in his position.

"We'll see what he's like in the morning," Mark said, "but I have to say, I'm extremely reluctant to release him immediately. He's had a pretty severe psychotic break. He had to be treated for self-inflicted injuries when he came in; it looks like he may have broken one of his fingers."

Mark *could* keep Kevin there for up to a couple of weeks, Tom knew. He really hoped that wouldn't be the case. Kevin would probably be furious with Tom for sending him there in the first place. If he was stuck there for a couple weeks, their relationship might not recover. Tom had promised not to force therapy on him, hadn't he?

What was I supposed to do? Tom wondered. *Just stand there and let him smash his hands to bloody pulps?*

"I know you'll do what's best for him," he told Mark.

"Why don't you go home and get some sleep? He's safe now. We have spot-checks on the patients throughout the night, and most likely he'll sleep until morning with the sedatives we've given him. I'll have someone give you a call when Kevin is awake."

SHADOW was a wreck when Tom got back to the house. The poor pup kept scurrying from room to room, searching for Kevin and whimpering. Tom finally got him to lie down on the bed beside him in the spot Kevin normally occupied. Then he stroked the dog's fur until Shadow fell asleep. Unfortunately, sleep didn't come as easily for Tom, and he lay there most of the night with the lights off, his hand resting lightly on Shadow's head to comfort himself as much as the dog. He finally drifted off as the sky began to lighten, only to be awakened by his cell phone vibrating on the nightstand a short time later.

When he answered, Mark Belanger said, "Kevin's awake and calm."

"Thank God."

"But he's not being very cooperative, Tom. He won't talk to me, and I can't release him if I can't do an evaluation."

Shit.

"He says he'll only talk to you," Mark added.

"I'll be right there."

AFTER he'd showered and taken care of Shadow, Tom drove to the hospital. He was dreading the meeting with Kevin, expecting him to be angry—furious!—at Tom for sending him there. Tom didn't think he'd had much of a choice, but Kevin probably wouldn't see it that way. Would this be the last straw? Were they about to break up for good? Tom's stomach was in knots over it.

But Kevin didn't look angry when Tom entered the hospital room. He looked frail and miserable, sitting up shirtless in the bed and picking unenthusiastically at a breakfast tray of oatmeal, toast, and juice with two bandaged hands. He glanced up as Tom came in and said in a quiet voice, "I wasn't sure you'd come."

"Of course I would."

Kevin looked away and cleared his throat. "I'm sorry. I know you didn't sign on for this kind of shit."

He thought I was going to tell him it was over, Tom realized. He'd been so worried about Kevin dumping *him* over putting him in the hospital that it hadn't occurred to him Kevin might be worried about Tom wanting to call it quits.

"What I 'signed on for'," Tom said softly, "was you. I'm still not sure what happened last night, and it concerns me for a lot of reasons. But if you think it means I'm going to turn tail and run, then... no."

Kevin's shoulders seemed to relax a bit at that, as if he'd been tensed up, waiting for Tom to berate him or worse.

"Are you mad at me for calling the ambulance?" Tom couldn't help asking. If Kevin needed forgiveness, so did he.

"You did what you had to do." Kevin held up his bandaged hands and looked at them in disgust. "I suppose I owe it to you that I didn't cripple myself for life. Jesus Christ...."

"Dr. Belanger said you might have a broken finger."

"Yep. And both hands look like I tried to stick them in a blender."

Tom winced at the image that conjured up. He came closer to sit in the chair beside the bed and noticed for the first time that Kevin's hospital gown was draped over the back of it. Recalling that Kevin never wore underwear, he asked, "Are you wearing anything at all under those blankets?"

"It's fucking ten thousand degrees in here, and I can't open a goddamned window." This was true to some extent, if not exactly literally. The temperature in the ward was far too warm, and Tom was finding it uncomfortable himself. "I'm keeping it under the covers," Kevin added irritably. "I'm not flashing anyone."

He glanced over at the second bed in the room when he said that. It was occupied by a young man who looked to be in his twenties, but the guy was asleep at the moment. Either that or he was faking it.

Tom lowered his voice when he said, "Dr. Belanger said you refused to talk to him."

Kevin sighed and shook his head. "If he gets one look at what's going on inside my head, he'll lock me up for good."

"He doesn't have that kind of power," Tom assured him. "But he does have the power to keep you here for a few days if he considers you to be a danger to yourself, just like he did three years ago."

Kevin snorted and held his hands up again. "What do you think, counselor? Am I a danger to myself?"

Tom wanted to say "of course not." He wanted Kevin to come home with him and for everything to go back to normal—normal for them, at any rate. But this wasn't about what *he* wanted. "What do you think?"

"I think I'm lucky I can still use my fingers."

Tom sighed and bit his lower lip. "Would you like to sign yourself in officially? It's an option. They can keep you safe and treat you—"

"Fuck no!" Kevin spat out. He glanced over at his sleeping roommate and lowered his voice again. "I want to go home."

"I want that too." Tom risked reaching out and touching Kevin's arm with his fingertips.

Kevin didn't flinch or pull away. He looked down at the hand resting on his forearm for a long moment before asking, "What do I have to do?"

"You have to cooperate with Mark—Dr. Belanger. Let him do the assessment."

"And then he'll let me go?"

"I can't make any guarantees. But if he doesn't think you're likely to hurt yourself, he may let you go, perhaps with a recommendation to seek further treatment."

"The last time, he kept me here for a fucking week."

"The circumstances were different then," Tom said. Then he added, "Look, I can't speak for him. He's the doctor here, not me. But you're not going to sort this out by refusing to talk to him. Just get it over with, and we'll see what we can do to get you home." And hopefully, he thought to himself, "home" meant the same thing to both of them now.

Kevin sighed and went back to poking at his cold oatmeal. "I don't remember any of it."

"What's the last thing you *do* remember?"

"Standing at the edge of the woods, feeling... I don't know. Fucked up. There was something about how dark it was and how much the wind was blowing that was freaking me out." Kevin frowned as if trying to concentrate. "Then you were there, yelling at me about something. And Shadow ran off—"

He looked up at Tom's face, alarm suddenly written on his features, and Tom reassured him, "Shadow's fine. He found you at the well and stayed with you until I found both of you."

Kevin sighed in relief. "Poor pup."

"And that's all you remember?" Tom couldn't help prompting.

Kevin looked uncomfortable at the question, so his answer was somewhat less than convincing when he shrugged and said, "I guess."

"You don't remember screaming 'He's in the well' over and over again?"

Kevin shook his head, but he'd gone suddenly pale, his eyes wide. When Tom continued to wait for a more detailed response, Kevin reluctantly added, "I don't... I don't remember that. But I had some kind of dream or hallucination or something when I was drugged last night. I kept seeing this... boy. He was naked, and he kept crying out and...."

Kevin's voice cracked, and he stopped talking. His eyes were glistening again, and he was forced to clear his throat a couple of times before he could continue speaking. "Jesus.... He was begging for help.... He was begging for *me* to help him...."

He lifted a shaking hand to rub his eyes clear.

"Who was he?"

"I don't know."

"Was he in the well?"

"What well?" Kevin snapped. "Jesus Christ! I've never seen a well anywhere. How could he be in a well when there's no goddamn well?"

"You didn't have one at your house?"

"No!" Kevin stopped himself and took a deep breath. Tom waited patiently until Kevin added in a calmer tone of voice, "He had black hair, kind of long. And huge, brown eyes. God, those eyes!" He rubbed his hand across his own eyes, as if to blot out what he was seeing in his mind. "Tom... we both know that I'm getting flashes of memory now, things I've blocked out because they were too awful to remember."

"Yes."

"So can you tell me this isn't one of those?"

"No, I can't. Not until we do some digging."

"And then what? What if it turns out there's some... dead kid...." Kevin broke off, as if too upset to continue.

Tom sighed and lightly stroked the hair on Kevin's forearm. "If this turns out to be real, then we'll go to the police."

"To do what? Report me as a murderer?"

Tom felt a chill crawling up the back of his scalp. "In these dreams, did you see yourself killing him?"

"No. But I seemed to be just... standing there looking down at him. I wasn't helping. What if I pushed him in there or something?"

"What did it feel like in the dream? Did you feel anger? Fear?"

"I was terrified."

"If it is a real memory, perhaps it's something you witnessed but couldn't prevent. It might have been an accident. For that matter, we don't even know if the boy died or was rescued. Not from what you've told me."

"I don't know," Kevin said, shaking his head. "I just saw him down there."

"How old do you think you were in the dream?"

"I'm not sure. It felt like I was a kid."

Tom was growing fearful—fearful that Mr. Derocher might have been even more of a monster than he'd already proven to be. He refused to believe Kevin had hurt or killed another boy. But what if he'd witnessed something? Had his father abused other boys? Abusers often did have multiple victims. But would Mr. Derocher have gone so far as to commit *murder*?

Until Kevin remembered more—assuming there was anything to remember, and this wasn't some kind of horrible hallucination—there didn't seem to be any way to answer these questions.

"Look, we need to get you sorted out first. If, God forbid, this is a real crime that you're remembering, it happened a very long time ago. Delving into it can wait until you're strong enough to deal with it, perhaps in Sue's office...."

Kevin raised his hand again, accidentally bumping into the plastic tray that straddled his legs and wincing. "Can you take this fucking thing out of here? I don't want to eat this shit."

Tom stood up and removed the tray from Kevin's bed, setting it on the floor. When he straightened up again, he found Kevin watching him intently.

"You win, counselor."

Tom found that comment unsettling. "What do you mean?"

Kevin sat back and closed his eyes as if he were completely exhausted. "I mean, you can do whatever you have to now: play me songs, grill me about my childhood, make me go back to counseling, whatever you need." He opened his eyes, and Tom could see the pain reflected deep within them. "I need to know if this is all in my head, or if there really is a well somewhere…." He glanced at the young man sleeping in the other bed and stopped, perhaps not trusting the guy wasn't faking it and listening to the conversation. But Tom knew what he'd been about to say:

…with a dead boy in it.

Twenty-One

BY THE time Mark did his assessment, Kevin was perfectly calm and rational. So Mark signed the paperwork to release him. He did insist that Kevin set up an appointment with someone outside the hospital, and Kevin promised to call Sue.

A short time later, Tom was driving home with Kevin in the passenger seat.

"Did you really mean that?" Tom asked him after they'd put Berlin behind them. "About me doing whatever it takes?"

Kevin looked out the window at the passing countryside. "Be gentle."

"I want to talk to your mother."

Kevin turned to him and gave him a sour look. "Christ! You don't waste any time going for the fucking jugular, do you?"

"I'm sorry. You're right. I said I'd let you have time, and then I immediately—"

"Why do you want to talk to her?"

Tom took a deep breath. "You know what's at stake here," he explained. "There's a chance you might be remembering fragments of something that really happened. If you did know a boy with black hair and brown eyes when you were young, maybe she'll know who he was."

Kevin looked away and thought that over for a long time before saying, "Fine. But not today."

"No, of course not."

"I'll decide when."

"All right."

SHADOW was so ecstatic to see the "fun daddy"—as Tom was convinced the dog viewed Kevin—back at home that he nearly knocked over half the stacked boxes in the living room as he tore around, wagging his massive Tail of Destruction. Tom made a mental note to finally get all the boxes either unpacked or put in the basement by the end of the week.

For a few days, neither of the two men had a strong desire to talk about Kevin's breakdown. They just wanted things to be normal and pleasant for a while. They went to work, they came home to each other and Shadow, they made dinner—though Tom was beginning to insist they occasionally eat something other than cheeseburgers—and they spent their evenings in the hot tub or just hanging out and chatting.

There were days when Kevin didn't like to be touched, but more and more often he would hold Tom's hand or reach out to give him gentle caresses. One night, as they were lying in bed together, both naked of course, Kevin spent several minutes running his hand softly along Tom's side and hip in a light, erotic caress that left both of them hard and wanting more. But Kevin wasn't ready to do more, and Tom accepted it when he stopped and said he wanted to go to sleep. Tom slipped out of the bed after a few minutes of lying there in the dark frustrated and went into the bathroom to quietly masturbate.

When he returned to the bed, Kevin asked him, "Were you just jerking off?"

"Yes."

"I'm sorry I'm so fucked up that I couldn't...."

Tom found Kevin's hand in the darkness and brought it to his lips for a gentle kiss. "I love you, Kevin. And I think you're incredibly sexy. So if I get so worked up that I sometimes have to... relieve the pressure... I don't see why either of us should feel upset or apologetic about that."

"I don't want you to be frustrated."

"Whatever frustration I was feeling is gone now. It felt great, and I assure you my thoughts about you a few minutes ago were extremely complimentary."

Kevin laughed at that. "Well, that's good to know. Did you have me up on trapeze or wearing a leather harness?"

"I would never put any article of clothing on you! You're perfect just as you are. And no—no trapeze. Just cuddling and caressing and making out... and I confess the idea of being fucked by you is appealing."

"I'm still...." Kevin hesitated and then went on. "I'm still hard from touching you. I think I'd be cool with you watching me. I mean, I think I'd like it. Do you want to do that?"

Tom felt a jolt of sexual excitement shoot straight to his cock and cause it to grow stiff again, even after his orgasm just a few minutes ago. "Yes. I'd love to watch you."

He knew he wouldn't be able to touch Kevin or himself and that would be frustrating, but that was completely overridden by how much he longed to see Kevin in the throes of an orgasm.

"Turn on the light," Kevin said as he pushed the blankets down below his hips. Tom obeyed and immediately felt a surge of arousal as the light fell across Kevin's naked body and Kevin's hands reached for his erection.

Tom had masturbated with other men before, but he'd never just watched as a man masturbated. He hadn't expected it to feel so... intimate. It was surreal. He would have thought the fact that he wasn't masturbating too would make him feel removed from it, the way a member of the audience at a play felt removed from the actors on the stage. But it wasn't like that at all. Instead he felt as if he'd been invited into something incredibly intimate. He was watching another man pleasure himself, watching Kevin do something intensely private.

And it was fucking hot.

Kevin wasn't performing for him, as Tom had anticipated. He was simply masturbating the way he would if he were alone, surprisingly unself-conscious. And Tom was taking mental notes. He saw how Kevin liked to play with his nipples a bit, liked to caress the taut muscles of his abdomen, and enjoyed caressing his inner thighs. He watched how fast Kevin liked to stroke and how he enjoyed alternating quick, short strokes with long, languorous ones.

Someday, Tom thought, *I'm going to make you feel incredible!*

When Kevin came, it sprayed all over his stomach and chest and even splashed against his neck.

"Wow," Tom said with a soft chuckle, "that was amazing!" His own cock was rock hard again, and he was beginning to think he might need another trip to the bathroom before he'd be able to sleep.

Kevin gasped and looked up at him through heavily lidded eyes. "Kiss me," he breathed.

Tom bent down and kissed him on the mouth, allowing Kevin to draw it out as long as he wanted. To his surprise, Kevin slipped his tongue into his mouth and kissed him deeper than they'd ever kissed before.

At last Kevin allowed him to come up for air, and Tom said with a lecherous smile, "You've got me all worked up again. I may need to leave for a few minutes."

"No," Kevin said. "Don't leave. I want to watch you now."

"Are you sure?"

"Yeah."

So Tom masturbated for Kevin. It felt a little uncomfortable for all of a minute or two, but with Kevin running his fingers along Tom's naked body in featherlight caresses and the scent of semen still in the air, Tom quickly got so turned on he got past his shyness. He couldn't come nearly as forcefully as Kevin—not after having just done it less than twenty minutes ago—but it was immensely satisfying. They hadn't quite had sex… but they almost had. And it felt wonderful.

Kevin kissed him again after it was over and told him, "I love you, Tom."

As much as Tom had grown used to the affectionately teasing nickname "counselor," it felt so much nicer to hear those words with his own name attached. "I love you too, Kevin."

KEVIN called Sue and arranged for a session with her, as he'd promised. But once he and Tom got there, it quickly became apparent he wasn't quite as ready to plunge ahead as he'd told Tom he was on the way home from the hospital.

"You won't listen to the song?" Sue asked him. She had her arms crossed and her right ring finger was tapping impatiently against her upper arm.

"I'm sorry," Kevin replied. "I know I said I would. I just… I can't right now. Every time I think about it, I start getting cold sweats."

"You realize, of course, that the most likely reason you're getting cold sweats is because the song is linked to a particularly powerful memory—one you're afraid to remember."

"I know."

"And this memory may have something to do with the boy you keep dreaming about." Kevin had been having more nightmares about the boy, waking up screaming in the middle of the night. But so far there was nothing coherent, just images of the boy calling out to him for help.

Kevin's leg was going a mile a minute again as he said, "Look, I know you don't like me, and you think I'm the worst thing that ever happened to Tom—"

"I've known Tom for over a decade, Kevin. You are not even *close* to being the worst person he's ever dated."

Tom snorted at that, recalling the last guy he'd introduced Sue to. It hadn't been pretty. Seeing him laugh appeared to ease Kevin's tension a bit, and he smiled.

"As far as whether I like you or not," Sue continued, "I suppose I do. But I'm not here to be your friend. I'm your therapist. Which means that sometimes I need to push you, where a friend might back off to preserve the friendship."

Kevin sighed. "Okay, I understand all that. What I'm getting at is, I'm not being difficult on purpose. There's just something about that song…. Even thinking about what might happen if I listen to it and it turns out to be the right one…. I guess it's not very manly of me, but it scares the shit out of me."

For once, Sue's voice was gentle. "I don't care much for manliness, Kevin. I care about what people feel—what *you* feel. And trying to be manly isn't going to help you get through this. Psychological problems need to be handled differently than financial problems or repair work around the house. They can't be solved by remaining cool and collected, or by being strong. They can only be solved by allowing ourselves to feel, even if those feelings are unpleasant."

"This is a little more than just 'unpleasant'," Kevin murmured.

"I know. So we'll let it go for now." Sue went to pour herself another cup of coffee. "Can you tell me anything more about these nightmares you've been having?"

Kevin described them again, but he couldn't remember any more detail than he'd given her earlier.

Sue took her seat again and looked down into her coffee cup for a long time before asking, "Have you ever been hypnotized?"

"No."

"It's not usually as dramatic as you see in films. A hypnotized person can't be forced to do anything he really doesn't want to do—"

"You mean there are people who *want* to cluck like chickens on stage in front of an audience?" Kevin asked.

"Yes, in fact. Those people accept the suggestions given them by the hypnotist because they want permission to act foolish or outlandish, while having the excuse that they weren't in control of themselves. Many people drink for the same reason."

Kevin looked over at Tom and raised an eyebrow at him, an irritating smirk on his handsome face.

"I didn't get drunk that night so I could behave like an idiot without being blamed for it," Tom said defensively. "I got drunk because I *was* an idiot. It's a completely different category of stupidity."

Kevin laughed and spontaneously leaned over to kiss him on the cheek. Tom felt his face flush for probably the first time in his life, and when he glanced over at Sue, he saw that she was amused by the exchange.

But the professional mask dropped almost instantly back into place. "Being hypnotized may allow you to recall some details of the dream that you've forgotten, Kevin. Would you like to try it? At no time will you be out of control. You'll be able to wake yourself the moment you encounter anything too frightening or disturbing."

Kevin agreed, if somewhat reluctantly. Tom moved to a chair so Kevin could lie down on the sofa, while Sue drew the blinds to dim the light in the office. Then Sue drew her chair closer to Kevin and told him in a gentle tone of voice, "All right, Kevin. Close your eyes and relax. Focus on my voice and let everything else go. We're going to start with some deep breathing…."

Sue walked him through a basic induction technique Tom was familiar with, though he rarely used hypnosis in his own therapy sessions. But when she told Kevin, "Your right arm is growing very light—so light that begins to drift upward, floating toward the ceiling…," nothing happened. Sue repeated the suggestion, but still Kevin's arm remained motionless.

"All right, Kevin. You can open your eyes now."

He opened his eyes without hesitation, looking a little sheepish. "I'm sorry. I guess I didn't do it right."

"Not at all. Some people just aren't very suggestible. We'll try something else next time."

Kevin sat up and rubbed his face with his hands. "Yeah, I guess."

"You are coming back, I assume?" There was a note of warning in her voice. Tom knew she was unlikely to give Kevin a third chance if he bailed again.

"Tom'll kill me if I don't."

"This isn't about Tom. It's about whether you want to work on these issues or not."

"Yes," Kevin replied irritably, and Tom was certain he'd bitten back a sarcastic "ma'am" at the end of it. But all he said was, "I'll come back."

"Good. In the meantime, I think Tom's suggestion that you talk to your mother is a good idea. If this boy was a real person from the years you have trouble remembering, perhaps she'll remember him."

Twenty-Two

IT WASN'T until the following Saturday that Kevin announced, "Okay, I think it's time to go see Mommie Dearest."

Tom was washing up the breakfast dishes and contemplating buying a dishwasher when the announcement came out of the blue. He turned off the water and turned to face Kevin. "Today?"

"Might as well." Kevin didn't look happy about it, but he seemed to have resigned himself to the idea. "We can drive over to Riverview as soon as you're done with the dishes, if you want."

"Maybe we should call first."

"It's not like she's gonna be out," Kevin said testily.

"It would still be polite."

"I don't want to talk to her on the phone. If you want to go, let's just go."

Tom decided not to push it. He finished up the dishes, and they took Shadow out before leaving. The weather was still too hot to leave the dog in the car for more than a few minutes, and Riverview was unlikely to let them bring him inside. But with the baby gate blocking access to the basement and any rooms that had doors closed, there wasn't too much trouble Shadow could get into, so Tom and Kevin had gotten into the habit of leaving him free to roam around while they were out of the house. Indoor "accidents" were infrequent now and as far as they could tell, Shadow mostly slept on the couch until they returned.

Kevin insisted on driving, even though Tom knew the way. Perhaps he wanted control over the escape route if he felt it necessary to get out of there. Tom didn't argue.

Riverview was a converted Victorian home that didn't house nearly as many elderly residents as some of the more hospital- or hotel-like facilities. It was rather expensive. Tom hadn't pried into it, but he knew the house didn't accept Medicare, and it seemed unlikely Mrs. Derocher would have collected any life insurance after her husband's obvious suicide. Somehow Mr. Derocher must have made certain his wife was well provided for.

The staff person at the front desk did not seem pleased to see them when Kevin mentioned his mother wasn't expecting him. But she said she would see if Mrs. Derocher was up for receiving visitors and then disappeared into one of the inner rooms. She returned a moment later, looking no friendlier. "Mrs. Derocher is in the garden, if you'll please follow me."

The garden was a small, pleasant area outside the dining room. French doors opened onto a flagstone patio with small metal tables surrounded by chairs. Gravel pathways led from the patio off in different directions through a large garden of roses and rhododendrons and other cultivated flowers Tom knew nothing about. This late in the fall, few of them were in bloom, but it was a clear, sunny day, and the space was serenely beautiful.

Mrs. Derocher appeared at the far side of the garden, walking toward them along one of the gravel paths, pulling gardening gloves off her hands. Kevin had been born late in his parents' marriage when they were both in their midthirties, which made his mother about seventy now. She was still a striking woman, straight and not at all stooped with age, though her abundant, braided hair had gone white, and her face was lined.

Her expression at seeing her only son was far from joyous. "What can I do for you, Kevin?"

"I just came to visit," Kevin said uncomfortably and not very convincingly.

"Well, have a seat, then." She gestured at one of the nearby tables.

"Would you like anything brought out to you, Ellen?" the staff person asked her.

"Could we have some coffee, Sarah?"

Sarah disappeared back into the house, while Kevin and Tom found seats at the table and Mrs. Derocher joined them.

"Are you planning on introducing me to your friend?"

Kevin fidgeted in his chair and said, "This is my friend, Tom."

He glanced quickly at Tom, perhaps to see if he'd angered him by referring to him as a "friend." But Tom didn't think a dramatic revelation about Kevin's sexual orientation was likely to help their cause much. That could wait for another time.

"I'm pleased to meet you, Mrs. Derocher," he said.

For him—a stranger—she could manage a gracious smile. "I'm pleased to meet you too, Tom."

"So how are you doing, Mom?" Kevin asked.

The smile faltered. "I'm fine. The people here are friendly; the food is decent. In the summer, I have the garden to keep me occupied." She paused as Sarah returned with a tray containing coffee cups and a silver carafe. Once the woman had poured them all a cup and left the tray for them to serve themselves sugar and cream, Mrs. Derocher continued, "I hear you've divorced."

"Yeah."

"That's too bad. She was a nice girl."

She'd either heard nothing about the suicide attempt and the miscarriage, or she chose not to mention them.

"Tracy's great. It wasn't her fault."

"Are you seeing anyone now?" she asked, opening a packet of artificial sweetener and emptying it into her coffee.

Kevin glanced at Tom, who gave him a barely perceptible shake of the head. Kevin looked down at his coffee cup. "No."

"Your Aunt Maggie called a few weeks ago. Do you remember Uncle Howard?" Kevin looked at her blankly, but she continued, "He passed away last…. When was it? May, I think. Pancreatic cancer."

"I'm sorry to hear that."

"You should call her. It would mean a lot to her."

"Mom," Kevin said, his impatience beginning to show, "I haven't seen Aunt Maggie since I was a kid. I barely remember her."

"Well, she remembers you. She asks about you every time she calls."

Kevin sighed. "Okay."

"It won't kill you to give her one sympathy call."

"I said 'okay'. I'll call her."

"Right after you stop by the cemetery to pay your respects to your father, no doubt."

"No doubt," Kevin replied coldly.

The three of them drank their coffee in near silence after that, mother and son apparently having no desire to continue the charade of polite conversation. Tom asked Mrs. Derocher a couple of harmless questions about the garden, which she answered, but the conversation failed to gain any momentum.

After they'd finished their coffee, Mrs. Derocher smiled and picked up her gloves from where she'd set them on the one empty chair and said, "Well, that was lovely. But I really should get back to—"

"I need to ask you something, Mom," Kevin interrupted.

She didn't look pleased, but she said, "Well, then ask."

Kevin glanced at Tom again, but Tom merely waited for him to continue. "I've been having really… strange dreams lately. I keep seeing this kid's face. He's probably ten years old or so. Kind of shaggy black hair. Big brown eyes. I don't remember ever knowing a kid who looked like that, but I thought maybe you'd remember if I had a friend coming around to the house—"

"Do you mean Billy?"

Kevin's face suddenly drained of all color, and his eyes widened. His leg, which had been tapping as it always did when he was agitated, froze in position. "Billy...," he said softly.

"He was the only friend you ever had over to the house that I recall. And he only came around for a few months when you were... I think eleven. I'd hoped you were beginning to come out of your shell, but... no."

Kevin seemed to have turned inward, saying the name "Billy" quietly to himself as if trying it out on his tongue. Tom had no doubt they were on to something.

He asked Kevin's mother, "Billy stopped coming to the house? Why?"

"Why?" She looked surprised at the question. "He ran away from home, if I remember. The police were asking everyone around town about it, asking all the kids in the school if he'd told them what he'd been planning. They came to the house, of course, to talk to Kevin. But he didn't know anything. Nobody did."

Tom looked over at Kevin and asked him gently, "Do you remember him?"

Kevin was staring blankly ahead, as if seeing something that wasn't actually there, but he merely shook his head.

"Do you remember Billy's last name?" Tom asked Mrs. Derocher.

She made a face, sort of a grimace with her eyebrows raised. "Oh Lord. It was so long ago. We really didn't know him all that long. I think it started with an *S*—Sherman or Shepherd or...."

In unison, both mother and son said the name, "Sherrell."

Twenty-Three

"THAT was it," Mrs. Derocher said with some satisfaction, apparently oblivious to the effect the name was having on her son. "Billy Sherrell. He was a very... almost *pretty* boy. I'm sure he grew up to be a very handsome man. I wonder where he is now?"

It was obvious to Tom that Kevin needed to get out of there as soon as possible. He didn't appear to be breaking down, exactly, but his eyes had become fixed in a sort of glazed stare, as if he was no longer processing what was going on around him.

"Unfortunately, I have to be somewhere soon," Tom lied. "I hate to cut things short...."

"No, not at all. It was very nice to meet you, Tom."

"It was nice to meet you." Tom stood and was relieved to see Kevin do the same. "Thanks for the coffee, Mrs. Derocher."

Kevin followed him out without even saying good-bye to his mother. That probably wouldn't help their tense relationship much, but Tom didn't have time to worry about that. He just wanted to get Kevin to the truck before he had a meltdown.

Once there, however, he came up against an obstacle. "Shit. I can't drive a standard. Do you want me to call a cab?"

"I'll drive," Kevin said quietly. "Just give me a minute."

They sat in the cab of the truck for much longer than a minute, while Kevin struggled to calm himself with the deep breathing exercises he'd learned from Tom and Sue. Tom remained silent, allowing him to take the time he needed until, at last, Kevin inserted the key into the ignition, and they pulled out of the parking lot.

To Tom's surprise, they didn't go straight home. Kevin pulled the truck into the lot at Lee's Diner and parked.

"You want lunch?" Tom asked.

"I want you to see if you can talk to Tracy for a minute. Her car's here."

"What for?"

"She went to school with me, so maybe she'll remember... this kid."

"I thought you were starting to remember him," Tom said.

Kevin shook his head. "I remember his face. And now the name sounds familiar. But nothing else. I want to know if Tracy remembers him. Maybe she'll know if his family is still in town." It was obvious Kevin was feeling overwhelmed at the moment. Tom would have preferred they deal with this later, when Kevin was in a better state of mind, but if this was what Kevin wanted....

"Are you sure you'll be all right while I'm inside?"

"I'm not fuckin' five years old. I just need to be by myself for a bit."

Tom left him there and went into the diner. As usual, the place was busy, but he was able to find a booth near the front window where he could keep an eye on the parking lot. He felt like an overprotective mother, but he knew he would be fretting too much about what Kevin might be doing if he couldn't see the truck.

"What's going on?" Tracy's voice cut through his thoughts, startling him.

He turned to find her standing by the table, one arm on her hip. She was looking out the window too, right at the truck. "Why is Kevin sitting out there by himself?" she asked.

"He, um… he's not feeling well. But he wanted me to see if I could talk to you for a moment."

"You're not gonna order nothing?"

"Um… no, I guess not."

She wrinkled her nose as she turned her gaze on Tom and gave him a sardonic smile. "I'm beginning to think his crazy is contagious, and you're starting to catch it."

"Maybe." Tom had to admit he felt foolish, if not exactly crazy.

"Well, what did you need to talk to me about? It's pretty busy."

Tom shrugged. "Kevin wanted me to ask you if you remembered a friend of his from his childhood—a boy with black hair and brown eyes. His name was Billy Sherrell."

Tracy slipped into the booth opposite him and frowned in concentration. "Billy Sherrell.…" She was distracted by the bell on the door as a family entered the diner. "I don't know, hon. Tell you what, leave me your number, and I'll call you if I remember anything."

W HEN they got home, Kevin brought Shadow out to pee, and it took every ounce of Tom's self-restraint not to follow them. But nothing dramatic occurred. Kevin complained about being tired a short time later and went upstairs to nap for a couple of hours. During that time, Tom did a quick search on the name "Billy Sherrell," using "Billy," "Bill," "William," and even "Will," as well as several spelling variations on the last name and trying to limit it to New Hampshire. The search turned up nothing interesting.

Kevin woke and had a cup of coffee. By nightfall, he seemed to be back to his normal self, wrestling with the dog and helping Tom measure one of the upstairs rooms to calculate how many bookshelves they could fit in there to make a library.

Tom wasn't sure if it would be a good idea to bring up Billy, so he avoided the subject. It was Kevin who asked, while they were sitting in the hot tub, looking up at the peaceful, starry sky overhead. "Do you think I'm capable of killing someone?"

"You're the only one who can answer that," Tom said and then kicked himself for being so cautious with the way he worded things. It was his training as an analyst. Of course he didn't believe Kevin was capable of it.

Before he could qualify himself, Kevin said with a sour expression, "I didn't ask you if I did it. I asked you if you *think* I could do it."

"No, Kevin. I don't think you're capable of killing someone."

Kevin looked contemplative, watching the stars in silence for a long time before saying, "It sure is hard for me to imagine."

"Yes," Tom said, reaching out to take his hand under the water, "it is. And we don't know what happened. If you're sure the boy you've been seeing in your dreams is Billy Sherrell—"

"I am."

"Then that's one piece of the puzzle. But Billy may still be alive somewhere. We'll find out."

"If he's dead," Kevin said quietly, "I may be the only person who knows what happened to him."

"Whatever it is locked away in your unconscious," Tom said, "we'll get to it. Just give it time."

His cell phone rang, interrupting the conversation. He climbed out of the tub to retrieve it from his pants pocket while Kevin watched him curiously. The name on the display was "Tracy Kimball."

"You remember that boy you asked me about today?" Tracy asked when Tom answered.

"Of course."

"Well, I talked to Lee about it, and between the two of us, we were able to piece some of it together. Now, it was a long time ago, hon, so we can't be sure if our memories are 100 percent. I'm still trying to figure out why Kevin wanted to know what *I* remembered about *his* friend."

"Because, apart from Billy's name and face, he can't remember anything."

There was a long pause on the other end of the line, but eventually Tracy said, "What we recall was that Billy was kind of a strange kid, kind of an outsider, and not a nice kid. If you tried to say 'hello' to him, he'd just tell you to fuck off—pardon my French. Everyone knew his father was an alcoholic, so we figured he had a rough time at home. Billy came into school with bruises on his face sometimes, but back then… well, too many people pretended not to notice that sort of thing."

"Yes, I know."

"Anyway, somehow he and Kevin became friends. I have no idea how they started hanging out together, but they were pretty inseparable for a while. Then one day Billy didn't show up at school. That was the last anyone ever saw of him. A cop showed up in our homeroom class and asked everybody if we'd seen him, but nobody had. Not even Kevin. And that was pretty much it."

"Did you hear anything about the police questioning his father?"

"I suppose I might have. Everyone was convinced the guy got drunk and took one swing too many at his kid. But nobody could prove anything."

"I couldn't find anyone named Sherrell living near here," Tom said.

"He left town after a while. I remember hearing that everyone was avoiding him and some of the stores wouldn't even serve him anymore, so I can see why he would. Not that I have any sympathy for the bastard if he really did kill his kid. As far as I know, nobody ever saw him again."

TOM watched Kevin closely for his reaction after explaining everything Tracy had relayed. But Kevin simply frowned and looked frustrated.

"Some of it sounds familiar," he said at last. "But I don't *feel* it. It's like I'm hearing about things that happened to other people, and I wasn't even there." Then he gave a long sigh and said, "There's no way around it. I'm going to have to listen to that goddamn song."

Twenty-Four

"YOU need to remember, Kevin," Sue told him, "that any memories that surface when you hear the song... they're just memories. They happened a long time ago, and they can't hurt you anymore."

"Sure," Kevin replied, though he didn't sound convinced. Memories had *already* been hurting him. He'd taken a sedative before the session—a prescription Sue had asked Mark Belanger to write out for Kevin since he didn't have a primary care physician—but he was clearly still agitated. He was clutching Tom's hand so tightly Tom was starting to lose feeling in his fingers.

"You're safe here. And we can stop any time you tell me to turn the music off."

That wouldn't stop the flood of memories, Tom knew—and he was sure Kevin knew as well—but at least it was some amount of control.

"Can I hold the remote, then?" Kevin asked, a slight smile quirking up one corner of his mouth.

"Certainly."

Sue handed the remote to him, and Kevin looked at it for a long time before sighing and saying, "All right. Fuck it."

He pressed Play and the song "Kyrie" by Mr. Mister began to play on Sue's stereo system.

Stark, New Hampshire, 1987—Billy

BILLY SHERRELL was the most amazing thing that had ever happened to eleven-year-old Kevin Derocher. He was strong and tough; he didn't take shit from anybody. And somehow, despite the fact that Kevin didn't feel at all strong and tough, that most of the time he felt frightened and overwhelmed, Billy had picked him—and no one else—for a friend. Perhaps it was because Billy had seen Kevin eating alone every day in the cafeteria and something in him had responded to his isolation. One day Billy simply set his tray down on the table across from Kevin at lunchtime and said, "I'm gonna sit here."

And that was it. They found a common interest in *The Karate Kid* and thought it would be cool to learn karate and go to Japan. They also liked a lot of the same music. It wasn't long before they were always together at lunch, and Billy started waiting after school for Kevin to catch up and walk home with him.

Mr. Sherrell frightened Kevin. The man was usually passed out drunk on the living room couch whenever Kevin stopped by Billy's house. He worked at the Berlin paper mill, and his usual routine after coming home from work was to drink himself into oblivion. On the rare occasions when he was awake, he was usually snarling at his son and calling him "faggot" for no particular reason.

"I fucking hate him," Billy told Kevin once, when they'd escaped from the tirade into Billy's room. "I wish he'd pass out and never wake up again."

Kevin had almost said, "I hate my dad too," but he couldn't bring himself to say it out loud. He didn't have any right to hate his father. It wasn't like his dad ever hit him or anything.

KEVIN was never quite certain how things turned sexual between him and Billy. It might have been his doing. Lately, once or twice a week, he'd been waking up in the morning with wet spots on his sheets. He knew what it was. He'd seen his father make messes like that more times than he could remember. It was feeling good to touch himself and make it happen on purpose, so he finally understood why his father liked it so much. But he kept it secret from his father. He didn't want to be forced to do it with him.

He did tell Billy about it, though.

"Yeah," Billy said with a soft laugh, keeping his voice down, as if afraid his own father might overhear, "that happens to me too sometimes." He was referring to the waking up in a wet spot part. He didn't know about touching himself.

Despite being tough and a little scary, it turned out Billy knew very little about sex. For the first time since they'd met, Kevin was the one who knew everything. He didn't tell Billy *how* he knew, but he explained how they could make it happen on purpose, instead of just when they were asleep. And when Billy wanted to try it together, Kevin didn't object.

For the first time in his life, Kevin enjoyed doing something sexual. And apparently, so did Billy because he kept wanting to do it whenever they had time alone together. When Kevin taught him how to kiss, Billy liked that too. And Kevin was happier than he'd ever been in his life.

Until the night of the storm.

IT WAS already beginning to rain as they walked to Billy's house that Wednesday afternoon. Their relief at getting in out of the storm was short-lived, however. Mr. Sherrell was tearing around the house, pulling out drawers in the kitchen and dumping the contents on the floor like a madman. When he saw the boys, he rushed up to Billy and belted him upside the head.

"Where the fuck is my new jackknife, you little faggot?"

Kevin couldn't stop himself from shrieking when Billy got hit, but Billy just gritted his teeth and glared back at his father. "How the fuck should I know?"

Mr. Sherrell growled and took another swing at his son, but Billy was prepared this time and ducked out of the way.

"I paid good money for that knife. You tell me where it is, or so help me I'll knock your fucking head off!"

"You probably got drunk and forgot where you put it!"

Mr. Sherrell made another lunge for him, but Billy dodged and shoved him hard, knocking him onto the floor. The man was a lot bigger than Billy, but he must have been drunk, as usual.

"I'm gonna kill you for that! And your little faggot girlfriend!"

Billy grabbed Kevin's shirt and pulled him out the front door. They ran as fast as they could in the rain until Kevin thought his sides would burst, but Mr. Sherrell didn't bother chasing after them. When Billy finally allowed them to slow down and look back, there was no sign of his father.

"Jesus!" Billy gasped. But then he grinned at Kevin and drew a large jackknife out of his pants pocket. He tossed it in his hand triumphantly, while Kevin stared in shocked admiration.

"You *did* take it!"

Billy shrugged. "He can get another one. But I sure as hell can't go back there tonight."

Kevin could understand that, but when Billy asked, "Can we go to your house?" he was hesitant. He'd brought Billy to his house a few times, but he didn't like to bring those two parts of his life together, his home life and Billy. And he didn't like the way his father looked at Billy. Mr. Derocher was always polite and friendly to the boy, but there was something… hungry in his eyes when Billy was around. Billy thought he was just a "really cool dad," because he was so friendly.

But the rain was getting heavier, and there was nowhere else to go, so Kevin said, "Sure."

KEVIN'S mother was away for the night, visiting her sister in Maine, but his father would be getting home soon. They would have the house to themselves for a while. But when Billy grabbed him in the entry hall and kissed him, slipping a hand down inside the back of Kevin's pants, Kevin pulled away.

"Not here."

"No," Billy agreed. "We can go up to your bedroom."

Kevin shook his head. They'd never done it there, and he didn't want to do it someplace that made him think of... him. "My dad'll be home soon. I know a better place."

He took Billy out to the gardening shed. Despite the rain, it wasn't very cold, and Kevin's mother had placed a kerosene heater and a radio in the shed for use when she retreated there. Kevin turned on the heater, and Billy switched the classical station on the radio to one playing Top 40 songs. Then Billy grabbed Kevin and pulled him close again. This time, Kevin didn't resist.

They were naked and not really paying attention to anything but each other when Kevin heard something that made his blood run cold—his father's voice. "Well, it looks like you two are having fun."

Kevin and Billy exploded apart, both looking at the man with horror while they clutched at their crotches with their hands in a desperate attempt to cover themselves. Mr. Derocher didn't seem angry. He was standing in the open doorway, rain pouring down behind him and water dripping off his raincoat and fedora as he regarded them both with an amused expression.

"Don't panic," he said softly. "You're not in any trouble."

When he entered and closed the door behind him, however, Kevin knew they were in for far worse than a scolding. They'd left their clothes near the door, and Mr. Derocher positioned himself so they'd have to go past him to get dressed. Billy attempted it, but Kevin's father blocked him.

"There's no hurry," he said. His voice sounded warm and pleasant, but Kevin could see that... look in his eyes. The one he always had when he came to Kevin's room late at night.

Billy stopped, uncertain. He glanced at Kevin, but Kevin couldn't look him in the eye.

I knew this would happen, Kevin thought, feeling sick inside. *I knew it! It had to happen sooner or later if I kept letting him come to the house. Why did I let him come here?*

"I should go home," Billy mumbled and made another attempt to reach for his clothes in the pile behind Mr. Derocher.

Kevin's father stopped him with a gentle touch to the shoulder. Billy flinched away from it, but Mr. Derocher acted as though he didn't notice. "You're a very beautiful boy, Billy. Very handsome."

"What are you? Some kind of—" Billy stopped himself before completing the sentence, perhaps because he didn't want to upset Kevin by calling his father names.

But Kevin knew the word he'd been about to say: *pervert*.

Mr. Derocher laughed softly. "I just caught you having gay sex with my son. Don't you think we're all a little...?" He left the word unsaid, just as Billy had.

No! Kevin thought, pleading silently for Billy to stand up to the man Kevin had never been able to stand up to. *It's different! Tell him!*

But Billy just stood there, apparently too confused to know how to react. He'd told Kevin that he liked Mr. Derocher, that he wished he could live with Kevin's family instead of with the monster who passed for his own father. Kevin had wanted to tell him then, to warn him. But he'd been afraid Billy would think he was a freak and not want to be his friend anymore. Now it was too late.

"I think all men get turned on by other men," Mr. Derocher continued good-naturedly. "At least a little. It's part of our nature. Some parents might be upset to catch a boy... playing with their son the way you were. They might call your dad to come get you."

At the mention of his father, Billy flinched visibly. Kevin had always thought of Billy as big and strong—he was at least an inch taller than Kevin—but Mr. Derocher was a tall man with broad shoulders, and he towered over Billy, making him look small and helpless by comparison.

"But I'm not like most parents. I know that boys need to touch each other. I have no problem with that. You and Kevin can use this shed whenever you like, as long as his mom doesn't find out. Women never understand these things."

Kevin felt himself flush with embarrassment, but Billy seemed to be falling for his father's smooth, easygoing manner and said, "Cool."

But Kevin knew that wasn't the end of it. His father wouldn't just turn around and leave them. It never happened that way, no matter what he promised. And this time was no exception. Mr. Derocher smiled down at Billy and asked, "Now don't you think I deserve a little something for being so understanding?"

Billy's brief expression of relief quickly flipped back to nervousness. "What?"

"That's only fair, isn't it? After all, I'm taking a risk by allowing this. Imagine what it would do to my career, if people found out that I allowed boys to have sex with my son?"

Billy's voice was small when he asked, "What do you want?"

"Nothing bad. I just want to touch you."

Perhaps unconsciously, Billy gripped his left wrist with his right hand, bringing them together defensively in front of his naked crotch.

Kevin couldn't stand it anymore. He had to *do* something—anything! "Dad, no, you can—"

"Don't look frightened," Mr. Derocher cajoled Billy, ignoring his son. "It won't hurt. We're all friends, aren't we? Tell you what, I can even give you a little money for it. How about twenty dollars? You could use that, couldn't you?"

Kevin saw some of the toughness he admired so much in Billy come back into the boy's expression, but it was moving in the wrong direction now. He appeared to have stopped resisting and was thinking about how to turn the situation to his advantage. "Okay, sure. If you give me the money first."

Don't.... You don't know how he is....

The sick feeling in the pit of Kevin's stomach grew stronger as he watched his father draw a twenty-dollar bill out of his wallet and hand it to Billy. This time, Billy was allowed to step past Mr. Derocher so he could place the money in his pants pocket.

Kevin couldn't watch what happened after that. He ended up sitting on the pile of clothes, not daring to leave or even get dressed, but unable to look directly at the scene unfolding in front of him. He'd pretended so many times in the past that what his father did to him was really happening to some other boy, but he'd never wanted that boy to be Billy. Billy had been *his*. He'd been the only part of Kevin's life that wasn't filthy. *God, why didn't I tell him he couldn't come over? Why didn't I warn him?*

Kevin held trembling hands against his ears, trying to block the sounds, but he could still hear too much.

He wasn't quite sure when his father began pushing Billy too far. He became aware that some sort of struggle was going on and when he could bring himself to look, Mr. Derocher was on top of Billy, trying to kiss him. The man's pants were down around his knees.

"Okay," Billy was saying, his voice beginning to sound frightened, "that's enough."

"I paid you, Billy."

"Please get off me."

Kevin's father had both of Billy's arms pinned to the plywood floor of the shed. "I'll pay you a little more."

"No—"

"Ten dollars."

"I don't want any more—"

"Twenty!"

"No!"

Kevin watched in horror as Billy started kicking his legs and one ankle came down hard on the back of Mr. Derocher's thigh. Kevin's father flinched, but he didn't let go. "Goddamn it!" he snarled, angrier than Kevin had ever seen him. "That fucking hurt!"

"Kevin!"

At the sound of Billy calling out to him, Kevin rose to his feet, but his father shouted, "Stay out of this, Kevin!"

Kevin froze in place. His eyes met Billy's, and he saw the growing fear there as Billy realized things were no longer in his control.

"Kevin, help!"

Kevin stood there terrified as the rain beat against the tin roof of the shed and a brief surge of static almost drowned out the song on the radio. Then Billy screamed in pain as Mr. Derocher thrust forward, and Kevin clutched at his ears, as if he could stop what was happening if only he could block out the sound.

"Don't," he sobbed. "Don't, don't, don't—"

"Shut up, both of you! You don't fucking lead me on, Billy, and then—"

"Kevin!"

Mr. Derocher yanked one of Billy's arms across his face and leaned his own muscular forearm directly on Billy's throat. "Shut the *fuck* up!"

Billy was choking now, unable to call for help. What little of his face Kevin could see was turning red as Billy kicked wildly at Mr. Derocher's legs and backside.

"Dad!" Tears were streaming down Kevin's face now. "Stop! He can't breathe!"

"Go sit down!"

Kevin remembered the jackknife in Billy's pants. *No*.... He forced himself not to think too far ahead as he went back to sit on the clothes and tried to feel around for the knife without his father noticing. *I can't....*

A song Billy liked—"Kyrie" by Mr. Mister—began to play on the radio as Kevin's hands closed on the knife. *I can't....*

Billy's legs had stopped kicking and were only moving slightly, but Mr. Derocher didn't seem to notice.

"Daddy, you're choking him!"

"Kevin... if you don't... be quiet...."

Kyrie Eleison down the road that I must travel....

As if he were dreaming, Kevin opened the jackknife, still keeping it out of sight. His father wasn't really looking at him anyway. The man didn't even notice when Kevin stood up and slowly moved toward him.

It was as if Kevin's body was disconnected from his mind. While his thoughts kept screaming at him to stop, at his father to stop, at the *world* to stop… still he kept moving forward, the metal and plastic inlay of the knife handle growing slippery in his sweaty hand.

This isn't happening. But he told himself that every time his father came to his room. It never worked. It always *was* happening.

Kevin no longer dared to call out to his father. The man was beyond listening to his pleas, and it would alert him to the fact that Kevin was standing over him now, gripping the knife tightly. *I can't do this….*

At that moment, his father grunted and stopped moving. The sound of electric guitars and synthesizers came to an abrupt halt, and Billy's head rolled to the side, eyes blank and staring lifelessly into Kevin's eyes, while the singers on the radio chanted:

> *Kyrie Eleison down the road where I must travel!*
> *Kyrie Eleison through the darkness of the night!*

Kevin half screamed and half sobbed as he realized he was too late.

"What the fuck?" Mr. Derocher panted, groggily, as if coming out of a deep sleep. He whipped around to see his son standing near him, and a split second later his eyes fell on the hand holding the knife. "Jesus!"

Some instinct for self-preservation took over, and he kicked out hard with his leg. It was still tangled in one leg of his pants, but he was able to connect hard enough with Kevin's hip to send the boy flying across the small room. Kevin smashed into the plywood wall, and the knife flew out of his hand. But he didn't care about the knife anymore. "You killed him," he choked out, the tears coming again.

Mr. Derocher stared slack-jawed at his son and at the knife on the floor, back and forth, as if he couldn't comprehend what he was seeing. Then he turned to look at Billy and whispered, "Billy…."

He tried to get to his feet, but his pants tripped him and dropped him down hard on his knees. He scrambled across the dirty wooden floor on all fours and shook Billy by the shoulder. When the boy didn't respond, Mr. Derocher slapped him hard on the face. "Billy!"

He checked Billy's pulse but apparently didn't find one because he dropped the boy's wrist and began performing CPR. For the next several minutes, Kevin watched his father's frantic fumbling as he tried to revive Billy, but Kevin knew it was hopeless. He'd seen Billy's eyes—the same eyes he'd always secretly thought were pretty, though he could never say so to Billy. They weren't pretty now. They were cold and dull and empty.

Mr. Derocher finally gave up his useless attempt at CPR and sat back, staring at Billy's naked dead body in horror. Only gradually did he seem to become aware of the choking sobs coming from his son, and he looked at Kevin with pleading eyes. "It was an accident."

Kevin was sobbing too much to answer him.

"You can't tell anyone about this, Kevin," his father said as he slowly got to his feet and pulled his pants up. "They'll arrest us and lock us away!"

"Us?"

"I'll go to prison, and they'll lock you up in juvenile detention. Then who'll take care of your mom?"

Kevin stared back at him in stunned silence. That wasn't true... was it? Would the police think it was *his* fault?

It is my fault! If he hadn't brought Billy here, none of this would have happened.

His father picked the knife up off the floor and held it in his hand uncertainly. When he glanced up at Kevin, the boy thought he saw something in his eyes—something that looked like fear. But the man quickly turned away, closing the knife and tucking it into his coat pocket. "We have to keep this secret. You understand that, don't you? We have to stick together."

Kevin didn't know what to say, so he just nodded mutely.

"Stay here for a minute. I'll be right back. You should get dressed."

Mr. Derocher left him alone with Billy's body as he stepped out into the storm. Kevin dressed slowly, dazedly, unable to think beyond separating his clothing from Billy's and wedging feet into socks, first the right and then the left…. All the while, the radio droned on and the rain battered the tin roof of the shed. Kevin wanted to turn the radio off, but he was afraid to be alone with Billy and no sound but the rain.

He kept watching the body out of the corner of his eye, as if afraid it would get up and attack him. It no longer felt like Billy to him. It was something cold and alien, something that terrified him and made his stomach churn with nausea. When Kevin finished dressing, he huddled in the corner, staring at the corpse, and whispered, "I'm sorry… I'm sorry…."

Billy's eyes stared back at him, blank and cold.

Kevin heard a car driving up to the shed and panicked for a moment. What if his mother had come home early? But he knew there was no reason she would ever drive her car across her immaculate lawn. After the sound of the car door opening and slamming, the door to the shed opened, and Mr. Derocher slipped back inside, water dripping from his coat and hat.

He hesitated a moment as his eyes once more fell upon Billy, and then he said, "Go keep an eye out. When I ask you if it's clear, you make sure there's *nothing*. Understand? No cars coming, nobody walking by, *nothing*!"

Kevin did as he was told, standing in the pouring rain, watching the road fearfully until the light went out inside the shed and his father cracked the door open. "Is it clear?"

"Yes," Kevin said, having trouble talking above a whisper. But it was loud enough for his father to hear.

It was past sunset by now, and the storm blotted out the moon. The only light came from the front door of the house and the light over the garage, but neither illuminated the backyard. Mr. Derocher carried Billy's body out, fully dressed, and tossed it into the truck. The sound of the trunk hatch slamming closed made Kevin flinch. Motioning for Kevin to get into the passenger seat of the car, Mr. Derocher jumped into the driver's seat.

Kevin was soaked through and shivering as his father drove to the driveway and then pulled out into the road in front of the house.

His father was gripping the wheel hard enough to turn his knuckles white, and his eyes flitted around as if he were watching for someone—perhaps the police—to chase him. When he spoke, his voice was agitated and clipped. "You've got to understand, Kevin. We've committed a murder. It was an accident, of course. If Billy hadn't... well, he shouldn't have gotten hurt. You always have fun, right?"

Kevin couldn't bring himself to answer that question. Fortunately, his father didn't wait for him to respond.

"It wasn't our fault, but nobody will believe that. It just... looks bad. So we've got to hide him somewhere where nobody will ever find him."

THEY drove for a while—how long, Kevin didn't really know or care—until they were bumping along a dirt road deep in the forest. He'd been vaguely aware the road skirted a lake and they'd passed several small lake cabins, but his brain had shut down. He'd cried himself dry and now he just felt numb all over. He barely noticed when his father pulled into a long driveway and stopped by a small cabin that had been boarded up for the winter.

"Come on," his father commanded, climbing out of the car.

Kevin followed him out into the rain and went around to the back of the car, where his father was opening the trunk. The sight of Billy's body sprawled on top of the spare tire chilled him yet again. His father reached in and hoisted the corpse up by the armpits, muttering, "Get his feet."

But Kevin couldn't bring himself to touch the body. He backed away in horror, his teeth chattering from fear and the cold as he hugged himself.

"I said 'get his feet'!"

Kevin looked at his father blankly until the man gave up in disgust. "Jesus Christ!" He scooped Billy up, cradling him against his chest with one arm under the boy's knees. "Close the trunk, you goddamned little pussy!"

Kevin flinched at the insult. His father rarely raised his voice or swore.

Kevin closed the trunk, the sound of it disturbingly loud against the background hiss of the rain. He couldn't resist a look at the cabin, but of course nobody was there. Reluctantly, Kevin followed his father into the forest.

They didn't go far, though without a flashlight Kevin was terrified they'd get lost. His father seemed to know where he was going, pausing only a couple times to check his bearings.

They came to a stop at a patch of brambles and witch hazel. Mr. Derocher set Billy down on the ground and shoved the brush aside, swearing as the brambles snagged his coat and scratched his hands. In the midst of all of it was a massive cement tube—just the end of it, rising up out of the forest floor. It was covered by a heavy wooden lid with iron handles bolted onto it.

"This well dried up a long time ago," Kevin's father said as he heaved the lid off it. "They had to have a new one dug."

In the dark night, Kevin couldn't see more than a few feet down into the black hole his father had opened. Mr. Derocher lifted Billy up again and held him for a moment, cradling him almost tenderly. Kevin couldn't believe how tiny and helpless that body looked now. Not at all the strong boy he'd admired so much.

Mr. Derocher sighed. "Sorry, kid." Then he dropped the tiny body into the dark pit. It must have bounced against the cement wall on the way down, judging from the dull thuds Kevin heard. Then once more there was nothing but the sound of rain and wind.

Kevin wanted to get as far away from this place as he could, but when he stepped away from the well, he saw his father frantically checking his coat pockets.

"Shit! What happened to the fucking knife?" Suddenly, he grabbed Kevin and pulled him close. "Give it to me!"

"What?"

His father angrily thrust his hands into all of Kevin's pockets, searching him. "What have you done with it, you little fuck?"

Kevin had thought he was beyond fear, but he screamed in newfound terror when his father spun him around and shoved him hard against the cement well, and then held his head down over the black pit. "You tell me where the knife is, or I swear I'll throw you in there with him!"

"No, Daddy!" Kevin sobbed. "I don't have it!"

"I don't believe you! You think I didn't notice you sneaking up on me to stab me with it, you traitorous whore? I thought you were innocent! I thought you loved me! But now I find out you're slutting around with other boys and planning on killing me!"

"No! Daddy, please!"

Mr. Derocher gave a roar of disgust, and Kevin screamed as he felt himself yanked backward. But his father didn't throw him into the well. He just threw him down onto the muddy leaves of the forest floor. Kevin sat there crying while the man turned his attention to putting the cover back on the well.

When his father stalked back to the car, not even checking to see if his son was following him, Kevin thought about running into the forest. Maybe he could find somebody's house, somebody who would take him in. But they'd ask who his parents were. Even if he didn't tell them, they'd just call the police and they'd recognize him—his father was well known in the area. Would they believe him if he told them his father was a murderer? He doubted it. And then the next time his father got him alone....

Shaking with fear but knowing he had nowhere else to go, Kevin stood and slowly followed his father through the pouring rain back to the car.

Twenty-Five

Berlin, New Hampshire—The Present

KEVIN was huddled on the floor in the corner of the room, wedged between the couch and the wall. He hadn't been coherent enough to tell Tom and Sue what he was experiencing, but the fragments of dialogue he'd murmured or shouted out had given them a fairly good idea.

Tom was sitting cross-legged on the floor in front of his lover, watching him anxiously. He was so sick with what he'd overheard that he felt like throwing up. How could any man do those things to little kids? Tom had thought molesting Kevin was evil enough, but this....

"I'm so tired," Kevin murmured, and it was a moment before Tom realized Kevin was talking to him. Or at least he was talking to both him and Sue—he was back in the present.

Tom heard Sue moving behind him, picking up her empty coffee cup from the table and standing up. She'd turned the song off the moment Kevin appeared to be losing control, and now the room was so quiet, Tom could hear every little rustle of clothing.

"You can go to sleep if you want," he said softly.

Kevin wasn't looking at him, and Tom wasn't even sure if he could hear him. He just stared into space, his expression as blank as a mannequin. When he spoke again, he sounded completely emotionless, almost robotic. "I should have killed him. I was too weak."

"No," Tom said, his voice breaking on the word.

He lifted a hand as if to touch Kevin, but Sue said quietly, "Don't touch him."

Tom turned to her and saw she was pouring herself a cup of coffee, her shaking hands belying her professional detachment. "In this state, he's liable to interpret any touch as coming from his father," she added.

Tom knew that, at least intellectually. He'd been researching flashbacks ever since that day at Kevin's old house. But it was hard to watch Kevin going through it without reaching out to him.

He turned back to Kevin and said, "You were eleven years old. And you're not capable of killing anyone. That's a good thing."

Again he wasn't sure if Kevin really heard him or not. There was a long silence while Sue approached and kneeled quietly on the carpeted floor beside Tom. Then Kevin said, "How could I forget all of this?"

It was Sue who answered in the gentlest tone Tom had ever heard her use. "Oh, sweetheart, how could you *remember* it?"

IT WAS a challenge to get Kevin into the car and home because he moved so incredibly slowly and didn't respond well to direction, but eventually Tom got him into bed. He slept the rest of the day away, with Shadow curled up protectively on the bed beside him.

Tom knew they would have to notify the police, but the crime was twenty-five years old, and one more day wouldn't make any difference. So he allowed Kevin time to recuperate. When night came, Tom climbed into the bed, forcing Shadow to relocate to his dog bed against the wall.

The clock read just past two when he woke to the sounds of sniffling. He was lying on his side facing Kevin, and Kevin had curled up against him so his hair was tickling Tom's chin and his face was nestled against Tom's collarbone. His breathing was labored, and Tom could feel dampness on his skin where Kevin's eyes touched him.

He whispered, "Are you awake?"

"Yeah." Kevin's voice quavered like a frightened child.

Tom rolled slightly away from him to reach for the bed lamp, but Kevin grabbed him and pulled him close again. "Don't turn on the light."

"Are you all right?" Stupid question. Of course he wasn't "all right."

There was a long silence before Kevin asked in a small voice, "Can you hold me?"

Tom brought his arm up to cradle him, caressing the back of Kevin's neck and stroking his soft hair. "You know I love you, right? Nothing will ever change that."

The only response was a tightening of Kevin's arms around his middle. He became aware of Kevin's erection pressing tightly into his thigh and his own body responded to it, but he knew Kevin didn't want sex. Tom simply held him until the tears subsided, and Kevin eventually drifted off to sleep.

Twenty-Six

THE Groveton Police Department served Stark as well as Groveton, but even at that, it was small—much smaller than the one in Berlin. The building looked more like a storefront to Tom than a police headquarters, and there was only one young woman in uniform at the front desk when he and Kevin entered a couple of days after the therapy session.

She asked what she could do to help them, and Kevin replied, "I have some information about a missing person."

"Who would that be?"

"His name was Billy Sherrell."

She looked puzzled and went to the computer behind the desk to type in the name. Apparently, her first attempt didn't find anything because she asked, "How do you spell the name?"

"S-H-E-R-R-E-L-L."

She tried again. "I'm not coming up with anything under that name."

"It was a really long time ago."

The officer looked at him curiously. "You say you know something about him?"

"I know how he died."

The young woman had them wait while she called Chief Burbank. He was out on patrol, but apparently she considered twenty-five-year-old murders to be *his* problem. He must have agreed to come in, because the officer instructed Kevin and Tom to have a seat in two of the cheap plastic chairs near the front door.

Kevin fidgeted while they waited, pumping his leg as if he were operating an old-style sewing machine in double time. But otherwise he seemed okay. He'd taken some of the meds Mark had prescribed, and they seemed to help a bit. Tom couldn't help watching him out of the corner of his eye for signs of a panic attack or another flashback, but he didn't want to embarrass Kevin by hovering over him. As it was, Kevin was irritated that he'd put his foot down about taking a day to rest before coming in to the police station.

After a while, the front door opened and Chief Burbank entered. His eyes fixed upon Kevin right away, and he wore a quizzical expression on his handsome, ruddy face. Tom and Kevin stood, and the chief came forward to shake their hands.

"Gentlemen."

"Hey," Tom said. Kevin was watching Burbank as if he expected the man to slap handcuffs on him at any moment.

"I've been puzzling over that name," Burbank said, turning his sharp gray eyes upon Kevin, "ever since Sandy called me. It sounded so familiar—'Billy Sherrell'." He paused. "We're talking about someone who disappeared over twenty-five years ago, aren't we?"

Kevin nodded, clearly uncomfortable. "Yeah."

He hadn't given them any details yet, but Burbank was regarding him as if he might be about to confess to killing Billy himself—which was a reasonable assumption, under the circumstances.

"There was nothing in the database on a Billy Sherrell," the officer at the desk volunteered.

"There wouldn't be," Burbank replied. "That case must've been closed before I graduated high school. I doubt the department even had a computer then."

He walked over to the coffee machine and poured himself a cup. "Would you guys like some coffee?"

Judging by the burnt smell, Tom estimated it had been sitting on the burner for a few hours. The thought of drinking it made his stomach turn. "No thanks."

Kevin just shook his head.

"Why don't we go into the office, and you can tell me what you know?" Burbank asked. Then he turned to the officer and asked her, "Sandy, can you take a look in the file cabinets downstairs and try to locate that case? I want to see what info we had at the time."

"Oh, that'll be fun," she grumbled. But she moved off to do as he asked.

Burbank gestured to a door behind the desk. "Gentlemen?"

TOM was worried that retelling the story would trigger another flashback, but Kevin seemed to be distancing himself from it, as if he were recounting something that had happened in a dream. All of the details were there, but he didn't appear to be upset about any of it. Which was probably why Burbank looked so skeptical.

"That's quite a tale," he commented when Kevin had finished.

"It's not a 'tale'," Kevin said, showing the first hint of emotion since he'd begun—irritation. "It all really happened."

"And after twenty-five years, you just suddenly remembered it?"

"No, I didn't 'just suddenly remember it'," Kevin snapped. "Tom and this shrink from Berlin have been dredging all this shit out of my head over the past few months. I had it all—" He made a gesture with both hands around his head, as if he were shampooing his hair. "—blocked. I didn't remember anything about Billy until Dr. Cross played a song for me the day before yesterday."

Chief Burbank looked confused for a moment, but then the light dawned in his eyes, and he turned to Tom. "Repressed memories?" He sounded even more skeptical than before.

Tom nodded. "Yes. He's been working through it with the help of my coworker, Dr. Susan Cross."

"Jesus." Burbank groaned. "I've read about that. Wasn't there a wave of people back in the nineties, remembering so-called repressed memories of satanic sexual abuse from their childhoods? And it turned out that they were just 'remembering' what the therapist *wanted* them to remember? None of it actually happened. And people went to jail for it!"

"Oh, fuck this shit! I don't need you telling me none of this is *real*!" Kevin made a move to get up, but Tom put a hand on his arm to calm him.

Tom was angered by the chief's attitude, but when he spoke, he kept his voice calm and reasonable. "I'm familiar with those cases, Chief Burbank. And yes, contamination of the recalled memories is a real danger. I don't believe that's the case here. Sue knows what she's doing. But the true test will be that well. If we can find it, and there *is* a body at the bottom of it… well, then we'll know."

Burbank frowned, but they were interrupted by a knock on the door. "Yes?"

"I found the case file," Sandy said through the door.

"Let's see it."

She let herself in and set a weathered manila folder on Burbank's desk. Then she let herself out while he flipped through it.

He withdrew a faded Polaroid picture—the kind that had been popular when they were all kids, where the picture developed after it fed out of the front of the camera. He placed it on the desk in front of Kevin. "Are you absolutely sure this is the kid?"

Kevin only had to glance at it before he nodded his head and looked away. "Yeah, that's him." His voice was strained.

The kid in the picture was about ten or eleven. Tom could see at once what Mrs. Derocher had meant when she described Billy as "almost pretty." He'd been a beautiful boy, with jet-black hair, large brown eyes, and a charming smile.

"The file says that was taken about a year before he disappeared," Chief Burbank commented, looking through the papers in the folder.

"I've seen it. Billy kept it on his dresser. I think his mother snapped it before she ran off. He told me it bugged him that she didn't take it or anything else to remember him by."

Kevin seemed to be remembering everything now, Tom observed. Or at least big chunks of it.

"The kid had a rough life," Burbank said sympathetically. "And if what you're saying is true, a very short one."

Kevin nodded.

Burbank sighed. "All right. You remember your dad throwing Billy's body into a well." He spread his hands out questioningly. "So where's the well?"

"I don't know," Kevin replied. But when the chief rolled his eyes, he added, "I'd never been there. But my father obviously knew the place. So I've been thinking... maybe it belonged to someone he knew."

"Your mother's still alive, isn't she?"

"Yeah. She's over at Riverview."

"Have you asked her about it? I mean, I get that she probably doesn't know about a lot of this—"

Kevin snorted. "Fuck, no."

"But she'd know if any of your father's friends had a place out in the woods, right?"

Kevin looked uncomfortable. "I suppose."

"But...." The chief waved his hand, encouraging him to complete the sentence.

"My mom and I don't really talk much."

"Are you concerned about her finding out what happened?" Tom asked him.

Kevin looked at him sharply, a frown creasing his brow. "She lives in her own little world, where Jack Derocher never did anything but dote on his wife and son and occasionally fart out some heavenly angel song. I don't know how the hell I'm gonna ask her anything about this without getting into a fight."

Burbank drummed his fingers on the desk, eyeing Kevin shrewdly. After a minute, he raised an eyebrow and asked, "Do you want *me* to talk to your mom for you?"

Tom expected Kevin to get annoyed again, but to his surprise Kevin just chuckled and grinned back at the policeman. "Be my guest."

CHIEF BURBANK left them alone in his office for a few minutes while he went out to talk to the officer at the desk, and Kevin muttered, "You're not here as my doctor."

"I never said I was your doctor," Tom said. Kevin had refused to have Sue come along.

"You acted like it. Just remember, you're my boyfriend—not my psychologist." The slight quirk of his mouth took some of the sting out of the reprimand, but it still made Tom feel defensive.

Tom leaned forward and lowered his voice, uncertain what might be overheard outside the door. "If you want to know the truth, I *am* a little concerned for your mental health. I mean, Jesus, Kevin! You had a total breakdown two days ago when these memories came through. Don't you think it's a little soon to be diving in headfirst? Are you really ready to go digging in a dried-up well for a corpse? I'm just saying, all of this could have waited a few more days."

Kevin took his hand and kissed it gently. "I'd be lying if I said my stomach isn't tied up in knots. But I can't just fart around the house for a few days now that I know Billy is rotting away at the bottom of a well somewhere."

"Kevin... after all this time...."

"Yeah, I know," Kevin said grimly. "There's probably nothing left of him. If it was damp down there, even the bones might've disintegrated. But... whatever's there, we have to find him. He deserves a decent burial. And if his father's still alive, he needs to know what happened to his son, even if he was a mean son of a bitch."

Tom sighed and asked, "Have you taken one of the Valium yet?" Kevin had promised to bring the prescription with him and take one before getting into all of this with the police. Tom hadn't seen him do that.

"I don't like that shit," Kevin complained. "It makes me groggy."

"I know. I don't like it either—I was given some a few years ago when I had an MRI. But I really think you should."

Kevin rolled his eyes, but he drew the bottle out of his pocket and took one of the tablets out. Then he held it up dramatically in front of Tom's face before popping it into his mouth.

Tom ignored the mocking gesture. "Aren't you supposed to take that with water?"

"I was hoping you'd lift your shirt so I could suckle off your tit for a few minutes."

Tom gave him a sour look, though he knew Kevin was right—he was being overprotective. Truthfully, he wondered if maybe *he* was the one who needed the Valium. He was a nervous wreck about all this. But he was the designated driver for now.

The conversation was cut short by Chief Burbank coming back into the room. "Okay, guys, let's go for a ride. I assume you'll want to take your own car so everyone in town doesn't see you riding in the back of my cruiser."

THE same staff person—Sarah—was manning the front desk at Riverview when they arrived, and she seemed even less enthused over Kevin and Tom's arrival than she had been the last time. But the presence of Chief Burbank forced her to at least pretend to be cordial.

"Is there something I can do for you, officer?"

"He's here to arrest my mom," Kevin stated flatly.

She looked alarmed, but Burbank rolled his eyes at Kevin. "No, I'm not going to arrest her. I'd just like to talk to her."

Somewhat relieved, but still clearly suspicious, Sarah escorted them to a small sitting room. She shooed out a couple of elderly men who'd been playing cards and explained, "This room is private. Make yourselves comfortable while I get Ellen."

Mrs. Derocher did not look pleased to see them when she entered the sitting room a short time later. "What's this about?" she asked Chief Burbank with only a brief glance at her son.

"Please sit down, Mrs. Derocher. I just have a couple questions for you."

"About what?"

Sarah entered with a tray of tea and coffee, and Mrs. Derocher curbed her obvious annoyance long enough to perch on the edge of one of the Victorian-style stuffed chairs while Sarah laid things out on the coffee table. After the receptionist left, Burbank took a seat on the sofa and said, "Kevin has been recalling some things that happened when we were in junior high school—some things that might give us some clues to the disappearance of a boy who lived near your house."

"Are you referring to Billy Sherrell?"

"Yes," the chief replied. "You remember him?"

Mrs. Derocher poured herself some coffee and spooned some artificial sweetener into it. "I've been wondering why Kevin and his friend—Tom, was it?" Tom smiled and nodded. "Why they were so interested in the boy. It was a very long time ago."

Burbank brought out the worn Polaroid of Billy and passed it to her. "Is this him?"

"Yes, of course." She glanced suspiciously at Kevin but continued to address the policeman. "What could Kevin possibly have remembered after all this time that could make any difference now?"

Tom was already familiar with the dysfunctional relationship between mother and son, but it was clearly beginning to make Burbank uncomfortable. He looked to Kevin for help, but Kevin simply gestured for him to go on. "Mrs. Derocher… did you and your husband know anybody at that time who owned a cabin out in the woods?"

"A cabin?"

Kevin sighed and finally spoke. "It was small. Red, I think, with green trim. At the end of a long dirt driveway. And it was boarded up for the winter or something."

His mother had lifted her cup to take a sip of coffee, but she hesitated, the cup poised at her lips. "You couldn't possibly remember that cabin."

"Obviously, I do," Kevin snapped.

Mrs. Derocher took a slow sip of her coffee and then carefully set the cup down on a coaster before once again addressing Chief Burbank. "The last time Kevin was at that cabin, before it was sold, was when he was only five years old."

"Whose cabin was it?" Burbank asked.

"Ours," she replied. "My husband bought it the year Kevin was born. It seemed a nice idea at the time, but neither of us really enjoyed spending our vacations that far out in the woods, especially with a young child to look after. It might have been different if it was on the lake, but it was too remote. We used it now and then, but eventually we just stopped going, and it sat there boarded up for years until we finally sold it."

"When was that?"

"Just before Kevin's father passed away. In the fall of 1988, I believe. Jack put the money into a mutual fund for me." She paused and took another sip of her coffee. "I think he already knew... what he was going to do... and he wanted to make sure I was taken care of."

"Where is the cabin located?" Burbank asked.

"Nowhere now," she replied, and Tom thought he detected an odd note of triumph in her voice. "It was torn down by the new owners."

But Chief Burbank was growing impatient with this dance. "Where *was* it, then?"

"It was near Christine Lake. But as I said, not very near the lake itself."

Burbank pulled a notepad and pen out of his jacket pocket and sketched something. When he placed it on the coffee table between them, Tom could see that it was a rough map of Christine Lake with

Percy Road and Stark Highway running parallel to each other in the southeast, and a road skirting the northern half of the lake which he'd labeled "Summer Club Rd." Tom was vaguely familiar with the lake since he'd gone fishing there as a boy. It was less than a half hour away from the Derocher house.

"Can you point to where the cabin was?" Burbank asked Mrs. Derocher.

"I can't recall."

"Just the general area."

"It was a very long time ago."

"Mom," Kevin practically snarled, "stop being difficult."

For the first time since their arrival, Mrs. Derocher turned to look directly at him, her eyes smoldering. "Difficult? For refusing to cooperate in slander? I'm not stupid. You're trying to link this boy's disappearance to your father. As if that wasn't the most *ludicrous*.... It's not enough that you refused to give him the respect he deserved when he was alive. Now you're determined to drag his name through the mud—"

"The respect he deserved?" Kevin asked incredulously. "The respect he *deserved*?"

"Don't you raise your voice to me, young man. Your father gave us a good home and—"

But Kevin had apparently been pushed too far. He jumped to his feet and shouted at her, "What he *deserved* was the goddamned electric chair!"

"Get out!"

"That son of a bitch started fondling me when I was five years old, Mom. *Five* years old!"

"I said 'get out'!" Mrs. Derocher called out, "Sarah!"

"Kevin," Tom interrupted, "perhaps we should—"

"Then he raped and murdered an eleven-year-old boy!"

"Shut up! *Shut up*! You *vile*—I won't hear any more of your lies!"

"That's enough!" Chief Burbank's deep voice reverberated in the tiny sitting room and startled mother and son into silence. He'd jumped up from his chair and suddenly seemed much taller than Tom remembered. "You two," he commanded, pointing to Kevin and Tom, "go outside. Now!"

Sarah burst into the room in a panic. "What's happening?"

"It's under control," the chief told her. "Kevin and Tom are on their way out. And Mrs. Derocher... you're going to tell me where that cabin is, or I'll book you for obstructing a police investigation. Is that clear?"

"I CAN'T fucking believe her!"

Kevin was pacing in front of the squad car, oblivious to the looks he was getting from people driving by. Tom couldn't blame him. His mother's willful blindness about what had happened to him as a boy was sickening.

"They barely spoke the last few years of his life," Kevin went on. "She spent all her time in that fucking shed, potting flowers and shit because he wouldn't give either of us the time of day. And all that time, she was working right where—" He broke off, unable to complete the sentence. "But now that he's dead, he's a fucking saint!"

"Perhaps she's remembering the way she wishes it was," Tom volunteered.

"Don't defend her!"

"I'm not," Tom said. "Really. I wanted to shout at her myself when we were in there."

That managed to get a faint smile out of Kevin. "Now *that* would've been something. My boyfriend versus my mom—the battle to end all battles."

"You always get annoyed with me when I act protective of you."

"Yeah," Kevin agreed, "but some things are worth it for the entertainment value."

Tom started to say something, but he noticed Chief Burbank heading for them, so instead he raised his voice and asked, "Any luck?"

Burbank held up the crude map he'd drawn. There was a small circle on the northwest side of the lake. "Kevin, your mother is...."

"A bitch?"

"I was looking for a more polite term." He opened the door of his cruiser and said, "I know the general area she described. There aren't too many back roads in those woods. So let's go see if we can find it."

Twenty-Seven

IT WAS late afternoon by the time their caravan headed down Summer Club Road—three cars in all, since another cruiser had pulled in behind Tom's car as they pulled onto Percy Road. At least Tom assumed it was part of the caravan because it didn't flash its lights for him to pull over and continued to dog him, even when Chief Burbank led them onto a narrow dirt road and on into the forest.

At one point, Burbank pulled over as far as possible to the right and stopped his car so a pickup truck could squeeze by on the left, heading toward the lake. After the truck passed, the chief got out of his car and walked back to stick his head in Tom's window.

"Kevin, does any of this look familiar to you?"

Kevin looked out the window at the stretch of dirt road with forest on either side and shrugged. "About as familiar as any dirt road in the back woods of New Hampshire."

Burbank chuckled and glanced up the road. "Yeah. That's about what I figured. Your mom said—under duress—that it was somewhere along this road, about three miles in. Keep your eyes peeled for a driveway on the right. It'll probably be overgrown and nearly invisible."

THEY drove for about a mile more before Kevin said, "There!"

Tom had to restrain himself from slamming on the brakes. When he did come to a stop, the cruiser behind him practically ramming up his exhaust pipe, he couldn't see any sign of a driveway. Chief Burbank pulled up about a hundred feet ahead of them. Tom and Kevin climbed out of the car while Burbank slowly backed his cruiser up. Tom recognized the police officer who got out of the other cruiser as the one who'd been with Burbank the night they pulled Kevin over at Recycle Road.

"What is it?" the officer asked.

Tom shrugged, but Kevin started walking back the way they'd come, searching the forest. A minute later he shouted, "Here it is!"

Burbank joined them, and all three walked to where Kevin was standing, pointing at something in the brush.

It was a wooden sign. After all these years, the green-and-red paint had nearly flaked away, and the exposed wood was now a weathered gray, but the name on the sign was still there.

Derocher.

"Well," Tom said, "isn't *that* fucking creepy?"

The driveway was nearly indistinguishable from the forest on either side of it. Fast-growing birches and aspens had claimed the space as their own, probably decades ago, and the ground between them was overrun with witch hazel and high-bush cranberry. The sign itself was nearly hidden behind one of the birch trees. Tom doubted he ever would have seen it if Kevin hadn't spotted it.

Without preamble, Chief Burbank pushed his way into the brush, and the officer went after him.

"Are you okay?" Tom asked Kevin, worried by how pale he looked.

But after a muttered "I'm fine," Kevin seemed to steel himself before following the two policemen into the woods. Tom had little choice but to go along unless he wanted to stand in the road by himself.

As often happened in New Hampshire forests, the brush was densest near the road and opened up a bit farther in, perhaps because it was dryer than the soggy ditches that tended to parallel roads—Tom had no idea. But the forest floor was dry and carpeted with dead leaves, leaving plenty of room to walk between the trees and clumps of brush.

The original path of the driveway wasn't hard to discern there since it was marked by deep gullies on either side. Where the cabin must have been were square holes, partially filled in with years of accumulated debris. Chief Burbank skirted it, telling Kevin, "Your mom said she heard that the new owners left the cabin boarded up for so long, the roof fell in. They probably tore it down to prevent kids from climbing around in the wreckage and getting themselves killed, but it doesn't look like anybody's done anything here for years."

Kevin was barely paying any attention to him. His face was pale, and Tom could see the muscles twitching in his clenched jaw as he searched the forest for any sign of the well. They all fell silent, watching him rotate slowly to get his bearings. "I'm not sure...," he murmured to himself, as if unaware of his audience.

He seemed to make a decision and began walking away from the cabin, deeper into the woods. After a short distance, he hesitated and looked around, then headed off in a slightly different direction. Tom and the two policemen trailed after him.

This went on for so long that Tom began to worry they would all end up lost in the forest. But he glimpsed the ruins of the cabin through the trees off to his left, and that reassured him. Kevin wasn't leading them too far away from it. Instead they were skirting it in a wide arc.

The sun was setting, turning the white bark of the birch trees orange, when Kevin muttered, "Goddamn it! I can't remember!"

"They wouldn't have put the well too far from the cabin," Burbank commented.

Kevin's face was screwed up in frustration. "It all looks the same!"

It did. Just birch and aspen as far as the eye could see, with white pine interspersed. Closer to the ground, clumps of hemlock, witch hazel, and other shrubs obscured any possible well covers. Kevin had said the well was buried within one of these, so they peered into them, but it was impossible to tell one from another without any other landmark.

They doubled back for a bit and tried to find patches they'd overlooked, but as the orange of sunset gave way to gray twilight, all four men were growing frustrated.

Then Tom kicked something in the leaves. It was partially embedded in the ground and came loose as his foot dragged across it, sending up a small spray of leaves and dirt. He bent down to pick it up, and a chill went through his entire body.

It was a jackknife.

It had obviously been there for a very long time since most of the metal had rusted away. But the plastic pieces on the sides, molded to look like bone, were still intact, though weathered and brittle from years of exposure to the elements.

"I found something!" Tom shouted.

The others came running, and he held the knife up for them to examine. "It was stuck in the ground right there." He pointed.

Kevin held out a shaky hand, and Tom dropped the knife into it. With an audible exhalation of breath, Kevin rubbed his fingers over the fake bone surface on the knife handle, rubbing dirt off it. "Yeah... I think this might be it. I only saw it that night, but...."

Abruptly he handed it to Chief Burbank. "Here. Use it as evidence or something. I don't want to touch it anymore."

Burbank took the knife and examined it. "Does this mean we're near the well?"

"Maybe. I don't know when that fell out of my father's pocket."

But they were standing not ten feet from a cluster of witch hazel. While Kevin and Burbank discussed the knife, Tom moved closer to the bushes, a sick feeling growing in the pit of his stomach. He brushed aside the broad leaves and felt the skin prick up on the back of his neck. "Oh Jesus...."

The cement ring of the well didn't rise up from the ground more than a foot, and the wooden cover was half hidden under a layer of dead leaves and twigs. The boards had nearly rotted through, and the entire thing sagged in the middle under the weight of the debris.

When Tom tried to call out to the others, he discovered his throat had closed up. But the two policemen were at his side almost instantly, peering down at the well.

"Kevin...?" Burbank started to ask him something, but when the three of them turned around, it was immediately obvious to them that Kevin wasn't going to be much help. He was crouched down with his hands over his head as if shielding him from something. "Are you okay?"

"I just need a minute." Kevin gasped. He exhaled slowly and then drew a long breath in through his nose. Burbank looked baffled by his behavior, but Tom knew he was going through the deep breathing exercises he'd learned, trying to calm himself.

"Let him be," Tom said quietly when he'd found his voice again. It wouldn't help for him to hover over Kevin like a mother hen, as much as he wanted to.

"We're losing the light. Joe, help me drag this off."

The sound the rotted wooden cover made as the policemen dragged it off was sickening, reminding Tom of breaking bones and tearing flesh as it snapped and popped and all but disintegrated in their hands. The debris on the cover rained down into the black hole underneath. He leaned forward, reluctant to see what was inside but unable to stop himself. It didn't matter. The gray twilight couldn't begin to penetrate the darkness at the bottom.

Chief Burbank pulled a Maglite off his belt and clicked it on. Tom leaned forward again as the chief shined the light down into the well. The bottom was dry and only about thirty feet deep, but with all the leaves and earth that had fallen in over the years, there wasn't much to be seen.

Burbank found a palm-sized rock nearby and threw it down. It thudded into the dirt at the bottom. "Looks pretty solid," Burbank muttered. "I wish I'd brought a rope."

Joe told him, "I have one in the trunk of my cruiser."

"Can you find your way back?"

The officer pointed out where the ruins of the cabin could be seen and said, "I'll go down if you want to lower me."

Burbank looked down into the well with a skeptical expression on his face. "You sure?"

"There's a tree right over there. We can tie one end of the rope to that. It'll be safe."

Burbank frowned but said, "All right. But hurry up. We won't have the light much longer."

While Joe set off for his car at a moderate clip, considering the terrain, Tom couldn't resist going to check on Kevin. He was sitting cross-legged on the ground now, his eyes closed as if he was meditating.

"How are you doing?" Tom sat down beside him.

Kevin opened his eyes and smiled wanly at him. "I'm okay, counselor." But to Tom's surprise, he reached out a hand and took one of Tom's in his, regardless of the policeman standing not ten feet away from them. They sat together like that for a while, not speaking, as they waited for Joe to come back. Chief Burbank glanced over but seemed to realize they needed a moment alone.

It wasn't long before Tom heard the leaves rustling behind him and turned to see Joe returning, a bit out of breath, with a coil of orange nylon rope draped on his right shoulder. The two policemen tied one end of the rope around a solid birch, and Joe fashioned a sort of harness out of the other end, looping around and between both legs and around his waist.

"Tom, I need you to help with this," Chief Burbank said, and Tom got up to join them.

The chief had Joe walk around a second tree once to wrap the rope around it. This would act as a bit of a brake, with Burbank and Tom feeding the rope out slowly on one side of it and Joe lowering himself down into the well on the other side. Tom suspected it wasn't necessarily the way a professional would do it, but Joe and Chief Burbank seemed to think it would be safe enough. Tom stood a couple of feet behind Burbank and held the rope taut as Joe climbed into the well. In the meantime, Kevin sat on the ground, staring at the well as if he expected... well, Tom couldn't really imagine what was going through his mind. He seemed to be holding himself together, at least.

After a long time of slowly feeding the rope out, it went slack between the well and the tree, and Joe called up to them, "I'm down! The ground is solid."

Tom and Burbank dropped their end of the rope on the ground and went to the edge of the well to peer down. Joe had brought his own Maglite with him, of course, and he was crouched down on the pile of debris, illuminating it with the light.

When he didn't say anything immediately, Burbank shouted down impatiently, "Well? What do you see?"

"There's something.... Looks like a sneaker."

Tom flinched at the words, and even Burbank had grown pale. Tom looked over at Kevin, but he was still staring intently at the well, his expression unreadable.

Then suddenly Joe cried out, "Jesus Christ! Lift me up! Lift me up!"

Burbank grabbed the rope and started hauling him up, demonstrating a surprising strength. "Get behind the tree and pick up the slack in case I slip!" he ordered Tom.

Tom did so and was surprised to see Kevin rush in behind the chief and start pulling on the rope too. With the two of them pulling and Tom picking up the slack, it only took a minute or so for Joe's head to appear over the edge of the cement enclosure. He struggled to find a handhold while Burbank and Kevin grabbed his clothing and hauled him up and over.

When he hit the ground, Joe hurriedly scrambled away from the well and stood there with his hands braced on his knees, catching his breath. "Jesus...."

"What happened?" Burbank asked.

Joe took a couple more breaths to steady himself and then answered, "The sneaker was embedded in the ground, so I started to wiggle it free. And then...." His voice cracked, and he had to swallow hard. "Christ, Randy! There was a foot in it!"

"A foot?" Burbank asked grimly.

"Well, there were leg bones sticking out of it." Joe winced at the recollection. "I mean, I know that's what we were looking for. I thought I could handle it. But the sneaker... it was so small. Like a kid's shoe...."

Burbank went over to him and clapped a sympathetic hand on his shoulder. "It's all right. We'll have to call in a forensics team to get him out. I'm going to catch hell for letting you go down there and stomp around as it is."

"You could've stopped me."

Burbank snorted. "If you hadn't volunteered, I would've had to come back tomorrow and do it myself. There's no way I'd call in the state boys without verifying there was really a body down there."

Kevin was still standing near the well, peering down into it, and Tom approached him, concerned. The bottom of the well was pitch-black again, now that Joe's flashlight no longer illuminated it, and Tom couldn't help shivering as he looked down into the darkness. The thought of young Billy laying down there, forgotten for twenty-five years, both chilled and saddened him.

The same thought must have been going through Kevin's mind because he spoke softly into the black depths. "I'm sorry. I'm sorry I took you to the shed that night. I'm sorry I couldn't talk that son of a bitch into taking me, instead of you. I'm sorry I couldn't *kill* him. And I'm...." His voice failed him, and he took a moment to take a breath. "I'm sorry I forgot you. Somehow... that almost seems worse than everything else."

He looked up and seemed to notice Tom standing beside him for the first time.

"It's getting dark," Tom said, unable to think of anything else.

Kevin nodded. "Let's go home."

Twenty-Eight

THE investigation went on for a few months. Part of the problem was identifying the body. Billy hadn't lived in Stark long enough to have gone to any dentists in the area, which meant there were no dental records to match up with the skeleton retrieved from the well. There were rotted fragments of clothing, but nothing that could provide a clue to his identity. A state forensics team had concluded the skeleton was most likely a young male, and it wasn't unreasonable to assume it had been lying at the bottom of the well for over two decades. The well appeared to have dried up long ago and there hadn't been any animals larger than mice down there, so things were fairly preserved. The labels in the clothing and the materials in them were likewise consistent with that estimate, though it was impossible to narrow it down more than a decade.

Chief Burbank appeared to believe it was Billy Sherrell, but he would have preferred something more concrete than Kevin's twenty-five-year-old—and somewhat shaky—eyewitness account to put in the case files. The partially disintegrated remains of a twenty dollar bill in the pants pocket did seem to corroborate Kevin's story, however.

It took time for the Groveton police to track down where Billy's father had moved to, but they eventually located him just over the

Vermont border, near St. Johnsbury. They brought him in to answer some questions and see if he could identify the scraps of clothing and what was left of the jackknife.

"He doesn't want to talk to you," Chief Burbank told Kevin when he and Tom stopped by the department one afternoon. Kevin had gotten it into his head that he needed to talk to Mr. Sherrell to somehow atone for his part in what had happened. "I don't think he blames you, specifically, but… to put it bluntly, he thinks Billy would have been better off if he'd never met you."

Kevin took the news stoically, though Tom was so used to reading his expressions by now that he could see it was a huge blow to him. All he said was, "He's right."

Sue Cross was also questioned by the police. Kevin had given his permission to discuss anything related to Billy's death that she'd learned in their sessions, as well as to provide information about the validity of recovered memories. The fact that a body had been recovered might have been considered proof enough by some, but as Chief Burbank pointed out, there was still the possibility Kevin had known where the body was all along and simply pretended he couldn't remember.

According to Sue, the chief barely survived that conversation with his testicles attached. "As if I couldn't tell the difference—after all the work I've done with survivors—between someone who's telling the truth and someone who's faking it!"

But the hardest part was bringing Mrs. Derocher in. Tom and Kevin weren't there during her interview, of course, and they weren't told anything about what was discussed. But the chief did tell them later that it was "very uncomfortable." And a few days later, Kevin received a letter from his mother in the mail at his trailer.

Kevin,

I have been tolerant. I have tolerated your moodiness and your hostility to me and your father. I tolerated your petty vandalism and your not-so-petty foray into arson. I tolerated the enormous expense of your treatment program. But my tolerance is at an end.

Your father doted upon you. He loved you more than I think he loved me. When you were young, I could understand. You were a beautiful, affectionate child. But why he continued to adore you through all of your misbehavior as you grew older is beyond me. I have no doubt that your hostility toward him in your teenage years played a part in his suicide.

And now you honor his memory with this slander—accusations of sexual depravity and murder! Why the police would choose to believe these disgusting lies about a man who served his community selflessly his entire life and gave his family everything is incomprehensible. I've heard rumors through the staff here about you and your "friend." I can only imagine you've projected your depravity onto your father, now that he's no longer here to defend himself. And as to the murder, perhaps the police should be asking more questions about why you were the only person who knew where the body was hidden.

You are no longer my son. I've already met with my lawyer to have you removed from my will, and I've informed the staff that you are no longer allowed to visit me.

Please respect my wishes.

Ellen

Kevin had brought the letter with all his other mail to Tom's house before reading it, and afterward he shoved it into Tom's hands and stormed out onto the back deck. Tom assumed that meant he could read it. He wished he hadn't.

He gave Kevin a few minutes alone to cool down, but he couldn't restrain himself for long. Kevin was in the hot tub by the time he walked out onto the deck, Shadow scampering along at his heels. It was midwinter, and the yard was blanketed in snow, but Tom had discovered hot tubs were a year-round thing, as long as he could survive being naked long enough to get in and out of the water. The deck had been shoveled and swept, so at least it was dry.

Tom removed his robe in silence, shivering a bit, and slipped into the water.

"I guess I was hoping," Kevin said quietly, "that when everything finally came out in the open, she'd come around. She'd finally see that I wasn't just an ungrateful little brat—there was a *reason* for the things I did, even if I didn't know what I was doing at the time. But... I guess there was never anything that would make her choose me over him."

Tom reached out and caressed Kevin's shoulder. "Some people invest so much of their time and energy into fabricating a safe, comfortable world for themselves they'll turn on anyone who threatens that illusion."

Kevin made a disgusted sound. "She chose a child rapist and murderer over her own son. Why do you have to keep defending her?"

"I'm sorry. That's the psychologist part of me talking, always trying to find reasons for why people do things."

"Yeah? Well, maybe I'd like to hear from the *boyfriend* part of you for once."

Tom wasn't put off by Kevin's irritability. He slid closer to him and said, "The boyfriend part of me hates that cold-blooded bitch for what she's done to you. For ignoring the warning signs when you were a boy, for distancing herself from you when you needed her, and especially now, for pulling this shit when she should be embracing you and trying to make amends."

Kevin smiled sadly. "Well, we're definitely not inviting her to the wedding."

That startled Tom, but he tried not to show it. They'd never discussed marriage. After all, they'd known each other less than a year. Tom didn't know if Kevin was serious about that or not. But it was a pleasant fantasy, and for now Tom decided it would be nice not to have his own safe illusions deflated. So he didn't try to get Kevin to commit to the offhand comment. He just settled back in the tub and let the jets massage his body while he gazed up at the clouds sailing by overhead and intertwined his fingers with Kevin's.

He was surprised when Kevin moved to straddle him, sitting in his lap with both hands braced on the edge of the tub on either side of Tom's head. Kevin leaned forward and kissed him on the mouth, long and passionately. As their bodies writhed against one another in the water, Tom could feel Kevin's growing erection rubbing against his stomach, and he grew hard in response.

Kevin had never been this bold before, and Tom wasn't sure how to react. But Kevin didn't seem to be changing his mind, and it felt wonderful, so Tom relaxed into it, kissing back and caressing the solid, sharply defined body he'd been presented with.

Eventually, Kevin broke the kiss long enough to chuckle into his ear. "We'd better move this upstairs, unless you want to spend tomorrow emptying all the water out of this thing and cleaning the filters."

"Ew. No, thanks. Let's go upstairs."

They climbed out and dried off, though Kevin made sure Tom stayed interested by making playful grabs at his erection and occasionally nuzzling his neck. Shadow still couldn't be trusted to stay outside unsupervised, so they brought him in with them but abandoned him at the foot of the stairs.

Despite Kevin's enthusiasm, he wasn't ready for anything as radical as anal sex. Tom wasn't sure if he ever would be. Certainly Tom was willing to be the "bottom," if it was a matter Kevin not liking the way it felt to be penetrated, but Tom knew there was more to it than that. Thanks to his father, anal sex was too closely tied to rape for Kevin. Tom still hadn't learned if Mr. Derocher ever forced himself that way on Kevin, but Kevin had witnessed his father raping Billy. It was possible he would never be able to enjoy it after that ordeal.

But they found other ways to pleasure each other with their hands and mouths. Kevin was squeamish about Tom ejaculating into his mouth, so Tom made sure he didn't. But he took Kevin joyfully, and when Kevin gasped, "I'm gonna come!" and tried to pull away, Tom held him there as he pulsed thick semen into his mouth, exulting in the taste of him.

Afterward, they lay together, kissing gently, and Kevin commented, "I can taste it in your mouth."

Tom laughed. "Sorry about that. I happen to like the taste."

"I don't."

"I can brush my teeth, if you like."

Kevin groaned and rolled over onto his back. "What really bothers me is that I can't get rid of *him*. Whenever you and I do something together, I can't stop remembering how *he* did the same thing. It's sick!"

Disturbing, certainly.

"We can't force ourselves not to remember things," Tom told him. "But remembering them drains them of their emotional power. You know this. Think about how much worse you felt when you couldn't remember what was making you feel this way."

"I guess."

"I hate to kill the moment, but… how did we go from discussing your mother's letter to 'Let's push our sex life to the next level'?"

Kevin smiled and shook his head. "We didn't. We went from discussing *marriage* to 'Let's fuck'."

Suddenly, Tom felt a wave of nervousness hit him. He lifted his head up on one arm so he could look Kevin directly in the eye. Those sleepy hazel eyes gazed back at him with open affection. "I thought you were joking."

"Well, I admit it kind of just popped into my head. I haven't had much time to mull it over yet. But is it something you'd be willing to consider?"

"Uh-uh," Tom replied with a smirk. "I'm not having you ask me on a whim. Especially right after sex. If you think about it for a while, and it still seems like a good idea, then you can ask me."

"Will you say 'yes'?"

"No cheating."

Now that they were cooling off, Tom became aware of the whining and scratching at the door. He grabbed a few tissues off the nightstand and wiped his stomach. Then he tossed them into the trashcan and went to open the door.

Shadow burst in and jumped up on the bed and half on top of Kevin, who suddenly found his face being bathed by a sloppy dog tongue. "Agh! Jesus! I don't want you French kissing me right after I've had sex!"

Laughing, Tom restrained Shadow long enough for Kevin to climb out from under him. Then he joined the two of them on the bed, Shadow lying contentedly between his two daddies while they both scratched his chest.

"Dumb dog," Kevin said, smiling affectionately at the pooch.

"Wait a minute," Tom said. "Didn't we leave him at the bottom of the stairs?"

Kevin laughed and bent forward to nuzzle the dog's chest while Shadow sighed in doggy ecstasy. "Looks like you're a stair-climbing pooch now. Look out, world!"

Tom scratched the dog's ear and mused, "He must have decided whatever he was afraid of wasn't as bad as being alone."

"Yeah," Kevin said. "I know the feeling."

Twenty-Nine

THE investigation into Billy's death was finally resolved to the satisfaction of the police and the New Hampshire District Attorney's office, and Billy was laid to rest in a proper cemetery plot. Since he and his father had lived in Stark only a short time, the family had no real ties there. The funeral ended up being held down in Littleton, NH, so Billy could be interred near his grandparents, and Kevin was informed through Chief Burbank that he would not be welcome.

Kevin respected Mr. Sherrell's wishes on the matter, but a week after the funeral, he and Tom drove down to St. Rose Cemetery to find the grave. As cities went, Littleton wasn't very large—only about five thousand residents—but St. Rose was still a fairly large cemetery with a number of recent headstones, so finding Billy's was an exercise in frustration. But eventually they spotted it.

Kevin stared silently at the grave for so long Tom finally felt compelled to ask, "Would you like me to give you a moment?"

Kevin looked up at the expanse of manicured lawn and headstones—it was early spring now, so the grass was green against the backdrop of pine trees that bordered the cemetery. "No. I don't really have anything to say. I know it wasn't really my fault, but I still feel like I should have... I don't know. Fought harder to save him." He held up a hand to silence Tom when he seemed about to say something. "Yeah, I know. I was just a kid. But Billy's father was right. If Billy had never met me, he'd probably still be alive today." He looked down at the lonely gray marble headstone again. "Maybe it would be me here instead."

Tom couldn't stay silent any longer. "I'm glad it's not! Not that I'm glad it's Billy, but.... It shouldn't be *either* of you!"

Kevin smiled at him and extended a hand to touch his arm. "It's okay, counselor. I'm still alive, and I intend to stay that way."

With that, he turned and walked back to the truck.

THE drive back to Stark was largely silent. Kevin was lost in dark thoughts that Tom knew better than to intrude upon. It wasn't until Kevin turned onto a side road Tom didn't recognize that he asked, "Where are we going?"

"I have a stop I want to make."

A couple of minutes later, he pulled over on the side of the road near Emerson Road Cemetery and got out of the truck. He strode purposefully through the cemetery, with Tom at his heels, until he came to an abrupt stop by one of the graves.

The headstone read:

Jack Kevin Derocher
Beloved Husband and Father
1942–1989

"The woman formally known as 'Mom' used to insist I come down here to pay my respects to you," Kevin said to the headstone. "So here I am, fresh from the grave of the only person you actually murdered. I just wanted to let you know, I finally figured it out. I finally pieced together why you killed yourself. It wasn't conscience. You didn't have one. You were too good at passing blame. It was always my fault for being too pretty, or Mom's fault for being too much of a bitch, or Billy's fault for leading you on...."

"No, the reason you never laid a hand on me after that night was because you were terrified of me. You really thought I'd find a way to kill you if you ever got near me again. And when I went away to Hampstead, you thought it was all over. You thought it was all gonna come out in my therapy sessions, so you did the only thing you could think of to escape everything coming down on you—you killed yourself. Poor Daddy. You didn't even know I'd forgotten everything. I couldn't give you away because I couldn't remember a goddamned thing from that night, you stupid fuck!"

He paused for a breath, but Tom knew better than to say anything. Kevin's eyes were glazed over, as if he weren't really seeing anything there.

"Pay my *respects*," Kevin muttered and spit on the ground. "If it wouldn't be disrespecting all of the *decent* people buried here, I'd whip it out and piss all over your grave. That's how much *respect* I have for you. You were an evil fuck, and you destroyed the lives of everyone around you. Not just Billy's, which I hope you're tortured in hell for, and not just mine. Mr. Sherrell was a bastard, but compared to you, he was an amateur. You took him out without even lifting a finger—stole his son away and had him railroaded out of town in one shot. And Mom? Was she always such a cold-blooded harpy or did decades of living with a man who preferred his own son to his wife do that to her?

"But I'm really here to talk about me. The sick thing is, I think you believed you loved me. You thought what you did to me was affection, and you thought I loved you back. I think you *needed* me to love you. But you stole my life from me. Not the way you did with Billy—you left me breathing. But I don't remember a moment of my childhood that didn't belong to you. Playing, going to school, trying to make friends.... Even when you weren't there, you were there, lurking in the back of my mind, the filthy secret I was afraid people would find out about. I didn't even dare tell Billy. I was scared to death he'd ditch me if he found out what I let you do to me. And then...."

Kevin paused and swallowed hard. "Twenty-five years. And even though I couldn't remember any of it, you were still there all the time—

every time I tried to have sex, every time I tried to get close to someone. Tom says I'll never be completely free of you, and he's probably right. But I'm telling you now, *I don't love you.* You tried to make me, but that was the one thing you couldn't force me to do. I stopped loving you when I was five, and no force on earth will ever make me say I loved you after that. I love Tom and Shadow, and I think I loved Billy. I'm pretty sure I love Tracy, and maybe I can even manage to love Mom a little. But not you. Not ever."

He stood there for a long time in silence until Tom, at last, felt compelled to reach out and take his hand. Kevin's fingers closed around his, and slowly Kevin turned to look at him. His eyes were threatening to brim over, but he blinked it away and said, "Let's go."

Still holding hands, they turned their backs on the gravestone and walked away.

Epilogue

THE next evening, as they sat in the hot tub with Shadow curled up on the deck nearby, looking up at a clear, star-filled sky, Kevin asked Tom, "Just how many days are supposed to go by before I'm allowed to ask you to marry me?"

Kevin laughed. "I suppose it's been enough."

"Do you want me to get a ring first?"

"No."

Kevin stood up, swaying a bit in the swirling water. Not for the first time, Tom marveled at the way water trickled down his thin, muscular back and abdomen. Kevin Derocher was the most beautiful man he'd ever met. And he was dead sexy. At the moment, though, he was more amusing as he crouched down in the water, struggling to kneel without being knocked over by the jets.

Tom laughed again. "You're not getting down on one knee!"

"Fuck you. That's the way it's done." Kevin extended his right hand. "Give me your hand."

Tom suspected he needed it as much for balance as tradition, but he put his hand in Kevin's. That's when he noticed how much Kevin's hand was trembling. "Are you all right? You're shaking."

Kevin rolled his eyes at him. "I'm not having a panic attack, counselor. I'm nervous because I'm about to ask my boyfriend to marry me."

"Oh. That's perfectly understandable."

"Thanks for the free analysis," Kevin said wryly. "Do you mind if I get on with it?"

"Not at all."

"Will you marry me, Tom?" Kevin asked.

Tom looked into those soft hazel eyes and smiled. "Yes, Kevin. Of course."

Kevin moved forward and slid his hot, wet body up the front of Tom's, making the latter groan in pleasure. "So... who do we invite?"

Tom kissed his neck before answering, "I don't know. My family, I guess. Though I don't know if they'll make it. Sue. That's about it for my side. I have no friends. What about you?"

"Tracy and Lee. Probably the gang at the diner. And my mom."

Tom pulled his head back in surprise so he could look up at Kevin's face. "What happened to 'We're definitely not inviting her to our wedding'?"

Kevin sighed and shrugged. "I don't know. I sort of realized yesterday that she's the only family I have left. And she's seventy. Maybe I should at least make an effort to patch things up with her. I mean, she hasn't actually taken out a restraining order... yet."

Tom wasn't sure he'd be as willing to forgive and forget, if he were in Kevin's place. After all, his mother had called him 'depraved' and implied he might be a murderer, all while defending the man who'd committed unspeakable horrors against him. But if this was what Kevin wanted, Tom would support him.

"Well, that's all fine," he said, "but perhaps you should send her a polite letter first, explaining that you'd like to patch things up and that you're in love with that nice man you brought to the home with you, before inviting her to your Big Gay Wedding."

Kevin chuckled. "Maybe."

"And now I'd like to get back to what we were doing before we started talking about your mother," Tom said, ducking under Kevin's chin to nibble his neck again.

Kevin pressed his crotch into Tom's and made a low growling noise. "Whatever you say, counselor."

JAMIE FESSENDEN set out to be a writer in junior high school. He published a couple short pieces in his high school's literary magazine and had another story place in the top 100 in a national contest, but it wasn't until he met his partner, Erich, almost twenty years later, that he began writing again in earnest. With Erich alternately inspiring and goading him, Jamie wrote several screenplays and directed a few of them as micro-budget independent films. His latest completed work premiered at the Indie Fest 2009 in Los Angeles and also played at the Austin Gay and Lesbian International Film Festival two weeks later.

After nine years together, Jamie and Erich have married and purchased a house together in the wilds of Raymond, New Hampshire, where there are no streetlights, turkeys and deer wander through their yard, and coyotes serenade them on a nightly basis. Jamie currently works as technical support for a computer company in Portsmouth, NH, but fantasizes about someday quitting his day job to be a full-time writer.

Visit Jamie at http://jamiefessenden.wordpress.com/.

Also from JAMIE FESSENDEN

http://www.dreamspinnerpress.com

Also from JAMIE FESSENDEN

http://www.dreamspinnerpress.com

Also from JAMIE FESSENDEN

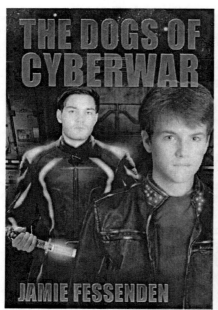
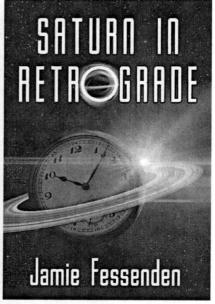

http://www.dreamspinnerpress.com

Also from JAMIE FESSENDEN

http://www.dreamspinnerpress.com

CPSIA information can be obtained
at www.ICGtesting.com
Printed in the USA
LVOW10s1115071117
555290LV00009B/111/P